Bill James

is a former journalist who worked for the *Western Mail* and *South Wales Echo*, the *Daily Mirror* and the *Sunday Times*. His espionage novel, *Split*, published by The Do-Not Press in 2001, introduced the mixed-race Intelligence officer Simon Abelard, born in Cardiff docks. James is also the author of eighteen crime novels in the Harpur and Iles series, which are published all over the world. The latest is *Pay Days*. The next, *Naked at the Window*, will be published later in 2002. *Protection*, fourth in the series, was televised by BBC 1 as H*arpur and Iles*, starring Hywel Bennett. Number three, *Halo Parade*, is under option by film makers in the United States.

James lives in his native South Wales and spends his time at his home near Cardiff and in a caravan on the Pembrokeshire coast. He also writes espionage and crime under the name David Craig. The Warner Brothers film, The Squeeze, with Stacy Keach, Edward Fox and Carol White, was adapted from the Craig novel, *Whose Little Girl Are You?* Bill James is at present working on a sequel to *Split*.

First Published in Great Britain in 2002 by
The Do-Not Press Limited
16 The Woodlands
London SE13 6TY
www.thedonotpress.co.uk
email: midman@thedonotpress.co.uk

B-format paperback: ISBN 1 899344 95 0
Casebound edition: ISBN 1 899 344 96 9

British Library Cataloguing in Publication Data. A catalogue
record for this book is available from the British Library.

1   3   5   7   9   10   8   6   4   2

Printed and bound in Great Britain by
The Guernsey Press Co Ltd.

Middleman

by

Bill James

THE DO-NOT PRESS

Author's Note

The geography of Cardiff dockland in this novel is broadly correct. There is a big development programme around Cardiff Bay and a barrage and a lagoon. The beach at nearby Lavernock, from where Marconi exchanged the first radio messages over the water, exists. So, of course, do the Welsh Assembly and its quayside HQ.

Some locations and all characters are fictional. There is no Gloria Complex. Bethel Baptist Chapel, which I attended as a child, became the Casablanca Club for a time before the building was finally demolished several years ago.

1

Don't, fucking don't, call me a middleman, right?

But he did not say it. He was alone, eating obnoxious bran for fibre at the breakfast bar, thinking about his trade. Henrietta had gone upstairs to get ready for work.

Middleman – it was a smear. Always lately this tag made rage hot up in his head, but the rage stayed there, inside, mute. There had been a time when he did not mind the term, had even gloried in it. Not now. Those words – Don't, fucking don't, call me a middleman, right? – the words were obviously like a yell or hurt scream, but were only a thought. He could manage thoughts.

The bran had skimmed milk on. A middleman berth in business made you careful about what you actually said. You built a knack of talking to yourself, and shouting to yourself occasionally. He more or less finished the bran and then washed the bowl. He went up to their bedroom. Henrietta was sitting at the dressing table, doing her face. Corbett opened a wardrobe. There were a pair of these, both mahogany, Victorian and ugly but all right for the job. He would have to wear a suit and collar and tie today. He had a meeting at the Complex.

He knew Henrietta was watching him off and on in the looking glass. 'Darling, Julian,' she said. She paused from lipsticking, her hand near her mouth but held there momentarily. It was not a deliberate pose, he was almost sure of that, and yet all the lines of her body seemed right: there was a lovely potential energy, and somehow the suggestion that she wanted to protect him. And somehow, also, the suggestion of the bully. Always these seeming opposites. That was how a living, lively marriage had to be, perhaps. Or their marriage. He would not have it any different, could not visualise it any different. They would repeatedly come back to each other, no matter where their wanderings took them. The wanderings were only that – wanderings; silly, fleshly digressions, boredom digressions. Her arms and shoulders had some weight, but nothing unsightly. 'I can always tell,' she said.

'What?'

'When you're seeing someone really mighty and frightening on business – if you let them be frightening, that is, and sometimes you do, don't you, Julian? Nobody does it better.'

'Does what better?'

'Cower. But I know, I do know, Jule, it's cowering in a good cause.' She brought her hand down slowly to rest on the dressing table.

'Oh, the suit and cufflinks.' He laughed. 'Yes, a uniform thing today. Sid likes that. Black lace-ups. Must blend.'

'No,' she said.

'What?'

'I didn't mean just the outfit.' He'd known this, but could do without a long tease from Henrietta. He'd have to go on with it now, though. 'What then?' he said.

'Nervousness. Uptightness.'

'I don't think so, Hen.'

'Terrified you'll speak out of line to one of these board-room ogres. Mr Middleman utters only what the client wants to hear.'

Don't call me a fucking middleman. He didn't say it, didn't say it again. 'I don't think so, Hen.' When he was in a power tussle with her he liked to stick to one calm, polite sentence as much as possible. It allowed no wavering and displayed assurance and control. It would put things right. She wanted them right as much as he did, but she had this need to show edge and this need to demolish him occasionally, in order to restore him – offer back his identity. That was Hen. He could be put off balance by her, but he also loved her for the clear way she saw things, and the hard way she could describe them. Yes, a true marriage had to be like this. 'They know me,' he said. 'They know my work, they—'

'Respect you?'

'Respect me.'

She half turned to Corbett and for a moment her voice softened. He knew, knew, that she did not really want to squash him, not flat. Acumen was a thing of hers. From somewhere he had a notion that women with fattish upper arms were often awkwardly bright. Possibly she had suddenly remembered he could be killed if he made a mistake, or was considered to have made a mistake. And a lot of very harsh considering went on in the Complex boardroom. Henrietta might realise he was all she had as a fixture. Perhaps widowhood was a dread: the drag of an autopsy and some solitariness for at least a while.

But, oh, it amounted to more than all that – more than just those bleak, legalistic, graveyard things. She was tied to him emotionally as tightly as he was to her, yet she did not always let it show. She said: 'I'd be so pleased for them to respect you, Jule. I'm not just scoring.' He believed this. Of course he did. They had to prop each other. She swivelled back to the looking glass and resumed making-up.

He sometimes wished she would leave the cosmetics alone. In Corbett's opinion she did not need all that. Her features were forceful and regular; yes, forceful but still altogether feminine, oh, marvellously feminine. Sometimes when he looked at her he was put in mind of Anjelica Huston, especially the way he had seen her lately in a television showing of *Prizzi's Honour*-dark-haired, getting on for statuesque, a face with some sadness, some devilry, buckets of intelligence. He revered Hen's eyes, when they were friendly to him. They were as dark as her hair and could be so lively and supportive and encouraging. He needed all that, could not need it more. Corbett believed he was unquestionably entitled to encouragement. At these friendly times he did not doubt she wanted him and only him. He lived for such fine spells with her. Hen was almost 5'11". He adored her tallness. There was a natural grandeur to her: not bulk, but what he liked to think of as presence. In a crowded room, people noticed her at once.

Now and then, of course, that could be a foul nuisance: men noticed Hen, saw some of the things in her that Corbett saw, and wanted to possess them. She might respond. Or – he had to admit this – occasionally, she would even go looking herself. Corbett tried to put up with it. He did put up with it. As a breed, middlemen often faced trouble from their women. But Corbett was confident none of the men who briefly intruded on their marriage could ever understand her as he did, and he was confident she understood this too and would never go from him permanently, as he could never go from her. Corbett himself might do some looking about from time to time. It did not matter. None of this could really shake the basis of him and Hen.

She said: 'Obviously, I know about some of what you've accomplished, Jule, and it's brilliant. Unique. I mustn't talk like a holy nincompoop.'

'They appreciate absolutely what an entrepreneur does, Hen. They know nothing could happen without people like me. Sid above all appreciates that. The Complex.'

Although Corbett preferred to be known as this – an entrepreneur – or possibly consultant, or Liaison Associate (Sites and Development) – any of these rather than a fucking middleman – yes, although he liked those terms, he never came out and insisted on one of them to the kind of folk he frequently dealt with, people like Sid. Stupid to offend clients by acting touchy; clients on all sides. This was the normal discipline of any profession – not to upset the customer. Although some clients could eye through a balance sheet with genius and had a true business status, they also had a true savagery aspect, particularly those in the sort of commerce Corbett did most of lately. Fees were highest there, and prospects, and risks. He had never actually picked that kind of work, but that kind of work had sort of come to him because of his talents and he had not turned it away. This was why a few of them referred to him as a middleman. He was in the fucking middle, wasn't he, and he could get trouble from any direction, all directions, and at the same time? If ever

Corbett incorporated himself he would call the company No Man's Fucking Land.

He fitted the cufflinks in a tailored blue-and-white striped shirt and put it on. There were drawers in the lower section of the wardrobe which ran beautifully and almost silently on old type craftsmanship and genuine wood. He admired first-class carpentry and good materials. They made high achievement in life seem routine. He knew they were not, or not until you'd already had some high achievements, when perhaps things did begin to get easier because you could put others to handle the tricky stuff: others like himself now. He loathed being named a middleman since middlemen had not much real self left, not much core to call their own, hardly any separate soul. Soul he valued, and he would take in a religious service at Bethel church now and then and sing the hymns at full volume. His father-in-law, Floyd, would be in the pulpit, frail and imperturbable. This was release for Corbett, but generally middlemen just thought their thoughts. They skipped about, bringing this big investor or developer and/or loot launderer to that big investor or developer and/or loot launderer, or an even bigger investor or developer and/or loot launderer, and helping them struggle and thresh and compromise to a kind of deal. The kind of deal was one that looked as though it might last a while. These were the conditions of progress.

Yes, although middleman might be a shitty name, in some ways it was spot-on. Middlemen had no home ground. They commuted facelessly between others' territories trying to be trusted and positive and, above all, unblamed, and therefore unhurt, long term and short. It could be hard to stay unblamed long term. There might be moments when even Henrietta, despite all her brashness, saw this. Long term was sometimes very long term. A project that had looked good, and which you helped on with all your soft-pedalled intelligence, eventually turned rotten. This could be an age after and, now and then, when an ex-middleman's body was found in the channel or a kiddies' pleasure park, you might not remember which transaction this death and obvious previous beating or defacement or scorching were actually for. Think how it had been with Boris Lowndes. God, yes; remember what Boris looked like when they found him on the beach? Boris had apparently been doing something intermediary for one of the big interests, but had offended. Nobody knew how, and nobody was sure which big interest he'd upset or when. It might even have been Sid Hyson himself. Well, not might. Boris had been a damn gifted, tactful fixer with almost enough built up to retire on. That was how he had finished, though. In retirement, he had intended writing a history of the refrigerator worldwide and had already done plenty of research. The waste of such knowledge depressed Corbett.

From the collection of ties hanging on a brass hook in the wardrobe, he chose one with a silver background and a motif of small red shields. He would wear a navy, double-breasted suit. A uniform, as he'd said. He liked to think it brought a flash of sameness with his hirers. They wanted you to look acceptable. They had a right to expect that. For now, this was his aim above all: to be acceptable. Henrietta said cowed, but that was just mischief. She did have a mouth on her occasionally, and lipsticked it into quite a bit of prominence, Corbett thought sometimes. But with it she would entirely spontaneously, and often in extremely unexpected settings, suck his cock to completion, and it would be perverse to think badly of a mouth like that. In the past, Corbett had never bothered greatly about clothes but, as things improved, he had decided to kit himself out with a few bespoke suits and shirts and some expensive, subdued ties.

While he dressed he watched Henrietta. He loved to be alongside her in this way, occupied with very ordinary things. It did not matter that she could be sharp. Such tolerance and relaxation were marriage, in his view. He definitely doubted whether she could get anything similar elsewhere. It did not matter, either, that her work with the make-up was half a botch. This made her pitiable, more lovable. He adored the long straightness of her back and the confidence of her hands as she worked the cosmetics regardless. There was a lot of powder about but he could still smell her skin; a nice, warm roundness, hygiene, like a very clean food shop where most produce was pre-wrapped.

Of course, anyone in Corbett's job was for ever liable to lose his woman. From close to, a wife or girlfriend saw her partner was nothing and might go looking for someone who did have a proper self and being and soul and, if possible, property, or its intense likelihood. Corbett had forced himself to treat this as understandable, although heavy with pain, and had welcomed Henrietta back twice after three- or four-week love wanders, staying silent about the tit bruises and new junk jewellery she'd insist on keeping, though he would offer to at least match this crap for value if Oxfammed. Christ, did Hen hang on in case she went back to who gave it, so he would remember her? Corbett had schooled himself to be patient and adult. Although she could give him terrible, enduring misery, there were also lovely pluses, and not merely sex: that would be shallow thinking.

He sat at the end of the bed to put on his shoes. His lace-ups were beautifully lightweight and narrow, with an interesting mottled pattern on the uppers. Always he felt nimble and ambitious wearing these. He aimed for some coup in his career that would really transform him and secure Henrietta properly. Continually he met persons who had changed themselves into solid figures through smartness, luck and the neat ability to down enemies for keeps – not just trivia like Boris Lowndes but really forceful, hellish competitors. These victors had to be his ultimate models. Buyable and blank and very quietly clever, middlemen scuttled between individuals of this sort who did possess a self and all the rest of it – who had made themselves individuals. They also had capital or, alternatively, illustrious, titanic debt and harsh, eternally increasing power: men like Sid Hyson, with his – what? – £100 million Gloria Complex at the Bay, named after Sid's beaky wife. Around that happy figure. The Complex included a shopping mall, hotel, helicopter port, nursing home, casino and huge indoor, domed botanic gardens, worth £40 million on its own – forty big ones for immigrant fucking vines! Botanic gardens would never earn their keep, of course, not even at £10 a ticket for entry, and Sid had collected enormous grants from the European Union sub-division whose brief was glasshouse trees and plants. He knew about grants. The hotel had been burned down once, just before completion; possibly arson. Sid had rebuilt. He used to speak of the hotel as costing £100 million itself, which was ludicrous. But he envisioned each part of the Complex as part of its essence and as integral to the total outlay. Sid thought in themes and schemes. He had a kind of dirty grandeur. He, personally, would not have seen to Boris. Things did not work like that. Sid had a rarefied side to him.

Maybe because of the powder cloud, Corbett sneezed and mucked up his tie. Henrietta saw in the looking glass and laughed outright, despite the layers of cosmetics. He did not mind. She had her problems to cope with. He could easily change his tie. He wanted her happy. Any sort of laugh was a help. It did not involve real venom. She swung around on the dressing table seat and undid his tie. 'We'll get the mark out, Jule, no bother,' she said. 'Wear the dark red one today – more assertive, but not foolishly defiant.'

'What I'd thought, too,' he replied. It was one of her favourite kinks, playing about with words like that. She might get it from her father. Floyd excelled at pulpit spiels. Corbett always felt excited by this skill in Hen. It was educated and indicated a kind of optimism and even innocence. She knew – well, clearly – she knew he routinely worked with people who would suddenly turn and have him crippled or slaughtered if they thought things were going the wrong way, yet Henrietta could talk as though the right tie was so vital, and not just the right tie but the right words for the flavour of the right tie. He might be nothing, but Hen was not. She had a whole structure of taste and values and civilisation to her. The lipsticking was a foul oddity, nothing more.

Henrietta had turned to the looking glass again now and, bending a little, he stroked her back through her silk jacket;

long, slow moves. She seemed to enjoy these for a little while, pressing hard against his hand, so notifying Corbett of something fine and wonderfully special to him, he felt almost certain. These moments of oneness would come like this, now and then. He prized them and knew they mattered more than anything else in his life, if his life were viewed in general. He knew he was reaching her core and spirit through her shoulders and back in a way that nobody else ever had or would. They could not get the measure of Hen in three or four weeks. She was too much for that. Corbett felt bucked by her statement that she recognised his achievements. He had handled much of what was referred to as 'mature period facilitating' for the whole Gloria Complex and kept violence around the negotiations to nearly zero from at least that stage, except for the fire, which might be regarded as an act of God, or of anything up to forty people who hated Sid. He had never accused Corbett of neglect or complicity. Sid could be reasonable.

Authentic skills had been required to get the Complex approved. Most of the Bay development was unbreakably honest. So was the Bay Corporation. Alone, Sid would never have reached final selection with his grandiose sprawl of a scheme and its wonky, hall-of-mirrors finance. Corbett's deep local knowledge of where the Bay possibilities were had turned out to be crucial, as it always did in such ploys. In fact, he realised he hated being called a middleman because he was one, and tops at it. He knew how to smile and how to agree, and how to propose vital little amendments or deletions without seeming to propose them, and how to be a slick nothing. Now and then, he told himself that being nothing was his prime flair. This was a kind of joke, but it was also something he spelled out in case Henrietta spat it at him on one of her fucking phrasy days. He wanted to get himself used to the poison and inured beforehand.

This flair helped him keep his best thoughts sealed off and only for the breakfast bar. This flair had let him take Henrietta back after her love saunters and act with kindness to her, as if what she had done when she was away was also nothing. He did not know who the men were, or whether, in fact, there was more than one. Often, Henrietta was a proud and niggling cow, but he revered her, depended on her, wanted to guard her skin and frame. She was the kind who did not realise she needed guarding. They needed it most, obviously. If he had peril, so did she. He would never let himself make her anxious, though, by stressing his fears and Sid and Gloria's deep unpredictabilities. Someone who made up her lips in the dauntless way Hen did had an unassailable faith in her destiny. He would like her to keep that if she could. Corbett did not wish to change her. He regretted the unfaithfulness but recognised it was linked to her fine vivacity and courage.

When Sid Hyson spoke to him at the beginning of this morning's special meeting at the hotel in the Gloria Complex, Corbett could not tell whether he had noticed his tie but hoped that, if Sid had, he would observe it was assertive though not foolishly defiant. 'This is your town and your country, Jule, and I trust I'm not one who'd have the crudity to say a fucking thing against them, even given present circumstances,' Hyson remarked.

'I'm sure of that, Sid,' Corbett replied.

'And what else I would never want to say a word against is you, Jule. I'd like to be able to go on thinking of you as almost a kind of partner, despite everything.'

'I try all I know to give a service, Sid.'

'Everyone in this room, not just self, accepts you really believed in it, Jule.'

One of the other board people, Jacob or Marvin, said: 'Oh, absolutely.'

Gloria said, 'Hear, hear, Sidney.'

'I think I can say I'd never take on a project I did not believe in,' Corbett replied. 'Couldn't. Against all my instincts.' Of course, by now he was almost dazed by fear, agonisingly shaken at the turnaround he felt coming in Sid's words. Corbett knew flattery from someone like Sid had to be the run-up to evil. This was not a situation to be affected by a tie.

'We want out, Jule,' Hyson said.

'I—'

'Gloria and I want fucking out of Cardiff Bay. We'll quit the development. Plus the rest of the board want it, naturally.'

'Sid, I—'

'When I say "naturally", I don't mean the rest of the board want whatever I want just because I want it. Are they nobodies, Jule? They want it because they've done their own thinking and happen to agree with me.'

'Certainly not nobodies, Sid,' Corbett replied. He could teach a course on what made a nobody. He said: 'Excuse me, Sid, but the Complex was so – so, well, central to you, to your thinking. Admirable. You saw it as an entity even before it fully existed.'

'Gloria's never felt the same since the fire. I don't say you should have prevented that, Jule, although you're of the area and hear the mutterings, but for Gloria this was an untidy experience.'

'Out,' she replied. 'We haven't decided this in haste. There's a spread of factors.' They were in the penthouse boardroom, which took about half the hotel's top floor. There was no table. People sat in easy chairs or on the two settees. A modern drinks cabinet stood against one wall, genuine timber, not veneer. Silver-framed class photographs of what appeared to be a very scruffy primary school hung near the drinks cabinet. Corbett imagined Sid or Gloria or both must be in them, but there had never been an explanation and Corbett felt it might be best to wait for one. Were Sid and Gloria sweethearts from school days? Corbett admired relationships of that sort: so sure, so total.

'Let's talk water, shall we?' Hyson said.

'Anything, Sid,' Corbett replied.

'And Henrietta – how is she?' Gloria asked. 'We've both been impressed by her over the months, Sid and I. She's a presence, that one. I don't mean burly. Majestic. We think of her quite a bit.'

'Impressed,' Hyson said.

'In her own right,' Gloria said.

'She's great,' Corbett replied.

'Very much in her own right. I believe she'd see the point of our change of mind,' Gloria said. 'A shrewdness there, a feel for the future. You chose well when you chose Henrietta, Jule – looking beyond the superficial. Oh, she moves around a bit, I hear. That's not fatal, though. Obviously. You still value her.'

'Would you say someone doing your sort of work ought to know about water, Jule?' Hyson asked. 'This is local water I'm discussing. We come in from Berkshire, Gloria and I, and buy a stake here, but you, you're a local boy, yes? One of your assets, all right? Son of the soil, yes? So, if you're truly local you ought to know about water that's local, is that fair?'

'I—'

Gloria Hyson slapped her chair arm playfully. 'But, all right, if Henrietta came sniffing and lipping around Sid himself, I expect all my tolerance and liberal instincts would disappear fast,' she said, chuckling. 'I'm sure you're thinking that, and I can tell you you're damn right, Jule. Sid's very mine.'

Hyson stood up and beckoned Corbett to join him. Corbett had been sitting on a long, blue leather settee. He went to Hyson. Sid took Corbett's arm in a sort of partner's, or asylum nurse's, grip and led him to the window that ran along the whole southern side of the penthouse. They looked down together on Cardiff Bay's 500-acre gleaming lagoon and the curving barrage that separated it from the sea. A couple of small yachts dawdled across the lagoon. It was a concept and more than that now. Sunshine glinted on the botanic gardens. The prestige they brought was especially welcome in the Bay, even though they'd cost only half what the Eden glasshouses project in Cornwall had added up to.

'You heard about this water?' Hyson asked.

'Beautiful,' Corbett replied.

'Beautiful's certainly one word, I don't deny. But a brochure word? You heard that some safety people – this is official safety people, qualified people – you heard they were anxious because this water could flood? You're local, yes? You heard this? I don't mean just this water, the lake, but too much sea water coming in through the barrage. You heard about the tides in the channel out there? Only one other place in the world with bigger tides. New to you? Have you thought about this fucking jolly tide getting itself together to smash my £100 million outlay? Well, £100K as starters. More like £180K, even £200 million now.'

'Certainly. It's all been sorted, as I gather, Sid – the flood danger,' Corbett replied.

'So, you heard of it? Did you mention it to me, I wonder?'

'This was denied as soon as—'

'So, you heard of it?'

'Very sensitive detectors in the sluices to make sure it won't happen, Sid,' Corbett replied. 'And even if there was a failure, the whole thing can be done manually. The detectors are overridden by an operator and the level kept down. Called fail-safe.'

'In many ways a personable and engaging woman, Henrietta,' Gloria said. 'A very unusual woman, not flimsy.'

Hyson said: 'Am I right they have to keep the level below full because they're scared what could happen if they go to max? You heard that, also, Jule? Tell me what you see over that way, by Windsor Esplanade. Are they mud flats?'

'Only for the time being, Sid,' Corbett replied. 'In months it will be different.'

'Those mud flats are supposed to be covered, aren't they? That's why they've got a lagoon, isn't it? This is supposed to be a beautiful stretch of water all the way across. They used to have mud flats but they built this barrage and made this lagoon so the mud flats would always be under. Have I got that right? That's why I wanted a site here, isn't it? That's why Rocco Forté put his St David's Hotel where it is, over there, wavelets lapping pleasantly just outside. Sir Rocco and family, 85th in the Sunday Times list of British rich with £300 million. All right, only 85th, but people like that probably know what they want. This water is what's referred to by planners as an amenity, Jule. Folk like to look out and see a fine stretch of water. Mud flats are not an amenity, except for ducks, which are admittedly part of nature but not a business factor.'

'Oh, they'll fill it properly very soon, Sid.'

'Will they? And? What happens? I have a nursing home in this Complex. Forgotten that? You ever seen a nursing home flooded, Jule? These are the elderly and sick, willing to pay for a waterside setting to help their cure. This is first-class medical equipment. Resuscitation gear, all that. Not pennies and it won't float. Have you thought what happens if it gets on TV about a nursing home flooded – rich, worthwhile, old people washed out to Steep Holm island in the night, their cries refined, desperate but unheard? Property values? Where the fuck are they then, Jule? I have this terrible ability for visualising disaster in detail. My father was the same. This channel can be callous. Do you recall that lad they recovered – like a Russian name?'

'Lowndes. Boris Lowndes.'

'Awful,' Hyson replied. 'Gratuitous was a word used a lot about his injuries and death. This is how water can be: ungovernable. It does not know the rules of behaviour. I'm with Prince Philip, Jule, about water, as about so much. He said he can't sentimentalise the sea because he's been a sailor. All he knows is that the sea is cold and dangerous, and I think of that opinion when I hear of someone like Boris.'

Hyson had on a very traditional, dark blue, pinstripe suit; double breasted, non-boxy shoulders, unvented, and not that lesser-breed, high-buttoned style chosen by loaded soccer players. He was handsome in a Scandinavian or German way, a bit beaky like Gloria, nose high-bridged and his cheek bones strong, short of flesh, persuasive. Corbett's mother would have described Sid as aristocratic-looking. By this she meant contemptuous.

Gloria said: 'I believe that with only normal good fortune, Henrietta will really excel. As a wife and so on. It might be possible to discourage the kind of man she goes to. After all, can they whistle when their teeth have been pushed down their throats? We don't want to be thought of as deserting the area, Jule. This is a financial readjustment only. We know you'll wish to help us unload in time and at a fair price.'

Corbett tried to keep his breathing steady and unostentatious; no gasping, nothing tremulous. After all, they were handing him just a minor chore, really, weren't they: simply locate some fucker with around £200 million on call, and find him fast? Then, after this formality, persuade him that Sid and Gloria were not on their way out because they feared for their money, but because… because what? Because they had decided from good nature to offer the market a bargain. So credible. Oh, Christ. And yet…. and yet what?

When Lowndes was found on the pebbles at Lavernock, he had no eyebrows and hardly any hair left – little face left, either – the whole area blackened by burning, not salt water. Lavernock was a distinguished spot, even before Boris appeared there: Marconi did his first radio communication over the sea from Lavernock Point. Boris Lowndes was another kind of communication. It was aimed at people like Corbett – middlemen. The state of him said: No errors, please. It said: Buy for me, or Sell for me, and, Do it spot-on right. Now it said: Sell for me. What did she mean about Henrietta's men?

Corbett said: 'If you're determined, Gloria, I'll—'

'Determined,' she replied.

'There's the usual fee plus – plus, Jule – one per cent of anything you get over the hundred and eighty mill,' Sid Hyson said. 'This could be retirement money.'

'Heavy enough to anchor even Henrietta for you,' Gloria said.

Boris Lowndes had had his retirement money piled and his refrigeration history nicely planned out. Fair price? What would Sid and Gloria really settle for to sell a thus far waterproof Complex? Were the banks leaning on Sid? They would have heard of the sluice scare, too. It made the national press and television. Communication had sharpened up since Marconi. Some of the banks Sid borrowed from were not main street and might be jumpy. Sid and Gloria appeared well ahead of Sir Rocco in the Sunday Times list of the British wealthy, but did the list concentrate on apparent assets and not know in full about debts? Was there interest as well as capital to be taken care of by the sale? Did Sid need £180 million, £220 million? And yet... and yet what?

And yet, one per cent of that extra £40 million would be £400,000. This, added to the standard half a per cent on the original £180 million, would take Corbett's commission to £1,300,000 if he could work something. Amounts like these had to be studied, and given at least as much weight as Boris washed ashore. Such earnings carried solidity and character with them. They might grip Henrietta, as Gloria suggested. Such earnings, such possibilities, were what made entrepreneuring potentially a magnificent, unique game; yes, even if it were called – by the coarse and ignorant – 'middlemanning'. These were the kind of fees that could mark the end of someone's status as a faceless nothing. Who asked a nothing to look after, on his own, a deal that might touch £200 million? Plus?

Hyson said: 'This Complex has my wife's name on it: the Gloria Complex. Does she want her... well, image... does she want her image tied up with a cruel fucking disaster like flooding, or this comical Welsh Assembly they've built close to the Complex with all its wacky people and little, parish rumpuses? They've messed up what was a sparkling ambience. Oh, look, regard anything we can do to contain Henrietta's heat and straying merely as a gift, Jule, an extra, thrown in. We'd like to see you comfortable. We need to have you comfortable and able to concentrate on our bit of business. What do you think's going to happen to property prices when people outside hear about this water and hear more about this fuckwit Welsh Assembly in its building going up there bold as buggery, farcifying the whole Bay with its splutters and yelps?' He pointed. 'You ever tried to sell a place that no insurance company will consider because of flood risks? This scheme used to look like the 21st century. Soon they might need divers to find it. I adore the notion of Atlantis, Jule, but not if I'm paying. Assembly members up to their belly buttons in creeping Bristol Channel. The Welsh are a short-legged people. Over some of their heads.'

'I'm assured the lake's entirely under control, Sid.'

'You've asked, have you? Why? You were bothered? Did you mention to me or Gloria you were bothered? But you might have been preoccupied with Henrietta and all that. This is what I mean, Jule – assistance there, to stop her sex-questing. Don't misunderstand. I consider it normal for a man, any man, to be concerned about his wife if she's banging someone else, or more than one.'

'Sidney's spoken to me about it with grief,' Gloria said.

'Certainly,' Hyson replied. 'Flood worries from far back, Jule. I knew about those, of course. The water table. You know about the water table, Jule? This is people not necessarily in the Bay at all, but waking up one day somewhere in Cardiff with tributaries of the lagoon in their cellars or drawing rooms. This is the water table. It means that under the ground there's buckets and buckets of water, but not like buckets, like a table. Now, if you put something on top of a table, say a box or garments, the top of what you put on there is higher than the table. Likewise, Jules, if you put water, such as a lagoon, on top of the water table, the water you put on there gets higher than the water table. So – those early worries. I gambled that would be all right. But now this as well – the channel ready to bulldoze through the barrage sluices and fuck up the Complex, victimise me and, so much more important, Gloria herself. I'd regard that as akin to rape. In the past I've always spoken well about your loyalty, Jule. "Jule is integrity." That's what I used to say, and was proud to say it. Many have heard me say it. A mantra. First class for your CV.'

'I've heard it. We would both praise you unstintingly,' Gloria said. 'We've undoubtedly been prepared to regard you as an asset, Jule, and Henrietta, despite the occasional wobble. Very correctable, believe me, Jule.'

Hyson said: 'Have you had a look at the botanic gardens at ground level, Jule? These are splendid, splendid constructions, thought up by a genuine architect that Gloria chose personally, who's in total harmony with leaves, branches, growth and useful insects, but in some ways the framework is frail. That's part of the beauty, this frailty. It's to symbolise man's brave but fragile attempts to create soaring beauty in a harsh world, like a filmy dress on a lovely model. Think of the sea banging through there, flotsam and refuse cascading, knocking stanchions. All right, not necessarily final. So, say it's repaired and restocked with rare plants from Botswana and Mexico, and it all happens again. Get us a buyer, Jule. Right? It's on you to arrange it. This is a real prestige site while they keep the water out. Unmatchable. Real. A gift at anywhere around £200 million in today's prices.'

Corbett said: 'Sid – your anxieties: I can swear none of this will—'

'We're keen to turn to another kind of investment,' Gloria said. 'Internet companies. Still promising despite a setback now and then. We feel our funds have been misplaced. This Bay scheme looked like something fine for the future, as Sidney says, but then …. Oh, I don't know – the gleam has gone – a whiff of catastrophe, an inescapable odour of clownishness, a stink of failure. So destructive of values. There's got to be a different kind of prospect for us. As Sidney also said, we know, absolutely know, that your motives were good, Jule, in bringing us here and sewing us so tightly into it. Yes, motives almost certainly good, Jule, and we're pretty sure you were not acting for any other interests. We're definitely prepared to believe that middlemanning has its ethics. We're never going to accuse you of playing for two sides or more at once, I'm nearly certain of that.' Wearing an amber, roll-top sweater and stone-coloured cotton skirt, she sat very erect in the middle of a long, beige settee. She gazed at Corbett with something like considerateness. He was grateful for that. Gloria would be about sixty, probably a little older than Sid.

'A buyer, Jule, before it all happens and while it's still insured and insurable,' Hyson said.

'For the botanic gardens?'

'The Complex,' Hyson replied. 'Toto. The whole fucking plateful. Think of flooding in a gambling centre, for God's sake. I've never been in a casino under water, I'll admit, but it's clear that if you've got a drowned casino there's going to be a total change of mood from when it was not drowned. There'd be less gaiety and sang-froid among punters. I worship this view, Jule, worship it.' He waved one hand in a lingering semi-circle, encompassing the lagoon. 'I worship coasts and headlands. Those would be suitable words on my gravestone: Sidney Hyson – Coasts and headlands were dear to him. And, of course, I love Wales. I'm famed for that. Oh, absolutely. That dragon on the flag. Symbolic, or am I wrong? Just get us out of this fucking trap, will you, Jule? I haven't time to be brought into the early negotiations myself. I'm going to be abroad quite a bit with Gloria so I'll ask Marvin and Jacob to handle all that – I mean handle it with you, of course, Jule. It would be nice if you could report to them, say, twice a week. That suit you, Marv, Jacob?' They nodded. Hyson went back to his armchair and Corbett returned to the blue settee. 'That suit you, Jule? Twice a week? I don't think it needs to be oftener, not at this stage. Let them know your progress, sift and sort the bids. All right, Jule? I don't want you to think of Marv and Jacob as nothing more than heavies.'

'Hardly,' Corbett replied.

'These are valid members of the board, fully accredited directors. They're documented in Companies House.'

Marv, in another armchair, nodded a couple of times again, but more slowly, to get some gravity.

Corbett said: 'What—?'

'Timescale?' Hyson replied. 'Soonest. The thing about tides and sluices – uncertainties involved, Jule. OK, there are tide tables in the paper and it all looks spot-on to the minute, but when you think of tides and sluices together, this is where the imponderables start. We don't want to hang about. We don't want to get caught. You wouldn't wish to be pinpointed as responsible for something like that, Gloria and I are certain of it. What I mean is that, having got us into this fucking dump, you'll see it as a real and urgent duty to get us out of it. But I've told Marv and Jacob, no thug pressure on you, Jule, nothing… nothing… well, gross… haven't I, boys?' Marv and Jacob nodded instantly.

'Thanks, Sid,' Corbett replied.

'They know how we esteem you, Jule,' Gloria said.

'Thank you, Gloria,' Corbett replied.

'And I'm sure they esteem you themselves,' Gloria said. Marv and Jacob nodded instantly again.

'Thanks, Marv; thanks, Jacob,' Corbett replied.

'They know, as well as Gloria and I know, that if you fuck up on this, Jule – if you are, say, less than committed or slow or can't get our price – anything like that and they know their future is fucked up as much as mine and Gloria's,' Hyson said. 'That's what Gloria means when she says they esteem you – you and your fine missus, Henrietta, in the background and variable, yet so lovely – they esteem you and would therefore be unbearably disappointed in you if you fucked up, Jule. I expect you've still got a whole list of people with funds who wanted to get in here and had to be refused. It will only be a matter of returning to some of them and saying it's a sweetly going concern now with brilliant appreciation, not just a scheme, and that you might be able to fix a deal for them. And then you start your auction, easing up the price to something in keeping. Marv and Jacob will be ready to advise on that – the level. Upwards of, say, that £180 mill. we mentioned.'

'Marv has done some research on at least the last man Henrietta slipped away to,' Gloria said.

'And the previous,' Marvin said.

'There you are, then, Jule,' Gloria said.

'It's all right now, Henrietta and me,' Corbett replied. 'No need for—'

'Research carried out in an entirely discreet fashion,' Gloria said. 'This is Marv's forté.'

'Entirely,' Marvin said.

'Secrecy,' Hyson said.

Corbett said: 'Regarding the—?'

'That we're selling?' Hyson replied.

'Certainly,' Corbett said.

'This information gets out, what happens to the price? The Complex suddenly on the market is enough to knock confidence, destabilise the whole Bay project,' Hyson said. 'Like unloading a ton of shares. Especially if you take it alongside Fred Karno's Welsh Assembly.'

'It would be an added reason for feeling bonded to us and giving us your best if we can do something about men who treat Henrietta like a come-hither-love-to-me slag,' Gloria said.

'I do feel bonded to you already,' Corbett replied. 'I hope there's never been any reason for you to think differently. And I'll act for you now as I always have – wholeheartedly.'

'Taking advantage of you, men like that,' Gloria said. 'Sidney and I can't watch you being degraded in such a fashion, Jule. We'd like you to be able to look after our business without the distraction of your wife's fits of "Take me, do."'

'It's resolved now, it really is,' Corbett replied.

'Marv has at least the one man's timetable and habits in remarkable fullness, should it come to a finalising interception and so on. I've glanced at the notes, mapping and photographs,' Gloria said. 'But we all know Marv to be like that, thorough, don't we?'

'And the previous one,' Marvin said. 'Educated. She might be fascinated by that. Women can be, I've heard. Affections may be back-burnered and then reactivated. It's wisest to know about more than the immediate. Two shafters given a really bad time by us would be more than twice as effective as one. It shows seriousness.'

'Think of it merely as a gift, Jule, if Marv does decide to intervene for you,' Gloria said. 'Oh, of course, we know we don't have to purchase your gratitude by helping with your marriage. That would be damn presumptuous. Your gratitude is there anyway, a constant, and much appreciated, be assured. This would be just a kindness to a colleague, to a friend.'

'Confidentiality absolutely vital,' Hyson said. 'Not just a matter of preserving values. If it got around that the board were losing faith in the project here, I could be in some peril. I mean, in person. People might think: Knock Sid Hyson over – I mean Sid in person – remove him, and what's left? What's left is Gloria, obviously, and the rest of the board – that's Marv and Jacob. They're all keen on the Bay, clearly, but the report would be around that they've grown uncertain about things here. Probably not so for me, yet. I, personally, am known as the one who was most strongly committed – my personal, intense love of the Bay and things Welsh in general. The dragon. Wipe me out and the value of the Complex crashes. Someone could take a pop.'

'Oh, don't talk like this, Sidney, don't, don't,' Gloria cried. 'Your death – as if it were just a commercial matter.'

'It would be a commercial matter,' Hyson replied.

'That's only a marginal concern. It would be you, you, Sidney,' Gloria said, 'a husband, a friend.'

'I'm handing you something tricky, I know that, Jule,' Hyson said. 'How do you sell and yet keep things quiet at the same time? Someone has to know we're selling, obviously, or where do the bids come from? But restricted, Jule, please. No general talk. That's why we're using you instead of property agents. And why we feel that a percentage for you shouldn't be the only reward. No, indeed. So, Marv and Jacob have been looking at these warm rambles of Henrietta's on your behalf.'

'Sid, honestly not necessary.'

'You value that woman,' Hyson replied. 'This weakens you.'

'Sid, if one of these men got... well, got badly hurt... or... got really badly hurt... the police are going to start sniffing around and they'll come up with Henrietta, most probably, especially if both men were done. This would be pretty conclusive, wouldn't it? She'd be the unifying factor. So, who are they going to suspect? You see where it leads, Sid?'

Marv laughed. Jacob laughed a few seconds after him. 'They're going to think you've killed someone? That what you're saying?' Marv asked. 'You? Or even two? Pardon me, Jule, but you don't look to me like a crime-of-passion lad.'

'Not the least cause for anyone to be killed,' Corbett replied.

'This would have an impact on Henrietta, you see, Jule,' Gloria said. 'She'd be impressed and, yes... impressed and a little afraid. No harm. She'd see you so differently. You become someone who does care and will ruthlessly act from jealousy, possessiveness. I think you'd find she'd cling much more willingly after this kind of signal; those sweet, considerable arms around you, rapturously. Obviously, she's not going to know it wasn't you who annihilated them. Marv's not going to broadcast who actually did it. She'd admire the way you had identified them and then... then pushed things to a conclusion. Ignore Marv's slur that nobody could think of you as a killer, Jule. She would, because she wants to.'

'So, it's important only to talk to interests where there's a likelihood of a bid, Jule,' Hyson said. 'Interests like that won't want to blab because it could bring competitors in. But, do I need to explain this? You're a brilliant star in these things, Jule. We're damn lucky to have you. I feel relieved at being able to hand it over to you and at knowing you'll be able to focus, because your sex angsts will be removed.'

2

Early that evening, Corbett went up to London by train with Henrietta. He felt... well, Christ, he didn't know quite what or how he felt, but most of it was huge, almost hysterical, joy. It had come to him, this delight, this glorious optimism, almost as soon as he said goodbye to Sid and the others after lunch in the hotel penthouse. All right, the assignment was tough. He could do it. He would do it. He would transform their lives, his and Hen's.

It had been a no-choice menu in the penthouse but a fine one: caviar – real beluga, not lumpfish row, Corbett was almost sure, though Sid would never childishly boast about something like that – mutton, with the veg at just the right level of hard-soft, sorbet, cheeses. Sid himself never ate much. He stayed slim. He used to say he had seen a Cary Grant film on television where the star played a business executive who kept telling himself to "think thin". Sid admired Cary Grant and possibly aimed to be debonair. He had a way to go. The wines were most likely decent. Corbett was learning about wines, but still had a lot of ignorance. None of these served now made his hair fall out, anyway.

Sid had not wanted to use the hotel restaurant in case someone spotted Corbett eating with the directors and wondered what was up. This had thrilled Corbett. He was a nothing, maybe, but a famed nothing. If Jule Corbett was on your property, getting fed in a suit and mild tie, things must be moving. He signified. Although some might look at him and see a nothing, and although he might see a nothing himself in the mirror, you could also look at Corbett and see the whole Gloria Complex: mall, botanic gardens, casino, hotel, nursing home. None of it would exist if he hadn't helped put it there. His work rated no plaques but was supremely positive. All right, the help he gave was help to a supreme villain – Sidney Hyson. Always there would be villainy somewhere in a scheme of this size. Even villains could be constructive, as a by-product to their greed. Corbett revelled in the way caviar stuck to the underside of his teeth, probably a sign of its quality. Eggs in the womb of a beluga sturgeon in fierce seas were bound to have a special, cling-on nature.

Hotel staff set a trestle table in the boardroom and brought food and drink on trolleys. Six flunkeys wearing white shirts and navy trousers arranged things speedily. It looked like a routine. Corbett thought Gloria groped the youngest of them from behind for a shortish spell while he was helping place the table and had his legs wide for balance. Gloria was supervising. The waiter did not waver or turn. He must be used to it. Perhaps they all were. Yes, a routine. Possibly Gloria also preferred some meals in the boardroom, rather than the restaurant. Women were entitled to their appetites and perks. Agonisingly, Corbett had learned this from Henrietta. After lunch, he left his car on the hotel forecourt and strolled in kindly sunshine around part of the lagoon, loving it: loving not just the grubby water but a long view over the barrage and past Penarth cliffs, then out to the channel and Holm islands. Gulls called in that genuine, neck-stretched, loony way of theirs. Sid regarded the channel as a likely enemy. He was still not used to the coast: Glorsid, his manor house and estate, lay in deepest Berkshire and he never really appeared at ease with the sea. To make his nervousness respectable he'd grabbed at that remark by Prince Philip. But Corbett had been brought up around docks, ships, the sea, the mud. This territory was a comfort to him. As a kid he used to scream back at the gulls, like talk.

Near the Pier Head building, he had rung Henrietta on the mobile and asked her to take a day's leave tomorrow so they could make the trip together. Instantly she agreed. London fascinated her. Once, she had told him she felt an eternal tug towards its big central streets, its multinationalism and

Formica sandwich bars, and its galleries – 'fucking pretentious, Jule, but often bright with quite passable stuff'. He
always enjoyed watching her grin responsively as they slipped
into the crowds on the pavement in Piccadilly. About
Henrietta there was a gorgeous promiscuity in the general
sense, not just sexual. She needed to interweave and mingle,
like a strung-out cloud on a windy day, or effluent in a river.

'Urgent, this visit?' Henrietta asked on the train. 'Key?'

'Not really.'

'If it were urgent – suppose – if it were, would you want
me with you, Jule?'

'Naturally.'

'It is urgent, isn't it? You've got that fizz to you, like a
would-be conqueror.'

'Not really.'

'I'm so glad you want me with you on something that is
obviously damn urgent,' Henrietta replied.

'Prospecting.'

'So what is it I bring to you when you're concerned with
something so damn urgent?'

Hen's mind was like this: very sure it had things right,
regardless of denials, very stage-by-stage methodical. It could
be a fucking drag. At university, she'd done philosophy. And
yet it was a mind needing reassurance from him, when she
was not away on a private jaunt. He treasured this mark of
dependence in her. 'You bring insight,' he replied.

'Ah, it is damn urgent. Why do you seem so pleased with
everything, then?'

'Because you're here.'

She turned so he could look at her profile against the
window and shadowy Wiltshire landscape. He liked that. He
felt a certainty this sales mission would work – not at once,
obviously: he did not expect to return with a purchase agreed;
but there would be a beginning and the rest must come. He
exulted. The history of the Bay would never contain his
name, but that was all right. He would know it should, and
his children would know, too, because Henrietta and he

would tell them, when children arrived. This was the thing about being an entrepreneur: the sudden helpings of zooming happiness it brought Corbett. These came not just because he could please Henrietta with the invitation, though that did count. No, the happiness, plus a wonderful excitement, were at the core of his job, part of it. Often, these would be powerful enough to wipe out for a while the stress and terrors his profession also carried. Oh, Jesus, yes, it did carry them, too.

Of course, in a sense the terror increased his excitement. After all, he was on his way now to see people about a possible millions-on-millions deal to do with magnificent properties familiar everywhere, through God knew how many media features on waterside renewal, architectural experiment, social transformation and brilliant civic progress. He might still think of himself as only a step up from a messenger boy, if that, but this messenger boy had uniqueness. This messenger boy was trusted to handle, utterly solo, the massive affairs of a truly world-eminent lout like Sid Hyson, and his strangely gifted old rough-house wife. No wonder Jule had felt so good during the lunch and during his walk at the lagoon and since.

All right, so he had to report to those couple of thug cruds, Marv and Jacob, twice a week. He was on a leash. Twice a damn week, like on bail! But could they have done this actual business themselves? Could they arseholes. Subtlety? Probably they'd heard of it – he didn't want to be unjust – but they would not actually recognise subtlety if it flew past them and waggled its wings. It offended him that someone as sickening as Jacob should have a Biblical name. Those two were good for threats and for nodding like minions at whatever Sid said, and for possibly knocking over with finality Hen's lover boys. Corbett would have to get the names of her admirers out of Henrietta and warn them, perhaps tell them to go abroad for a while. God, some job for a husband: "Look, excuse me, gents, but Henrietta Corbett is my wife. You recall having it away with Henrietta? Please, please, watch your backs. I fret about you." He did not want them dead or even badly disabled. That could only bring difficulty on Corbett, either from the police or from Henrietta. Gloria thought something that resembled jealous revenge might improve his status with Hen. No. She was more likely to be grieved and angry; an endless, very focused anger. 'You're not going to tell me what's so damn urgent?' she said.

'Prospecting. Feeling out.'

'I like it when you're secretive,' Henrietta said. 'It makes you seem strong. I say to myself then…' Her voice grew thin. 'This is sort of harsh, Jule, I admit… but I say to myself then, when I see you so strong and solid, I say to myself that none of them would ever hurt or kill you, you're too major to the scene.'

'With your help, Hen.'

'I don't even know what it's all about.'

'With your help, Hen.'

Corbett must not let any of his worries spoil the London outing now. There might still be time to deal with all of it after this trip, depending on how ready Marv and Jacob were for the hunt back in Cardiff. Marv was probably the more savage one; white, smaller than Jacob, edgier. One thing, if they saw off Hen's longcocks while she and Corbett were in London, Henrietta would at least know he could not have done it, and so would the police. Corbett never regretted marrying Hen, no matter what cruel dilemmas she brought. He had always wanted a woman with her own powerful identity and fire. These shone from her.

'Are you too major to be hurt, Jule?'

'I'm getting there. We're getting there. I don't like speaking of myself without you, Hen.'

'Will you get there before?'

'Before what?'

She had been facing him in the carriage but turned away once more now towards the window, not to give him the profile but because she obviously felt sensitive again about what she was going to say. Occasionally she could be like this, so much more than just raw mouth. At these times, he thought her firm, jutting, perfectly symmetrical features partly disguised a supreme tenderness. 'Before they hurt or kill you,' she replied. 'I think of Boris Lowndes.'

'Oh, Boris. Clumsy.' He stroked Hen's back through her clothes as earlier, to show he valued her anxiety. She did not press back, seemed weakened by her thoughts. He quite liked the dominance that sitting on information gave him. It was probably best she did not know what the urgency was. Henrietta had never been good at silence, except about the fancy chums she left him now and then, to fuck. Back at work in a day or two she might gossip. Sidney would be damned upset if he started hearing rumours around the Bay that he meant to quit. He would guess how it happened.

Corbett had the use of Hyson's London flat in Knightsbridge. At a rush, they dumped their luggage, then went straight out. Henrietta loved the theatre and she had managed to get them seats in a West End revival of the Harold Pinter play, *No Man's Land*. Did she understand what the words meant to Corbett? No Man's Land was where he lived. No Man's Fucking Land. He felt a kind of awe and gratitude for how thoroughly she seemed to know him. There were deliberate, long pauses in the play's dialogue. Bored during one of them, he put his mouth close to Henrietta's ear and said: 'Sid Hyson wants out. He's looking for a buyer.'

'Darling,' Henrietta replied, 'your responsibility? You have to find someone?'

'My kind of job.' It was not just the tedium of the play's silences that made him blurt. He had found he could not block secrets off from her after all. It felt like treachery. He would ask her to keep quiet but bugger it if she did gab: once you started talking possible deals with people, leaks could come from anywhere. Secrets gave him dominance, yes, but he was not used to that with Hen, and now had decided he disliked it. If there was a superiority for one of them it had to be Hen's. Always, she led. This was a play about power battles: fine for drama, not for a marriage.

Henrietta said: 'The urgency, you see! I knew I had read things right.'

Talk and action on the stage abruptly resumed. People around them in the theatre began to shush her. She turned on an oldish Japanese man sitting behind. 'Fuck off, you skinny tourist bastard,' she said. 'This is important.' She switched back to Corbett: 'Wants out why?'

'I'll tell you later,' he whispered. He did not mind this play too much. As the words were on the go again it might be clever to listen.

'No, say now,' Henrietta replied.

'The water,' Corbett said.

'Ah, that smart old schemer. The famous table?'

'Plus sluices.'

'Please, silence.'

'This is the big one for you then, Jule?' Henrietta said.

'For us,' he said.

'Terrific,' she replied. 'You can sell it. My own Jule. Mud, anything. You know my mood now?'

'What?'

'I want to fuck you. There's an aura to you, Jule. I need it aboard.'

'Fuck, fuck, always fuck,' the Japanese man muttered.

'Later,' Corbett said.

'Would I mean now, here?' she cried, laughing.

'I don't know,' Corbett replied.

This was the sort of dazzling uncertainty with Hen that always got to Corbett, made him prize her. She was unreadable, irreplaceable. Someone from a distant culture, say Oriental, might not know how to appreciate her fully. Understanding Pinter must be tricky enough. Stage dialogue set the audience laughing suddenly and Henrietta looked about and smiled. Probably she thought they'd heard her and were as amused as she at the saucy notion of a blatant, total shag in the crowded stalls while a modern classic was on and the auditorium rich in overseas visitors.

*

In the morning, Corbett would have liked to take Hen with him to see people at one of the companies he had shortlisted, but this was impossible. Although her wisdom and quickness of brain might be important to Corbett, she would have no standing with the developer he was visiting, and they would decline to talk essentials in her presence. They would not understand, and would not want to understand, why she was with him. Her kind of charm might not reach them. In any case, he disliked drawing attention to Henrietta. Negotiations like these could turn dangerous. It was stupid to let the powerful see who was dear to you and possibly make her a target. Of course, some in the business knew of her, anyway. Corbett had not much liked the way Sid and Gloria insistently talked about her. He judged the repetition to be an oblique threat. Most threats in this work were oblique, until the final one.

Henrietta accepted that she could not accompany Jule and said she would have a session at the shops and then possibly look in at the Chardin exhibition. She approved of Chardin's still-life groupings and the use of shade. Corbett took a taxi to the Holborn offices of Ivo Vartelm. Jule knew what the difficulties were. Naturally he did. Ivo had wanted to develop in the Bay from the very start, and before the very start, back in the early nineties. He had tried to buy Corbett's help then and, obviously, Jule had been courteous and friendly, but he was already commissioned by Sid and Gloria and had, in fact, believed Sid and Gloria and the Complex were the best prospect for the Bay. Although he had listened to Ivo's proposals, as he had listened to the proposals of other would-be participants, he put his chief effort and influence behind Sid and Gloria. He still thought he had been right. The Complex was complete and looked brilliant. He had known Sid's money was dodgy but Ivo's money had appeared dodgier, from what Corbett had been able to discover about it; likewise the capital of another main contender, Philip Castice-Manne. The kind of people who sought out Corbett for aid were always liable to have rocky and impenetrably

mysterious capital. Choose the least chaotic. The term middleman signified more than putting one business head in
touch with another. In the areas where Corbett worked, the
law sometimes had a look-in, but sometimes not at all. He
moved between legitimacy and banditry: another meaning
for No Man's Land. Nobody equalled his sly skills.

Corbett found it bracing now to cross the wide pavement
to the stately entrance of a mock brick office block where
Ivo had his quarters on two complete floors. In the road,
almost every other car seemed a luxury job: Daimlers,
Bentleys, Mercs. Corbett was proud to have a part in this
scene, and a decent part, not just walk-on. His breathing
was so excited it burned his chest. He wished Hen could see
him. At the same time, he realised Ivo might still detest him
for favouring someone else when the Bay was young. If
there been more time, Jule would certainly have looked
around to find new likelies. But when you were instructed
by Sid, best act at the pace he expected, or he might decide
you were neglecting him and perhaps deceiving him. He
could be sudden then. With Boris he had been sudden.
Corbett needed to get to companies he knew were interested, or had been.

In one way, people like Sid and Ivo and Philip Castice-
Manne were themselves also middlemen, inhabiting this
vague, wide region between raw criminality and the almost-
OK. They directed things from fine dens – like Sid's in the
Complex or Ivo's here in Holborn – and built magnificent
properties which revitalised derelict urban areas. They had a
great yearning to be above board and probably thought they
were on the way to it. But part of the money they used at this
stage came from God knew where: drug trading, protection,
porn, robbery of some kind or another, and not necessarily a
subtle kind. Their office suites were show-places, testaments
to respected business triumphs, but they could call on brutal
hood help if things looked to be going wrong. Ivo had that
kind of back-up, in the same way as Sid and Castice-Manne.
If Corbett came to seem treacherous to Ivo – treacherous

again, in his view – Corbett might be in peril. These were serious, thoughtful business folk.

Corbett said: 'Yes, Ivo, the Complex. This is – I mean, at this stage – this is wholly unofficial. It's even possible I'm right out of order, but I pick up this intimation – and no more than an intimation, I mean, at this point – I pick up this intimation that Sid, by which I mean Sid and Gloria – which is important to be clear about, as you know, she having big, undefined influence – an intimation that Sid and Gloria might be feeling some restlessness.' He knew his words were tumbling a bit. His nerves would ease back soon. 'This is a personal intuition of mine and fallible, fallible, fallible. Oh, "intimations", "intuitions"; you'll ask what the hell is all this about, anyway, and are we in the shifty land of wool and concealment? And yet, intimations, intuitions – these are not totally to be despised, I think you'll agree, Ivo. In fact, some would argue it is in the realm of guesswork and uncertainty that the truly great business decisions are made – decisions ahead of the certainties and therefore ahead of the competition.'

'Restlessness?' Ivo Vartelm replied.

'Sid's a great man, clearly, but not used to long-term captaincy of a project.'

'You kept me and mine out of that sodding Bay, Julian.'

Corbett waved a hand, as if to brush away the charge, and as if to beckon sense. 'I realise it could appear like that, Ivo, appear and appear only. Oh, yes. It's really a misunderstanding, believe me. All my influence was behind you, but – look, in a way it's damned humiliating to say this, undermines my status – but I admit my influence was limited. I could recommend, I could to some extent lobby, and I did, rest assured of that. What I could not do was make decisions, or you and your companies would be installed there now. I still don't know where Sid Hyson put his pressure, or if it was legal, or even if it was bloodless, but it was pressure that worked. I have to say it, Sid was irresistible then. No longer.'

'When you rang asking for a meeting today, do you know what I thought, Julian?'

'Well, I imagine you'd—'

'I thought: Some fabulous fucking nerve after the way he betrayed me at the—'

'No, not betrayed, never, Ivo. I can't allow that word. Would I, after all the—'

Vartelm said: 'Maybe scared shitless by Hyson.'

'Sid Hyson is, admittedly, formidable, but I think you know Julian Corbett better than—'

'And to a degree I can understand that,' Vartelm replied. 'You smoothed the way for him and picked up your nice, ribbon-tied package.'

'I hope I've never acted out of fear, Ivo. I hope I've always preserved my integrity.'

'What symptoms?' Vartelm asked.

'Of what, Ivo?'

'Symptoms of this restlessness.'

'I know him well, have had many chances to observe him well.'

'Sure you know him well. You hear me argue? That's why he's in the Bay and I'm not.'

'Body language,' Corbett replied. 'The odd word. The odd glance at Gloria.'

'I heard he's like an emperor down there – penthouse, yachting shoes, tropical plants.'

'The Gloria Project is certainly prime,' Corbett said.

'So what body language? Are you talking about Boris Lowndes in the fucking water. That body?'

'Everything's gone exactly to forecast, commercially speaking,' Corbett replied, 'and yet – oh, a slight but developing stoop, as if things are too much. That's what I mean, Ivo; he's not used to this kind of role. Others would relish it, as a constant challenge and stimulant. You would, for instance, I'm wholly certain of that.'

'So you shut me out.'

'Not I, Ivo. Whenever I spoke of you in the pre-contract

period – and this was at every chance I had – it was your durability I stressed, among other strengths, naturally. I told
people the Bay was not some PR scheme that could be
brought into being by a bit of spin and flash and then left to
look after itself. I said when it came to durability, look at your
track record. But Sid could mobilise all kinds of leverage. I
don't mean just local. Westminster? Sid had an acceptable
aspect to him. Has even now.'

Ivo was still youngish, say forty-three or -four, smooth-
skinned, bald, placid-looking but unplacid, small-eyed,
small-nosed, small-mouthed, big-chinned. Neither Chardin
nor any other artist would risk drawing a face like this
because the finished work would look like a composite of at
least two people, possibly more, and done on different days.
There was an unpredictability to Ivo, as if he had two or three
internal engines to match his two of three faces. He wore
casuals most of the time. Today, he had on a magenta tracksuit top, with some kind of emblem at the breast – perhaps a
javelin in flight – navy combat trousers and suede desert
boots. They talked in Ivo's minimally furnished suite at the
top of a tower block up towards Farringdon street. From
here, Ivo ran operations in Manchester and Liverpool, possibly Birmingham too, and perhaps London itself. It might be
clubs and/or the protection of clubs, possible video porn and
print porn, plus, of course, the basic drug trading. Corbett
had done as much inquiring as he could when Ivo first
approached him back at the beginning, but the information
was not on a plate and you didn't push too hard. That was
nearly a decade ago. His network might be wider and bigger
now. Corbett did not believe it was smaller, and so he gave Ivo
priority. This was a considerable man: expansion and
absolutely no jail during almost ten years.

'The lot?' Vartelm said.

'What?'

'He wants to dump the lot? Not just slimming down –
looking for someone to take the dud bits? That fucking dead-
loss fucking greenhouse.'

'An impression, as I said, Ivo, and only that. But I feel he regards the Complex as very much a unit.'

'Some old folks' refuge there, too, I heard.'

'A nursing home, right up to date.'

'How close to the water?'

'Water?'

'This is a lakeside development, yes? How it's advertised, the Bay. There's tide out there, isn't there – waves, all the usual?'

'Lovely lakeside views, yes. Some real visionary planning.'

'That's one thing about a penthouse,' Vartelm replied.

'What, Ivo?'

'They'd be above it.'

'What?'

'The tide. Helicopter takes them off the roof,' Ivo replied. 'Could Gloria get up to the roof, those old legs?'

Most probably his name was not really Ivo. Although Corbett had never done deep research on Vartelm because of the danger, he looked more like a Neville or a Vernon. His eyes were right for a Neville or a Vernon. 'My own assessment – again very unofficial, Ivo: Sidney's under-financed.'

Ivo was the sort of high-grade name you saw in Court Circulars and big funerals when someone stood in for the Queen. Vartelm could have lifted it. A name like that would be useful every time he needed investment capital. People would think he knew dukes and had old-fashioned integrity. Many folk longed to believe the best. Crookedness wouldn't get anywhere otherwise.

Corbett said: 'Loans to Sid being called in?' It was good Vartelm wanted a name that seemed to make him time-honoured and bursting with repute. This showed depth. It had to be possible that one day he, or more likely his great-grand-children, might corner repute. 'Everything in the Complex is working beautifully – the hotel booked right up, all the mall franchised, the nursing home with a waiting list from loaded chronics, the casino, very professional – so there's beautiful, multi-source, long-term income, but if someone's under-financed to start, or borrowing from off-Broadway banks that are up and down themselves, there could be a squeeze on Sid.'

Of course, Corbett would not be talking to Ivo now if he were already bursting with real repute. Only very rarely did Jule get to deal with people like that, and he felt uncomfortable when it happened. They seemed to sense something off-colour in him and, because he was so damn sensitive, he could sense them sensing it. This affected his poise.

'When I say Sid's restless, Ivo, one thing I mean is literally that – broken sleep for thinking about the bailiffs. But nobody would want to let it go that far because, all right, it might be knock-down cheap if there were complete financial collapse, but then a swarm is after it, and the Complex would be let go in bits. A serious buyer, in my view, wants the glow and prestige, a very real prestige, which comes with ownership of a complete project. I think it's fair to say you recognised very early the… well, position and dignity that's attached to a unified, substantial holding in the Bay, but were unfortunately thwarted at the last moment.'

'I never got a fucking look-in. You know that. Hyson, Philip Castice-Manne – these were the ones you pushed for.'

'Ah, yes, there's Philip.'

'You're seeing him as well about this?'

'About the Gloria Complex?'

'Don't piss me about, Julian.' It was spoken without too much malice, almost deadpan, a kind of weariness built in.

'Philip already has his stakes in the Bay, elsewhere.'

'Of course he has. You fucking put him there. Are you going to ask him if he'd like to buy Sid's Complex on the profits?'

'I—'

'Listen, you won't suck me into some damn auction, Jule. You trying to play me against Castice-Manne?'

'Didn't I think of you at once, Ivo? Didn't I come here straight off?'

'Did you? Did you?'

'That's what I meant by intuitions, impressions. I've sought you out urgently, Ivo, while all I have is suspicions about Sid's intentions, so you – if it's still your wish, obviously – depending on your judgment and current situation, clearly – but if it's still your wish and is in line with your current situation – so you could begin thinking about this early and making such provisions as might seem appropriate.'

Corbett judged the timing of that – the 'current situation' references – to be sweetly right. It meant: Could Ivo Vartelm and associates raise the money? This turned the talk away now from potentially vicious water and tide, and away from the blame Vartelm wanted to load on Corbett for allegedly keeping him out of the Bay first time around. Well, not allegedly. Corbett was saying to him: and Vartelm would know Corbett was saying to him, Never mind the pique and shows of doubt, can you and yours get the price together, and if not I'll move on to Castice-Manne or play it even wider? Ivo must know Corbett would not be fooled by the Ivoism of Ivo's name – all that supposed built-in class.

Always there was due pace to deals of this kind. You took the scepticism and the shit for a while from someone like Ivo so as to let a bit of confidence build in the dim, profitable sod, and then you started gently to kick the confidence away, so gently that chummy hardly knew it was happening. Are you a player, old chummy, or just a big-mouth spectator? Is your interest real? Ivo was jumped-up and sensitive about being jumped-up, unlike many these days. Of course, he knew he was not old money, but at the very least he would want to be thought genuinely jumped-up. Any suggestion that he might not be able to raise funds – either personal cash or from trusting backers – would infuriate him. Ivo did feature in the Sunday Times list, but very near the tail. Corbett found it touching to observe the confusion and would-be rage in his pink and healthy features now. This bluster-boy would never cope with someone like Jule. Corbett said: 'Obviously, my anxiety is that some party I might know nothing of gets a hint the Complex is for sale and decides to move.'

'You mean Castice-Manne?'

'A superior, variegated site, already in great running order, doesn't come up often in the Bay. Never. Not necessarily Castice-Manne. I was thinking more of, say... well, say European or city of London or Irish interests – lots of money around Dublin these days, buying control of our newspapers, God knows what – interests with no... no, well background, Ivo.'

'Background?'

'These would be firms with impeccable records.'

'Totally clean?'

'It has to be possible, Ivo. They wouldn't be on their own. Many, even most, firms in the Bay have nothing suspect in their history. Nothing discoverable or provable.'

'Smart fucking sods. They know how to spin. They know how to draw veils and keep them drawn. They know exactly where to put their backhanders.'

Corbett nodded, to show he understood about competition. 'We can counter them, Ivo, as long as we don't delay. I hope I find my way about the Bay scene better than most. Well, I do find my way about that scene. It's how I manage to be here, telling you so early of this opportunity, isn't it, Ivo?' More tactics, that 'we.' It said he and Ivo were already allies, had formed a new team. Corbett could watch himself use these skills and could analyse them, but this did not mean he despised them, nor himself for employing them. They were positive. They concerned the wellbeing of a fine development, the Gloria Complex, which brought daring architectural brilliance, jobs, hospital care and botanical distinction to the Bay. It was how business had to be done. He was a salesman but also a visionary, part of a bold, creative force. Yes. Hen recognised this in him sometimes. Basically, she did admire him. He was convinced of it. She and he knew the Bay needed Corbett, and he was proud to be of use. His skills were even more vital now Boris Lowndes had been removed like that. Although Hen teased Jule, he was sure she appreciated his guts in not allowing the death to unsettle him.

Her regard for Jule would swoop almost devastatingly sometimes. After the play last night, when they were back in Sid's flat, she wanted to fuck standing and with nearly all their clothes on, although three beds were available. This fuck was urgency and based on one she revered in The Godfather, when Sonny Corleone has a bridesmaid against the bathroom door at his sister's wedding: you could see where the word banging came from. Hen needed Corbett's strength on show last night, his 'warrior mode' as she called it. She jumped up with her legs around his waist and he clasped her buttocks, taking her weight on his palms. He knew she wanted everything of him rigid, not just his dick but his back, arms, legs as they supported two writhing people, also his neck and shoulders which she clung to. He was her hard man for now, her through-and-through man, the man she might mock occasionally and often betray, but ultimately and always her man of abiding efficacy who would come in from his no-man's land and be her man, her man. That was how he had seen it, screwing against Sid's wall like kids in a lane or a young James Caan in the bathroom. The walls were duck-egg blue wash. Hen and he were beneath a framed still-life that had looked to Corbett as if it might be something genuine and, all right, maybe even Chardin. Sid had a lot of advisers. This painting could be worth tens of thousands, even more. It would be entirely like Sid to let a business colleague use his place regardless of valuables there. Now and then he could show a holy disdain for possessions. Small-mindedness he loathed. Perhaps Boris Lowndes had shown small-mindedness. As well as his admiration for Cary Grant, Sid had once or twice told Jule he fancied life as a monk. Just the same, he would want his price for the Gloria Complex.

Everyone had personality fluctuations. Behind his miniature desk, Vartelm began to chuckle suddenly. This was how it could be – one of those other Ivos was breaking through, or perhaps a Neville or Vernon.

'You handle things damn well, Jule,' he said. It was a comrade talking to a comrade, someone who saw Corbett's problems and sympathised, might even help. 'You come in here alone, unafraid. It doesn't matter to you that you pissed on me and my hopes last time. This is coolness, Jule.'

'I come because I might be able to correct an obvious wrong, Ivo. It wasn't my doing, not in the least, that you were overlooked, but I knew of the disappointment, clearly, and here was a chance to rectify. That's my opinion.'

'I've always appreciated you, Jule.'

'Thanks, Ivo.'

'In a hell of a tricky occupation you maintain openness.'

'Thanks, Ivo.'

'I say to myself: This is someone I can do deals with.'

'My own feeling about you, Ivo. With some others I might have been... I might have been hesitant in coming back. There could have been childish but real and bitter resentment.' When these changes in Ivo turned up you had to adjust, get the new tone fast.

Vartelm said: 'A useless feeling, I always say – resentment.'

'Unconstructive.'

'The word.'

'So negative,' Corbett replied.

'I'm going to ask some colleagues to join us. Do you think that's reasonable, Jule, and positive?'

'Now? These will be colleagues of what kind of—'

'I believe in discussion within our companies,' Ivo said.

'Oh, certainly.'

'Colleagues with responsibilities for very specific areas in our business structure.'

'Discussion is obviously fine,' Corbett replied, 'but—'

'Time. You're thinking of time, Jule.'

'The need for speed. I'd hate to see you lose an opening at the Bay again.'

'We're counting on you – my colleagues and myself, Jule – we know you wouldn't let anything like that occur once more. And Henrietta – how's dear Henrietta? She's a boon to you, Jule, anybody can see that.'

3

'So here's Jule Corbett,' Ivo said, his voice loud and companionable and worrying. 'Laura, Peter, he'll be new to both of you. Not to me, obviously. New to you face to face, I mean. You'll have heard of Jule, I know. But that deceitful little chapter involving the first Complex bids would be before your time with the companies. Jule is very close to Sid Hyson now.'

Corbett saw he would have to look after himself here, every step. That was all right. That was the career: if he'd wanted safety he would have become a lion-tamer. 'Well, I wouldn't say close, Ivo,' he replied gently. 'And certainly not *very* close. In contact with. It's a matter of geography as much as anything.'

'I'd say close,' Ivo answered. 'Very.'

'Location. Neighbours in the Bay,' Corbett answered. 'The sort of village.'

'I don't think it's an exaggeration to say Sid prizes him,' Ivo replied. 'And understandably.'

'I expect I'm useful now and then,' Corbett said. 'A consultative capacity.'

'Useful now,' Ivo replied.

Corbett said: 'Oh, I'm acting without Sid's—'

'And useful then, too,' Ivo said. 'The first contracts.'

'This must have been such an exciting period,' Laura replied. 'Forefathering.'

'The making of Jule,' Ivo said. 'Would you say the making of you, Jule?'

Corbett had a smile. 'If so I haven't noticed.'

'Plus there's his very remarkable wife,' Ivo said. 'When you think of Jule you have to think of her as well, isn't that so, Jule?'

'Is it Henrietta?' Peter asked. He seemed to glance at a notebook, an old scaring dodge.

'You've been browsing the file, have you, Pete?' Ivo said, a sort of naughty-naughty tone to his voice. 'She's always there to back Jule. Almost always there. A definite underlying loyalty if you look deep enough. Jule says he's not close to Sid but he also says he has been observing him lately. From close.'

'Ah,' Laura said. 'This could be interesting. I wonder if you noticed a certain… a certain let's call it restlessness, Jule.'

'Jackpot!' Ivo cried, beaming. 'Laura, my dear, how do you do it? That is exactly what Jule did notice.'

This was set up? He wished he'd done some research himself: on Laura and Pete. He did not mind the looks of Laura, but she was on Ivo's board, so to be regarded as a hazard.

'I'm no magician,' she said. 'It would be natural. Haven't we heard Sid wants to move on, sell?'

'You've got this fucking room bugged, have you, Ivo?' Corbett replied. 'They eavesdropped our earlier chat?'

Ivo said: 'As soon as word reached me that they'd had enough, Sid and Gloria – this is a month ago, five weeks? – anyway, I at once asked Laura to get down there and do a rough evaluation of the Complex, Jule. That seemed ordinary business procedure. I felt I might be asked to offer. And now, lo, a bit late, here you are, Jule.'

'That's impossible,' Corbett replied. 'They've only just decided – if they have. And it's confidential.'

'Laura, love?' Ivo said.

'Yes, about five weeks. I could get my work diary, to check.'

So, who had been leaking, if it was true? Marv? Jacob? Sid? Gloria?

Laura opened a ringbinder on her lap. 'I have to stress that it is rough, Ivo, Jule. This is a walk-around survey only. No floorboards lifted to find if the sea's in the basement yet! And I didn't stay in the hotel. I'm pretty anonymous, I should think, but with someone like Sid and his information service you can never be sure. We didn't want him scenting a possible instant buyer. Up, up, up would go the fucking price. It might reach fifty, even sixty million.'

'Sid's got cheek, even when he's slipping,' Ivo said.

Corbett saw he was being dragged down, down, down, even before the proper money talk started. He was here to begin at somewhere around £180 million and she said under fifty.

'You've been promised real goodies, have you, Jule?' Ivo asked. 'I loathe discussing with someone who's already bought.'

'I'm go-betweening, as ever, that's all. Why?'

'We're going to settle important hopes on you, Jule,' Ivo replied. 'There's a true fee if you can get us accommodated this time.'

Fees? Corbett could wonder sometimes whether he should be above fees. Why didn't anyone ever offer him a slice of the business, a piece of the action? Fees were for hacks.

Ivo said: 'I think you know, Jule, we're the last people who'd want a drift into brutality, either to you or your wife. Gross. We try and try to avoid the Sidney Hyson mode.'

'I bring just a presentation of how things are, Ivo,' Corbett said.

'Laura's actually been in the greenhouses,' Ivo replied. 'Escaped without getting assaulted by one of those man-eating African clematis or such.'

'In some ways quite adequate,' Laura said. 'It would need to be brought up to at least the standard of the Norman Foster bot gardens at Middleton Park in West Wales, or where are we? The Bay job won't draw if it's seen as second string. We won't even talk about the £80 million bubble hothouses for the Lost Gardens of Heligan project in Cornwall. Nowhere near that league. I'd say another big spending on the Gloria greenhouse scheme might get us to respectability. And I'd certainly be prepared to value it as it stands at seven or eight.'

So, what had Corbett expected? Did he think they'd rush to give Sid his capital gains dream figure? Some capital gains and some doesn't. Corbett giggled but very mildly: 'We've got an estimate of £40 million on Sid's botanical gardens.'

'Which "we" is that, Jule?' Ivo asked. 'You and someone you're very close to?'

'When I say "we" – what I mean, obviously… there was a general view that the gardens were at around this worth, even when they were only half stocked,' Corbett replied. 'The structure. Sid knew he had to knock that Middleton Park job out of the picture. Now, all kinds of remarkable stuff from all kinds of jungles and countries are actually growing there; rare, priceless exhibits.'

'I'm not an expert on botanical gardens, I'll give you that,' Laura said.

'Well, exactly,' Corbett replied. 'Which of us is? But I know Sid's had advice and, yes, around the forty.'

'We want you to be reasonable, Jule,' Ivo said. 'You're key in this. We know Sid will listen to you. We'd really like you to explain to him and explain and explain that he's down the fucking chute with this Project and he can't expect generosity, even from friends, and I'd certainly count myself as an eternal friend to Sidney.'

'He couldn't think more highly of you, too, Ivo,' Corbett replied.

'But what we've got to ask, Jule, is: would I take peaceably another attempt by you and your master to shit on me? I honestly don't want to send people looking for you and your wife, Jule, on account of a replica black treachery, if I'm priced out this time instead of just ignored – well, same effect, isn't it? I'm excluded. No, I don't want crude hired hands dogging you. On the contrary, I'd like you to come looking for me with some lovely, sane proposals that you'll guarantee to put with all your influence to Sidney and Gloria. All right, you've made a start, I'll accept that. You called. You're here. Fine. I'm waiting for some of that sanity to show itself, though, Jule. I do not wish, absolutely do not wish, to be pushed into frustration and hatred. Pete could tell you that he and I both detest briefing the contractors we can't avoid using sometimes for dark work. It's tainting, Jule. Distasteful. And you'll ask how can I plan damage to someone I hardly know, except from the dossier – your wife. Probably you'd understand my possible disgust with you if things went askew for me again, but you'll say: Why Henrietta also? And I can't give you an answer to that, but you're right, it is how it is, I'm afraid. Somehow she would seem to share the blame. She's a thinker, isn't she? She's valuable to you.'

'A general lack of grandeur in the bot gardens,' Laura said. She and Pete were sitting on plain, straight-backed wooden chairs. Ivo was behind the desk on another. Corbett had the only armchair in the room.

Laura said: 'What I'd call a suburban tone to things. There's a dignity, a natural dignity, to many of the plants and trees, I wouldn't question that. You're correct to speak of their distinction. But the setting, Jule. The setting is made to seem mean by the very magnificence of what the glasshouses contain, you see. And yet, because of potential, I'd still be willing to go to seven. Yes, even possibly eight.' She studied a page in the ring binder. 'I see I've actually got it noted as "seven plus", which would be my shorthand for seven and a half or at an extreme push, eight. But this would be for Ivo's judgement, clearly. We'd have to keep in mind that it would need at least thirty or forty spent on it to get serious. Would we be buying a forever problem?'

Peter said: 'I don't actually know Sid Hyson, but my feeling is he'd see Laura's point about the greenhouses if someone skilled and tactful put it to him.'

'What I've been trying to say,' Ivo replied. 'You express it much more economically, Pete. Jule is certainly skilled and tactful. He can get people's ears, can't you, Jule?'

'What I've heard about Sid Hyson and read in profiles is that under the roughness there's a basic ability to grasp reality, even when it's not wholly favourable,' Peter said. 'He knows that what he's asking for here is not much more than a salvage operation. We're faced with a possible wreck.'

'The words!' Ivo cried. 'Salvage. Wreck. God but it's humbling to hear one's own thoughts so much better framed.'

'This is someone who's lost faith in his own creation, the Complex,' Pete said. 'That might be wise, given the uncertainties. He'll appreciate he can't get out at anything like the original figure for getting in. That was about a hundred, as I understand.'

'Pete really has been going through the files,' Ivo said. 'We'd like you to talk to Sid for us along these lines, Jule. Urgently. A genial but measured offer.'

Laura said: 'The hotel plus casino are supposed to be around twelve. I've seen that quoted.'

'This was the original, for the buildings alone, without furnishings and its established reputation and goodwill,' Corbett replied.

'The hotel reception area is magnificent, I wouldn't argue,' Laura said.

'Redesigned after the fire,' Corbett said. 'Sid thought the original didn't do justice to Gloria – her name being on the Complex. He guards her dignity. It's touching.'

'Yes, the fire,' Laura said. 'This is a place that has been targeted.'

'Probably an accident,' Corbett replied. 'No arson arrests.'

'A fire like that, a notoriety like that, they're bound to drag down an evaluation, aren't they, Jule?' Laura asked. 'Even if the building itself, apart from the vestibule, wasn't in any case so un-state-of-the-art – those rat-run little corridors and the tired lifts. Enemies know now that it's flammable, and Sid has enemies. I was glad not to be staying there.'

'Views – the hotel outlook is so brilliant,' Corbett replied.

'If you like water and it's water that can be trusted, I agree,' Laura said.

'I don't mind taking on this oldies' coughing Rest Centre if I have to,' Ivo said.

'No, it's a proper nursing home, virtually a hospital, high-grade facilities,' Corbett replied.

'I don't mind doing a service to the aged, but not at a tear-away price, obviously, Jule,' Ivo said.

'In any flooding the shopping mall would get the worst,' Laura said. 'The layout – they could have designed it to welcome an inrush.'

'There'll never be any flooding,' Corbett replied.

'And then we'd have an enormous area virtually derelict,' Laura said. 'Sid and Gloria are not going to stay there, are they, and there'd be no replacements.'

'Which means we've come to a very decent overall figure, Jule,' Ivo said. 'What I like about dealing with Jule is he doesn't arrive here brandishing a price tag, screaming what we've got to pay. That would seem vulgar to him, I know. He can be slimy, sure, and devious, but not vulgar. You'll have noticed this, Laura, Pete. But also he's smart and he's informed. He knows we're cash-rich just now, owing to one or two very productive mergers and business successes generally. Yes, we're looking for investment openings.'

Pete said: 'As I see Sid and Gloria Hyson, they—'

Ivo began a kind of oration; slow, unstoppable, viciously fluent: 'I can imagine the fucker up in that penthouse he created for himself, looking out and down and thinking he would be there for fucking ever, like the sun or Table Mountain, the anorexic jerk. He thinks he's got himself above all the processes of change and decline that affect the rest of us. He'd forget about the fire. He'd think he owned the whole lot, not just the Complex, everything he could see, Channel included, and the islands. That's how he is. Coloniser. He'd build high and believe this brought him personal height and majesty and honour. Oh, I'll love to get him out of there. I'll keep it, the penthouse, even if it's a roaring fucking waste when it could make four or five suites for guests. It will be Ivo Vartelm then gazing from those windows, suitable absolutely to this role because of upbringing, background and flair. I don't know what I'll call it as a Complex, but not fucking Gloria, believe me. Not my own name. Self-promotion I detest.'

Corbett glanced at the other two while Ivo spoke. They looked sympathetic and unshocked. Perhaps they had heard it, or something similar, from Ivo before. Possibly this kind of envy was what drove Ivo's companies and made them work. It had become an obsession for him, had it, this acquisition of the Complex, the rectifying of history, the annihilation of Sid? So, don't knock it. It would not do just to displace Sid. He had to be humiliated financially, obliterated financially, strangled by his borrowing and mortgages. Corbett realised that as many dangers reached out from Vartelm as from that meeting with Hyson. There was the special 'Ivo' concept to cater for: people with that kind of name were not made for defeat, and certainly not defeat twice. Corbett felt stupid now for imagining he could manage Vartelm. There was nobody able to manage Vartelm in his present state, possibly not even Vartelm. Jule wished Henrietta could be here to help him. And yet he also felt relieved she was not here to be stared at and memorised by these people so that a fuller description than they had in their fucking files could be passed on to the day-wage heavies. God, but the threatening was crude. Unreal? Farcical? You couldn't rely on that.

Corbett said: 'This is really an opportunity to place substantial, possibly, well, possibly *difficult* funds into a development that could not have more prestige and spruceness, Ivo,' Corbett said.

'Dry cleaning,' Ivo said, 'as long as the fucking grubby water stays back.'

'I mean funds that are hanging about and perhaps drawing attention, the way cash does, inviting questions about where it came from,' Corbett replied. 'Damned intrusive curiosity everywhere. But a good property portfolio, that's not the same at all. This has a solidity to it – something beyond the solidity of the constructions themselves.'

Peter said: 'The Treasury's getting wised up about laundering.'

'But there's an aura to property, unmatchable,' Corbett

replied. 'Ask some of the lads who've bought bits of Mayfair or Knightsbridge for committing, well, awkward money. The Bay is of that category. And the ownership documentation – the intricacies – so much more difficult to penetrate than a stack of money in accounts. I can understand your urge to disburse. This is classic in my kind of work. I'd like to congratulate you, Ivo, for being in that position – cash-rich.'

'As to a totality, I'd definitely go to £38 million,' Laura said. 'This involves taking the hotel and casino at the full twelve evaluation. That's probably generous, but we could recover it all, given superb management and no water devastation. I can itemise, if you like. Twelve for the hotel and casino, say eight for the botanicals, seven the nursing home, one the heliport, ten the mall.' She would be about fifty, round-faced, her hair in an oh-let-it-go-grey, apparently insecure mound, her eyes large, steady and untroubled. Her skin was smooth and youthful, troubling under the grey hair. Corbett felt convinced she had never done time. Peter, a little younger, seemed also free of jailhouse shade, and Corbett knew that Ivo himself had no record. These were accomplished folk. They knew how to delegate anything dubious.

Peter said: 'I have the feeling Jule's not impressed with your global figure, Laura.' He was small, thinnish, wearing pale-framed spectacles. He blinked a good deal. Corbett thought it was supposed to be disarming so he kept sharp.

'Did you have a figure, Jule?' Ivo asked. 'Did you and Sid have a figure?'

'I jumped on a train, that was all, Ivo.'

'But maybe some figure in the air down there – the buzz. You mentioned gossip about the botanical gardens and its price. A mad idea, yes, but if it's around there's probably a sum-up figure, too. Mad as well?'

'No, nothing of that sort,' Corbett replied. 'Clearly, Sid and Gloria will reach a figure, if what I hear about their wish to sell is confirmed.'

'I'll confirm it,' Ivo replied.

'I've certainly been no party to that kind of discussion,' Corbett said.

'Good,' Ivo replied. 'It gives us a nice open situation to start from.'

4

Now and then, when Corbett was up in London alone on business missions, he had been taken out as a facility by the men he was visiting to what were known as 'afternoon girls'. He felt the need of an afternoon girl now. It was a particular taste. The meeting with Ivo, Laura and Pete had elated him at times and crushed him at times. Mostly, though, elation: Corbett never stayed crushed for long. He believed in his education and drive. His mother used to say Julian always came up smiling. He would wonder if it made him sound like a moron.

He wanted to share his triumphant mood now with a girl, and he wanted the girl to give him admiration for his good humour, clothes, his body, probable wealth and easy-going charm. These afternoon girls were ready with such a response. Didn't they live by it? Their scents and lotions seemed to get into his veins and make them bristle. The girls had to assume that men who could take time off in the middle of the day to see them must be established pretty well. He wished his nails were better shaped. Manicures he did not go for, but perhaps he should. Afternoon girls were an exceptional group: elegant and caring, uncoarse. He hated roughness in women. Sometimes Hen upset him with her systematic swearing. Her big teeth flashed like neon when she said 'fucking.'

There had been no suggestion from Ivo that they should go out together to girls. He had not even proposed lunch. By this, the snobby sod might want to suggest he lunched regularly at a sensationally OK gentlemen's club such as White's or the Carlton and did not wish to be seen with someone from the darker end of business, however decently dressed. It showed how shaky Ivo's social confidence was, the bonny nouveau prick. Corbett would make his way alone. He had more than one address, all in very fine streets; streets where almost any man would be proud to get close to a responsive girl.

His arrangement with Henrietta was that they should meet for tea at the Connaught hotel at five, so she could have a long saunter around the galleries and shops before. She liked the Connaught for its good furnishings and the many unnoisy Americans in outstanding leisure clothes who stayed there. It excited her to name the Connaught to a taxi driver. She always pronounced the 't' at the end very heavily, as if to repel argument.

Corbett should easily be able to make it for five o'clock and would still have some of his elation then, perhaps even more. He was approaching a pretty large decision about the future and he might want to break it to Henrietta. Or, at least, he thought he was approaching a decision. It contained some hazards. This process began soon after he left Ivo and the other two and let his mind go thoroughly, bit by bit, over the contents of that meeting. The conference with Sid and Gloria also had a bearing, of course. Obviously, he would not discuss something major and confidential like this with the afternoon girl, or possibly more than one if things grew really high-spirited, but not more than two. The talk would be happy and general. Conversation in detail about his possible new plans must be for a wife only, a valued and frequently helpful wife, as Vartelm had suggested in his dark way. Corbett was delighted he had brought Hen to London with him this time. They might need to stay at least one extra day while he carried out further negotiations; negotiations of a completely different sort. She could telephone her office and let them know.

Corbett did not expect to be remembered at Omdurman, the large house in Kensington which he set out for by cab now, the preferred one on his list. It would be comically arrogant to think he had made an impression on the management or girls there during earlier calls. This house had a portico.

The girls probably changed about quite often, and it was months since Corbett and London contacts last visited. In a house like this, staff would see many men of Corbett's kind: youngish, audacious, fit, successful. He loathed places where the girls were already half-undressed when you arrived. It was discourteous, screaming the reasons for a man's visit. At Omdurman the girls sat in a good, well-lit, square reception hall and wore fashionable clothes. Garments like this, as well as the girls themselves, could burnish Corbett's soul. He did not ask for formality but he liked procedures and thought appearances certainly mattered. He felt sure that if you asked any of these girls she would know that the name of this house referred back to a battle in the North Africa region when Britain was still unquestionably great, a name probably attached to this Edwardian property from the start. These afternoon girls were like that: always ready with conversation and knowledge. He prized such qualities in any woman. Hen was wonderful at both. More and more women seemed capable of sensible conversation these days. It pleased him. Why should women have to talk only about garments and kitchen layouts? Afternoon girls tended to be students who could arrange their academic work so they had daytime hours free to do a stint at Omdurman, or single mothers, or partnered mothers whose children were at school or nursery during Omdurman spells and whose menfolk were at work.

Almost at once this afternoon at Omdurman, Corbett saw a girl he remembered from last time or the time before. She was in blue and this suited her brilliantly. Blue, he thought, always brought an admirable coolness to a woman, and yet the richness of the colour could also suggest good, hidden vitality. It thrilled him to realise the girl did after all remember him, too. Her eyes brightened and she raised a hand and waved, a small but very genuine sign. 'Julian,' she said. It was not a question.

'Why, Grace,' he replied. He liked the plainness of her name. In places like Omdurman, girls would give themselves all sorts of ludicrously extravagant names, as if that increased mystery: Cora, Velda, Zelda, Cordelia, Persephone. Corbett went to sit by her. He thought two or three of the other girls looked disappointed. Unfortunate. Grace was exactly the sort of girl he had come here to see. He felt he knew her so well and she him that it would be heartless to continue mooting a threesome. Her Red scent jostled his balls. He was wearing a custom-made navy pinstripe suit, one of four outfits he had ordered and been fitted for on previous London trips. He thought he was probably in one of the others last time he met Grace, possibly dark grey. She would remember it. Perhaps she had even spoken of it then. These were girls who would know a fine, non-reach-me-down suit in best wool. It was great that she'd see he had more than one of this calibre: that such clothes might be usual wear for him, rather than just special-days showpieces. Not too long ago Corbett used to go to multiples for his clothes, but lately he had begun to believe in quality. He'd worn a handmade suit, of course, when calling on Sid and Gloria in the penthouse the other day.

It had been a lovely impulse to come to Omdurman. He felt he had a kind of stature. These days he let his hair grow longish and it was brushed back almost straight over his ears. There had been no difficulty getting into Omdurman, though he did not think the people on the door had recognised him. What they recognised as he stood relaxed in the portico was that he shimmered with a natural entitlement to admittance, an obvious rightness. It might be part the suit but also part his manner and dauntless selfhood.

'Julian, I was thinking of you only last week, yes,' the girl said, excitedly, '— well, I think of you often, naturally – we all do – but last week we were watching on television a programme about botanical gardens, one in Cornwall, one somewhere in South West Wales and one in Cardiff Bay, which I remembered was your patch, you told me, and you mentioned a Complex you'd helped create had a botanical gardens, and suddenly there it was, on the screen. So beautiful and interesting. I felt sort of sort of amazingly proud, yes, proud, to know somebody connected with it. And the cost! They said maybe £40 million!'

Yes, fucking maybe.

'I thought this is really something to know someone who's into deals worth 40 mill, Julian.'

She was talking quite loudly and the figure caused a flutter among the other girls. A couple of them seemed automatically to loosen their legs. There was much more to these girls than good limbs and bodies and an awareness of money, but they were aware of money, probably. Corbett said: 'Property values – they just soar, particularly when there's a degree of architectural distinction.'

'Which there is,' Grace replied.

'Oh, yes. I don't touch developments that lack beauty – beauty and… yes… daring, no matter what the fee. I couldn't.'

'Daring, oh, yes, Julian, I said daring when I saw those soaring greenhouses.'

Corbett said: 'Daring – to be associated with something daring makes the mind sing.'

'The responsibility!' Grace replied. 'And yet you're so untroubled. Happy. So young.'

'It's the only way to be. Untroubled, I mean. Happy. Can't control the other, can we? Keep ahead of things, keep ahead, keep ahead, and you'll always be untroubled and happy. That's my philosophy.' A couple of hours ago, less, he was with people who believed he, personally, could bridge a price difference for them between £38 million and something like £200 million. Of course, Ivo and Laura and Pete would not know this figure – or would they? They knew a hell of a fucking lot, so they said – but, anyway, they'd certainly know there was a mighty gap between what they'd told him they could offer and what Sid would want. They made their pitch madly low, just as Sid's might be madly high, because they had faith in Jule somehow to find a compromise. This was a terrifying fucking commission. But it was also a gorgeously flattering commission. Ivo believed in him, just as Sid and

Gloria did. They revered his powers. No wonder Grace could sense the ferocious glow in him. And the other girls had noticed it, too, he was sure of that. Girls like this would never go in for the sort of evil teasing and belittling that Hen liked now and then, especially when Jule felt especially strong. Elated. Hen was lovely and clever and there were times when he considered giving up for ever girls like these because of the disloyalty to her and disease risk, yet there were difficulties with Hen – he could not always draw what he wanted from her. He hated negativeness in life. Wasn't he entitled to due recognition? She wandered a bit herself, but Jule did not turn to other girls as mere retaliation. Simply, he needed due, unalloyed recognition now and then. It did not matter that his time here had to be paid for, at Omdurman's damned pricey rates. He was sure these girls, or at least some of them, would be won by him even if no money were involved. Style could accomplish so much. Even while talking to Grace, it almost unnerved Corbett suddenly to get a mind-picture of Hen's body, washed up on a pebble beach in office clothes.

Upstairs, Grace was delightful with Jule, admiring the symmetry of his shoulders, his strong but by no means gross neck, and the fineness of his nose and cheek bones. He liked the room. It was wide and light, the floor done with thin, gold-coloured, varnished boards. There were small vivid rugs, possibly Egyptian, on each side of the bed. These rugs seemed exactly harmonious with a house called Omdurman, referring back to that battle more than a hundred years ago when Kitchener reclaimed the Sudan for Egypt. Out of her surplus brilliance, Britain could handle such deeds on other countries' behalf in those days. All that was over now, obviously, but Corbett liked to think of himself as connected to such a stout tradition. The furniture in this room was all Victorian and mainly mahogany. This also seemed suitable for such a room and such a property. The mattress and springs of the bed were modern, of course, but the head- and foot-boards looked genuinely old and also mahogany.

It was the same room he used with Grace the last two times he visited, and Jule felt thrilled about that. The Omdurman management were sensitive. To have the room as a fixed feature gave the connection with Grace a kind of enduring significance. He could imagine this was their own room and that Grace never came here with other men. That was daft romanticism, of course, and she and the others would certainly shag rotten in this bed with all sorts, afternoon after afternoon, many of the clients probably wholly indifferent to the board floor and furniture and rugs, and ignorant of the meaning of Omdurman – though some might be Arabs. Corbett today could think of this room as 'our room' regardless, and he would treat her praise for his body and general character as entirely personal to him. He considered her epic groaning and passionate upthrusts could not be more genuine nor more uniquely brought on by himself. A standing fuck with Hen was fine, too, he would never deny that. Jule liked to think of himself as multi-faceted in expressions of love.

Grace would not let him bite her tits to the point of bruising, but he was certain that, if she were due a sabbatical from Omdurman, and also did not have to return to her husband in the evening, she would have encouraged Corbett to chew unrestrictedly on her nipples. That was the kind of respect she had for him, unquestionably. She adored giving him adoration, this was so apparent, yet he did not merely take her praise as if it were owed. No, he spoke praise to her, also, extolling her eyes, underarms, loins and sweetness of breath. These were unforced tributes, not just a matter of squaring for the good things she said about Jule. He despised that kind of quid pro quoism in a love encounter.

When she was putting the lovely short, blue dress back on, Grace said: 'Those three pals of yours were in lately. I shouldn't tell you, but I think of you as so much more than a client, Jule – the usual professional secrecy rules seem wrong.'

'Pals?'

'The ones who brought you here first – Karl, Andy and Clark the American.'

'Business acquaintances.'

'What I meant. They're on a real roll, I'd say.'

'Yes?'

'Oh, yes. They mentioned you, Jule. Well, talked about you a lot. All of it nice and more than nice. Really great stuff for a CV!'

'Good.' They were people he'd middled for on a property thing, nothing to do with the Complex. He'd forgotten what it was to do with.

'They said you'd really put them on the way, Jule. Set things up for them.'

'Good.' He resented this. He thought it damn presumptuous of men he hardly remembered to talk about him in his absence to a girl like Grace. Also, it pissed him off to hear her say they had brought him here. It was true, but sounded like kindly taking a toddler to the Christmas grotto. And what they seemed to have said lately angered him, too. He had put them on their way and set things up for them. Oh, gorgeous! It made him sound what he was, a bloody middleman. He owned nothing, had no capital. All he did was help others towards proprietorships and capital and a roll. Those three were buildings and land and real money now, cars on the firm. Probably they had their own office block with a nameplate and company pennant. And Jule? He was fees. Wages. He needed a fucking C.V. He was faceless. Naturally, Grace would have picked up the difference between them and him. These girls were as smart at spotting true wealth as at recognising handmade suits. He'd been reduced. Grace had behaved all right to him, because that was the nature and training of afternoon girls. So, in bed she bounced back off her arse with seeming sweet commitment and stuck her finger possessively up his own arse to proclaim foreverness. But any girl could learn that. Suddenly, his glow and uniqueness were shattered. He said: 'Oh, those days with Karl and Andy and Clark – I was just at the beginning. I was what's known in business as a middleman then, that's all. Heard of that – middleman, Grace?'

'But a middleman handling deals in millions. Tens of millions.'

'Still only a middleman. It looks pathetic when I glance back. A messenger boy, allowed to open his mouth now and then, or not so often, with a fraction of a suggestion. And the major lads would probably ignore it. Mind, it was good preparation, I wouldn't argue, Grace, but that's all it was, preparation. I decided I mustn't stay there too long. Since then, I've moved into ownerships myself. I had to get a stake in things, not just show others how to get a stake in things.'

It was rot, of course. He had no ownerships, no stakes in anything. All right, after those meetings with Ivo and Sid Jule he had begun to wonder about getting into ownerships and somehow landing himself a stake in this or that, a piece of the action. He had decided, half decided, quarter decided, to give it a try. Or try to give it a try. This was as far as he had moved and he knew it was no movement at all and might never be. The change would be enormous, and most likely impossible. Hen would giggle if he proposed it. But could he let himself remain diminished in the mind of a tart, for God's sake? He felt like the spot labelled YOU ARE HERE on a publicly displayed town map. The suggestion was that you wanted to be somewhere else. Corbett wanted to be somewhere else.

'Karl said you were sure to come out on top somewhere,' Grace told him.

Yes, somewhere. Somewhere else. Patronising shit. 'Which did you fuck?' he replied.

Standing before the beautiful, narrow, mahogany-framed cheval mirror, Grace adjusted her hair.

'Not the three of them?' Corbett asked. 'Not in this room?'

Probably Corbett liked the Connaught just as much as Hen did. Yes, the quietness of the Americans. You could not imagine any of these women thigh-flashing as drum majorettes, even when younger. There was a novel called *The Quiet American*, a title obviously indicating that most

Americans were not. But those who came to the Connaught possibly wanted to learn how to be British – British in the old, un-soccer-mob mode. Some of the American men wore, with their leisure clothes, good brogues, perhaps bought at Lock's, the famous London shoe shop. He liked to think of them getting some quality to justify the journey from the States. Jule and Henrietta found a table in a crowded lounge. It would be hard to talk privately here, yet he longed to. They must be discreet, that was all. Corbett was fond of the decent, mild wallpaper in the Connaught and the polished wood. It was not the same character as the Omdurman, but there *was* character. Who owned Omdurman and all the other Omdurmans around London and any other city? A house that size in Kensington was plump money. So were the takings. He said: 'My aims have changed, Hen.'

'Which?'

Typical. She had to hammer away for exactness and knock all the sweet spontaneity from a statement. She could not let a policy hint build naturally. He often wondered if she was like this with other men, or was she someone else then, just frantic under duvets?

'My business aims,' he replied.

'Oh, right. Those.'

'The sort of status I want. The sort of status I believe I can get and should get now.'

'You been fucking someone else?' she replied. 'Are you on an after-shag high?'

This was like her, too: the slovenly, prole way of talking to make him seem bogus and high-falutin. He did not mind this too much. Corbett said: 'I don't see it any longer as enough just to bring off deals. I've got to be taken into a firm, given a major holding.'

'Some girl, girls, been telling you you're the greatest piece of dick since the Maiden's Prayer and suddenly you're the new JD Rockefeller, right?'

'It can be done, Hen.'

She ordered tea and pastries from a Filipino waiter. They sat quietly for a while, very serenely observing the other folk in the lounge. He tried to work out how much money was involved just in teas. Corbett and Henrietta had taken the last place. He loved the subdued, decently mannered bustle of the big room. It might impose some restraint on Hen. This should have been possible, but suddenly she said: 'Yes, you fucking reek of euphoria, Jule. I smell blood from lust-scratched skin.' She reached over and forced her hand hard between his back and the chair's and pulled up his suit jacket a foot or a foot and a half. Then she would have tugged his shirt and vest out of his trouser waistband and up also, to examine his shoulder blades for love furrows. Perhaps it showed a bit of surprising ignorance in Hen: girls at a place like Omdurman would never nail-dig clients unless this was particularly asked for, and Corbett was not likely to ask when, even in the natural course of things, his wife could soon be seeing him stripped.

He twisted quickly like someone who had detected a pick-pocket or felt a flea bite his body and fixed a hand on her wrist, holding it firmly. 'We'll cause disquiet, Hen,' he muttered. Corbett loathed any untowardness, especially in a tidy place like the Connaught. His mother had taught him to make no fuss in public rooms. The waiter brought their tea and food and set it on the table. Hen let Corbett's jacket fall into place again and sat back, her breathing bitter and tinged with threat. She lived on victories.

Corbett told her: 'From now on, yes, from today, today, I say to people: "Don't offer me a fee, offer me a part of the business free or at heavy discount as long as I'm successful, and if necessary I'll get a bank to finance my share." We'll have some of the most desirable new building in Britain as security. God, the opportunity, Hen. Sid's panicking, because of the water. We know his fears are crazy. I've even told him his fears are crazy. He doesn't hear, so I won't tell him again. I've behaved right. We pick up an entrée to his properties instead, in partnership with whichever firm I choose for the Complex.

We could be strutting around that penthouse. Think of it as a sea change!' Corbett valued a pun now and then.

'I don't see Sid as a man who panics,' she said.

'The sea wrecks his brain.'

'It could wreck more than that.'

'We know it won't, don't we, Hen?

'Perhaps.' She ate and drank. Although she niggled, Corbett could see Hen was impressed. She had not laughed. The quibbles could be taken as routine from her. It was Hen's magnificent, sceptical intellect. This could be a fucking pest. She gazed about the room again and smiled at people who'd grown obviously troubled when she grabbed at Jule's jacket in the flesh hunt. For the Connaught at tea time, she might look a bit too much like real life. Overseas folk here, or the Japanese man last night, must regard her as an exceptional British feature. But Corbett knew she was thinking and getting constructive. On the whole, he loved this brain-box ability in her, to some extent leaned on it, he'd admit that. It was one reason why a vision of her dead appalled him so much, her body disorganised and tumbled in by the brown waves onto rocks and pebbles at Lavernock. On a roll.

He said: 'Hen, you must tell me the names of the men you've shacked up with lately and where to find them. I regard these episodes as episodes only, lapses. Forgive the bluntness, but it's vital. This might be their lives. But as well as that, I don't want any disturbance now.'

'What disturbance?'

'I've got to look a flawless Fauntleroy if I'm going to banks for big funds.'

'Why shouldn't you?' she asked.

'I don't want any shadow – no inquiries from the police.'

'Why should there be, for fuck's sake?'

He said: 'Hen, we should try not to shout, not to confront. These folk are on vacation.'

She poured more tea and bit into a cake. The strength in her long face and sculpted features, which he could worship sometimes, now seemed oppressive.

Corbett said: 'They might assume I've killed – a jealousy thing. This would upset the situation. Word travels.'

'You? Kill? You?' Marv and Jacob had reacted in this dismissive, sarcastic way. Hen's question was not a bellow, but it carried, despite the food in her mouth. She could manage a sneer around the fragments. He did not believe she really felt contemptuous. It was only the need to win here, now, in a chintzy setting.

'I don't want you thinking the wrong things about me either, love,' he said.

'What wrong things?' Her voice was rising further. People who had looked anxious before began to watch her again in that open, American, gun-lobby way.

'Sid's going to have your boyfriends seen to, Hen. He regards it as a duty to me. There's a Puritan streak in him.'

'Which boyfriends?'

'I can't help you on that.'

'I don't have boyfriends,' she replied.

'No, I know this, obviously. Sorry. Not actually continuing relationships. But recent contacts, Hen.'

'You asked Sid to do that, to do a vendetta for you? You've farmed out cock vengeance?'

'Christ, no, no. I'm trying to stop him, Hen. It's his way of binding me to their firm. Gratitude. He wants me to concentrate on work for him, not get distracted by hates.'

'You've handed something like that over to heavies instead of doing it yourself? What the fuck are you, Corbett?' She seemed about to weep. He couldn't tell if it was because she feared for her lovers, or because she considered he had conspired against her. Didn't she realise he could never do that? He almost wept himself. She said, with power and edge: 'Jule, you come here direct from some furtive joy session and want me to name names of people—'

'Hen, it's better to soft-pedal.'

'Name names of people I've slept with in my sad, desperate, attempts to realise myself and to seek personal therapy and reassurance while there's time? Is this wholesome of you?' She gazed about, her face a plea, as if longing for people in the room to aid: to come in on her side against him and male dictatorship.

'We can be big together, Hen,' Corbett replied. 'We can be strong together. You and I, we can progress.'

She did not weep and nor did Corbett. 'What happens when these people you're supposed to be acting for find out you're in it for yourself?' she asked. 'God, we're actually using Hyson's flat. He gives us our base and we try to destroy him from it. Suddenly you're a competitor. Suddenly you're the enemy, Jule.'

'Yes, some difficulties, maybe. Initially.'

'They'll kill you from all directions. Ever think of yourself jetsamised on a beach with your face gone?'

He tried to get her voice down by keeping his own lowered almost to nothing, his cup up in front of his mouth. 'Not myself,' he replied.

'What? Who?'

Hurriedly he said: 'I mean Boris, obviously. Yes, he's relevant, an indicator of possible pressures. We'd have to keep alert.'

'Is that what he tried,' she asked. 'Getting too pushy, going for a chunk of the equity?'

'He was nearly ready to leave the game altogether and write his history of the fridge. He thought it a niche market.'

'But he wanted to take something solid with him?'

'We really can be big together, Hen; strong together.' She chewed for a while. Then, Henrietta leaned forward, hand out again, but this time not to yank at his jacket. She half-circled his wrist with her fingers, the way Corbett had held her, yet this was affectionate only now. 'Yes,' she said. 'Yes, I know it, Jule. Deep down you're a lovely schemer. Grab. Vision.'

'Thanks, Hen.' This was what he cherished Henrietta for: the fight in her, the speed of recovery, her belief in him regardless, the grip on the future, the go-for-it grip on his wrist.

'When?' she asked.

'What?'

'When will they attack my acquaintances?'

'Your men?' Corbett said.

'Acquaintances.'

'It could be immediately. You must give me the names. I'll see them as soon as we've finished in London.'

'No,' she replied.

'Please, Hen, this is urgent.'

'I know it's urgent. It could be now, couldn't it? I mean NOW.'

'I think a day or two.'

'Why?'

'They'd have to get organised, Marv and Jacob.'

'We might not have a day or two. I'll tell them myself. To disappear. I'll go back to Cardiff tonight. Get them out of the way.'

'No, Hen. It's for me to do.'

'No,' she said. She stood up. 'There's an evening train.'

Corbett also stood. He took her arm. He could feel a tension around them in the lounge. Conversations had been cut as people concentrated. 'No,' he said. 'Look, I don't want my wife going back to these swordsmen, do I?'

'I'll be there to tell them they could be killed, not to fuck them, for God's sake,' she stated.

'Re-fuck them.'

'Please don't harass.'

'Well, phone the warning,' he replied. 'If you go to them you might run into Sid's people. His thug unit.'

'You said they'd take a while to get ready.'

'Possibly.'

'This has to be face to face.'

'Yes, I should do it.'

'No, Jule. It's not your kind of task any more, is it? That's a middleman's errand; in the middle between Sid, me and them. I won't have you pipsqueaking again. You're bigger than that now. You've just told me. You're a man of property. Will be. It's important I think of you like that. This is a man I can devote myself to, give myself to, exclusively. I don't want a husband who goes on caring jaunts to men who've been up his wife. I will visit these others and say: "Clear out. It's safer for you. I shan't ever need you again."'

'Thanks, Hen.'

'Never need them.'

'Be watchful. Be watchful around their places above all, but also around our place and your office. They have you charted, in case they have to turn on me. They know you're my weakness, because I prize you.'

'I'll be there for you when you return from your grand works, Jule.' She left the lounge then, her face blank, disregarding the spectators. Corbett had to wait to pay and when he left the hotel she was gone. He took a taxi to Sid's flat, thinking she might have called there to collect her things. He did not find her, though. She must have made straight for the station, leaving him to bring her luggage later. She could be like this now and then: fiercely decisive, wholly brave, wholly devoted to Corbett. He yearned to be worthy of her, and to be regarded by Grace and the other afternoon girls as equal in business stature to Karl, Andy and Clark.

In the evening he had two phone calls at the flat, the later one from Sid on behalf of himself and Gloria. When Corbett answered the first, a woman said: 'Mr Sidney Hyson?'

He did not recognise the voice. 'Mr Hyson is not here,' he replied.

'Oh, it is Mr Hyson, is it?'

'Who's speaking?' Corbett replied.

'It's important I speak to Mr Hyson personally. Something to ask. Something I must ask.'

'Perhaps I'll be in touch with him. I could pass on a message.'

'You are Hyson, are you? This pretence is for your protection. You'll ask how I got this ex-directory number.'

'You're a friend of Mr Hyson?'

'No, not quite that. I wouldn't say that.'

'Is there a number he could call you at?' Corbett asked.

'Will he be there later?'

'He might be abroad,' Corbett replied

'Who are you, then? You're an assistant? Perhaps you're the butler?'

'Like that, yes.'

'Mrs Lowndes,' she replied. 'Boris was my son.'

'I knew Boris.'

'Of course you knew him,' she said. 'What had he done to you that you should treat him like that? This is what I wanted to ask you. Only that. For my satisfaction. So I might understand.'

'It's not a question for me, Mrs Lowndes.'

'I can see why you don't want to admit you are you when it comes to a question of this kind. Your number is around, you know. People have traced you. Boris had friends.'

'Certainly.'

'I've got all these entirely harmless notes of his. They are an insight on his nature.'

'About the fridges?' Corbett asked.

'This is what interested him. I don't see why he should have been treated like that. Many don't. What is the answer?'

'Did he suddenly want property for himself?' Corbett asked.

'Are you saying he wanted property?'

'To move on from being an entrepreneur and get into capital? It's one suggestion I've heard.'

'His real interests were always elsewhere. He was a studious, kind man.'

'Did he want property?' Corbett replied. 'Did he try to fix himself up somehow?'

'Is that what you're saying, Hyson? Is that why you had him burned and disfigured and so on? You ask it as a question, but really you're telling me, aren't you – he was slaughtered and so on because he wanted property? A rival? Is this call being recorded so you can gloat? What if he did?'

'What?'

'Want property. Is that so unforgivable? Countries are built on property ownership.'

'Did he?'

'The history of fridges was only a hobby. Clearly. He knew that. We both knew that. There had to be something else to live on – for us both to live on. He was a responsible boy. He was determined to look after me. People do reach out for property as they get older. Why not?'

'Well, I agree,' Corbett replied.

'So, is that the answer?'

'To what?'

'I need the answer. I can't rest.'

'Which answer?' Corbett asked.

'Why he was killed.'

'I don't know. I have to guess, Mrs Lowndes. Yes, it's frightening.'

'Why are you at this number if you have to guess?'

'Boris has been on my mind and the mind of someone dear to me,' Corbett replied.

'I'll keep searching, you know. I want to know what happened, why it did.'

'Admirable persistence,' he said.

'If you are an assistant or the butler, were you involved in it? Ruining his face and so on. That knowledge was about, affecting the funeral. Friends wondering how far he had been patched up by morticians. The feeling is Hyson would not do such violence himself, only give instructions.'

'I'm only passing through.'

'Who dear to you?'

'Everyone thought well of Boris.'

'Most did; only most, or how would it have occurred? That's why I'm ringing to find out. Some thought he'd gone soft, I know – the history of the fridge a few regarded as ridiculous. But this couldn't account for such action against him. Would you like it?'

'What?'

'To be on the end of it if you'd done nothing at all and had a dependent mother.'

'Terrible.'

'You're just playing with me, are you? You *are* Sidney Hyson.'

'I just happened to pick up the phone,' Corbett replied.

Hyson rang not long afterwards from Malta. 'I tried earlier, Jule. You were busy.'

'I'm trying to set up meetings. More meetings. We want a range of offers so we can play them against one another, Sid.'

'Who?'

'Ivo, so far.'

'That prick.'

'I know. This is the beauty of using a middleman.'

'What?'

'You don't need to meet him, Sid.'

'All right, so you're invaluable. You boosting your fee? Valetta. I like to look at the port and think of our naval ships here in the last war. Grey hulls, possibly shell-scarred. I can visualise. Convoys. All that. George Cross Island.'

'Right.'

'Malta was ours from right back, you know. Gone now, like nearly everything else. Did he offer?'

'Ivo? Not so far, Sid. Preparatory talks, but favourable. He's interested.'

'He's got colleagues.'

'Laura, and Peter or Pete.'

'They're important, Jule. The woman. She knows values. She's fucking dangerous.'

'I have her in mind, Sid.'

'Did Ivo ask about the fucking water?'

'He has no anxieties.'

'Are you saying I'm a fool?' Hyson asked.

'Obviously I don't make a big thing of the water with prospectives, Sid.'

'Who else?'

'I might see Philip Castice-Manne. He knows the Bay.'

'Ivo's doing porn, girls and possibly un-Customed tobacco. The loot's up to his Adam's apple. He'll be looking for laundry facilities.'

'I've pressed that. Does this phone do a record, Sid?'

'Why?'

'I might want to play over what you said, to give attention to points. At more leisure.'

'There's only one point. Get the fucking price.'

'No recorder?'

'Why you so bothered? Does it look as if there's a recorder?'

'No, but some phones—'

'Are you into something private, Jule? I might not appreciate that.'

'To get the tone of your advice, Sid.'

'After all we're doing for you. Those boys who were giving it to your wife. This is very much in hand, Jule. That will be dealt with very nicely. Marv can cut loose, sometimes, but I've told him to handle it very nicely. This is what I mean, Jule. We're entitled to look to you for gratitude, even devotion.'

'Of course, Sid.'

'Ivo will try to bring it right down. And the woman. That's Ivo's way. Don't be surprised. He might say something as low as £120 million, just to panic you. He believes in cheek, always has.'

'I'm ready for him.'

'And Castice-Manne. He'll pretend they're cash-short. Bollocks. Every sort of substance and he's running girls in all the big towns in Britain. London included.'

'Yes?'

'Do punters pay with tokens, for God's sake? Henrietta with you?'

'Oh, yes, Sid.'

'Good, I like that. Give the girl a decent outing and keep her away from those hard-timers. And it will keep you out of the wrong pussy.'

'Hen's very aware of your kindness, Sid – the flat, making things so easy and pleasant. We saw a play, *No Man's Land*.'

'That's from the earlier war. Mud. Craters. Star-shells. They'd be good in the theatre. It's all part of our heritage,

Jule. This will help bind her to you, Jule – sharing glimpses of our history.'

'Right, Sid.'

'Don't worry about the bed sheets. It's all spruced professionally. Use the time for a cementing of things between you and her. I can't stand it when my people have private troubles.'

'Right, Sid.'

'Gloria sees her as extremely suitable. Those were her words: extremely suitable.'

'Thank her for her concern, Sid.'

Corbett searched around for anything that might show the phone was recording or bugged but it seemed clean. When he rang Henrietta at home he got only the answer machine. That might mean she had not arrived yet or was out on her missions. He left no message but tried her mobile. She answered at once. 'Hen, they're moving already on that matter,' he said. 'Where are you?'

'Good job I came back then, isn't it?'

'Where are you?'

'I think I've a very fair chance of getting to them first,' she replied.

'Marv can be undisciplined.'

'I always say best not use names on mobiles when it's a sensitive topic. Next to no security.'

'Are you on your way there now? To one of them?'

'As long as they'll both believe me. It does sound a hell of a tale, doesn't it? Drop everything. Vamoose. They'll ask why. I say: A purge. They'll swallow that?'

'It's you I worry about, Hen.'

'But why? They want to look after you, don't they? And looking after you means looking after me.'

'Marv can get confused and hasty.'

'There you go again with names.'

'He can get confused and hasty and very vindictive. He enjoys that sort of work.'

5

And then Corbett had a visitor, though one who did not stay and would not even enter the apartment. The front door voice-box sounded and when he switched on the screen Corbett saw Ivo's property valuer, Laura, waiting; round-faced and benign-looking, lumpily dressed in a heavy fleece, very middle-aged, very unremarkable. Perhaps she was more like fifty-five than fifty. This was Chance. This was the future, was it? 'Come up,' he said on the intercom. 'I've unlocked. I'll meet you at the lift.' He spoke gently, as to someone's mother or Ivo's hatchet woman.

'Better if you could come down,' she answered. It was hesitant, uneasy, determined.

He enjoyed seeing her so jumpy. 'The doorstep?' he said. 'Like selling mops? It's comfortable here.'

'Could we just drive for half an hour? '

'Where?'

'Around. I have to pick up my grandson from Cubs at 9 o'clock,' she replied. 'Caspar. Important they join things, don't you think? Extend social awareness. We could cruise until he comes out. I wouldn't be happy talking in a place furnished by Hyson. I sound squeaky and upper-crust on tape. And I'm on double yellows.'

In the street, she led him to one of the smaller, black Mercedes, walking a bit stiffly, he thought: ah, Time. Once she might have been great in her university long jump. He climbed in and she took them out into the traffic. 'Were you ever a Cub?' she asked.

'Naval cadet.'

'Knots?'

'Some. And sailing a small boat.'

'Ah, of course, sea-girt, your childhood. Mine, too. I'm in

favour of the Cubs,' she said. 'A uniform without quite being a uniform. I was brought up with uniforms. I'm not totally sure about them, though.'

'How did you know where I was staying?' he replied.

'A guess. If you're up here for Sid, Sid's place seemed logical. And Sid's place is known about, to us. Pete's damn good at charting.'

'Sidney might have been here.'

'No harm. I'd say I'd heard rumours he wanted to sell.'

'There shouldn't be any rumours,' Corbett replied.

'Whatever.'

She talked as if they both recognised that Sid was someone to be guarded against, perhaps fooled. Odd. As far as she could know, Corbett was in London only to act for him. God, until very lately he was in London only to act for him. She said: 'It seemed worth a call, while I was waiting for Caspar. These are matters that should be kept up regularly or they lose their purpose.'

'Which?'

'Cubs. Regularity becomes a part of their social conditioning. Discipline. As much as anything, I wanted to apologise for this morning – the absurdities.'

'Which?'

'The valuation figures, naturally. It's probably good, also, that Cub meetings should be in a church hall, regardless of one's actual beliefs – or not. Churches, church halls, are central to a tradition, and it's useful for children to absorb some of that: the odour of respectable grime, and comfortable clanks from old heating systems. This is continuance. My own sons were Cubs, then Scouts.'

'The figures were low,' Corbett replied.

'Fucking mad.'

'Sid warned me Ivo would start down and down.'

'This was more that just his standard bargaining ploy.'

'Oh, some venom there because of what happened with the first contracts? I can understand a grudge. I have to dispel that. It can be done.' This he believed. It could be managed by skill and sweetness, and managed to a point where Ivo would see that someone with the skills and sweetness of Corbett should be taken aboard his operation.

'All venom,' she replied. 'Ivo is someone short of discipline, without background. An appalling shallowness. Have I made this sound a class matter? I'd hate to do that. I trust one has contempt for such incidentals. Ivo certainly is deepest crud with no class, but this isn't necessarily a failing. All sorts climb out of shabby backgrounds. What I suppose I do believe in – what I was brought up in – yes, what I believe in is an officer class, a leadership class. This is ingrained. Daddy retired as a Commodore, RN, and might have gone further but for the cock thing. Ivo's always been defective in OQs.'

'Sorry?' He was asking about 'the cock thing' but she answered otherwise.

'OQs – officer qualities. He's not capable of separating personal concerns – say, damaged pride, trampled ego – he's not capable of separating these from the overall needs of the outfit. He's a throwback to Thatcher days – Ivo's got huge drive, a sparkling ego, but no sense of the group, the crew. Oh, he can create businesses, of course he can. And they soar. He makes a load for all of us. We have brilliantly profitable activities nationwide. And they operate without any serious crassness from the police or Customs. Nobody – certainly not I – nobody would dispute Ivo's skill at spotting easy, heavy cash returns and at annihilating or squaring possible hindrances. Ivo's name attached to an enterprise is an undoubted boon – enterprises in the special categories that interest us, I mean, clearly.'

All this was to be undone, naturally. He waited.

Laura said: 'Yet there will come moments like this current situation where his vision and sharpness falter – or are crushed by something dark and preposterously trivial. He cannot see that, for the sake of the companies, he ought to ditch his chickenfeed hates, forget the heavies he employs. We look to him for something else now. There's a supreme lakeside laundering service on offer and, for the sake of the firm, he should ensure we get it. We have these non-stop tons of money that could do with purifying. All right, so there's a drive against laundering, but the Complex would still come out all innocence. The Complex might also produce legitimate revenue in its own right. OK, OK, so there'd be a tax liability. But revenue like that, even net, would still be a plus, an extra plus.'

'He went with you to the Bay to do the costings?' Corbett asked.

'I've never been to the Bay, never seen the Complex. Neither has he, lately. These were just off-the-wall figures, meant to insult and humiliate Hyson and you. It's supposed to be a smart ploy but we think Ivo's mind-balance has gone. Tragic, sad. Such balance as he ever had. This is what I mean about membership of Cubs or something similar when a kid. Can give stability. Only to some. But some is all we're interested in, as long as it included Ivo. He's never going to be a Commodore RN, but he might have learned the obligations of command.'

'Who think?'

'What? she replied.

'Ivo's cracked.'

'Peter and I.'

The idea of them in alliance against Ivo shook him. 'Is this visit part of a putsch? The chief's gone nuts, so get rid. Like *The Caine Mutiny*?'

She negotiated a turn, driving slowly. 'I'm very much in favour of proper command structures and due respect to a leader,' she said. 'My upbringing. This is something Cubs and scouts and sea cadet training would probably implant. I suppose Ivo's the captain, yes. He's 76 per cent of the companies – always insisted on not just more than half, more than three quarters. No breeding, so he's constantly nervous, scared he has no right to be where he is, like Stalin. But there can come a stage where—'

'Which companies are those?'

'Various interests. Didn't Sid tell you that, as well?'

'Of course,' Corbett replied.

'Pete's 14 per cent, me ten. The middle-classing of porn, thanks to the Internet – you've heard of that? Perhaps you're part of it, you're middle-class enough. It's been respectabilised. Anyway, I look after that side for us and have my capital mainly there. This was inherited cash. It has grown by a factor of eleven, going on twelve, last time I counted. I don't know what Daddy would say if he knew my share of his little loot had finished up in porn, but he couldn't really complain, not after that cock thing.'

'Which was that?'

'We see very plump returns. These days – and nights – you have bridal suites in top hotels – I mean real deluxe places – top hotels offering the happy couple video hard porn in their room. There's a classy magazine called *Erotic Review*.'

She drove with neat, instinctive efficiency, like someone considerate who was used to carrying a child or children in the car and didn't want to shake them about.

'So, Ivo does what he likes,' Corbett said.

'Don't give up on us, Jule.' Suddenly, her voice was shrill and desperate. Laura's words gripped Corbett – the words themselves and the plaintiveness of tone. He felt power piped into him. He was ready for it, knew he was fit for it. She said: 'That's why I'm here so soon. We were scared you'd write us off and go elsewhere for offers. To Castice-Manne? He's next? You'd have fall-back. We realised this. And I have to say it might be natural for you to go there or somewhere similar. My God, you hear an apparently itemised, careful, idiotically small bid of £38 million and would be justified in deciding: These fuckers are a nonsense and a fucking grief, I'll move on. Of course, Ivo thinks he can push his offer up once he's had the pleasure of hurting Sid, and you, for old times' sake. Vendetta, vendetta. He believes you can't do without him. Pete and I are not certain of this. No, not certain at all. Please, show us patience. We're right for the Complex. More right than Sid and more right than Castice-Manne. Pete's working something out with his financial people tonight – his own financial people, not the firm's. Obviously. He'll call on you tomorrow morning with a proposal, if that's acceptable.'

'But Ivo's not going to—'

'Oh, it's difficult, certainly.' She was back to her measured, mild way of speaking.

Corbett said: 'You could have misread him. Perhaps he just wants to keep playing things for malice, revenge. It might take an age to get his offer to somewhere sensible. I'm not going to wait that long. Can't. How do you vote him down? There's two of you to one of him, yes, but I assume it's not one man one vote. He's 76 per cent and you're 24 between you. You're slaughtered.'

'Voting doesn't come into it.'

'What's that mean?'

She gazed ahead at the traffic.

'How else?' Corbett said.

'You do know the nature of our companies?'

'Of course. But there's always a proper ghost structure – in your firms, Sid's, Castice-Manne's. The procedures have to look right. You work behind a front but that front is important.'

'There are resentments against Ivo in various parts of the outfit, not just at board level,' she replied. 'I mean real, grown-up resentments.'

'Yes?'

'Pete's in touch with some of these people this evening, as well as the financial side. They are people who will sometimes operate... well, who operate outside the narrow business mode, the genteel mode. Not mere heavies like Ivo's, but definitely inclined towards action.'

'Action?'

'It's hard to restrain them if they're determined on change by their own methods, however regrettable.' She glanced from the road and at Corbett for a moment. 'Oh, does this sound like a blood threat against you, in case you go elsewhere? No, no, honestly. Mainly, I'm speaking of their attitude to Ivo. Oh, almost totally.'

'What kind of resentments?' Corbett asked.

'There's a lot of detail still to be covered, you'll understand, but our thinking is that you, personally, must be involved with Pete and me in any new ownership of the Complex,' she replied. 'You'd be beyond middlemanning. Plainly, this offer is intended, above all, to keep you with us now, a bit of bait – keep you with us tonight, tomorrow, the next few days, while we try to arrange things. We see this as probably better than threats against you. Almost certainly. You're used to threats in your role, can cope with them. In any case, on the practical, selfish side, we also think we would gain by having your know-how built into the companies, not merely on call. We feel at least a 15 per cent stake for you, if you want that kind of deal, Jule. And if you couldn't raise the capital against your holding as security, we might be able to assist. Pete knows the City. But, then, you do yourself. Together you'd bring in true backing. Do it as seems most suitable.'

She changed tone again – became seemingly offhand: 'But perhaps you're content middling away. Possibly you're not interested in ownership. Some are not – regard it as a burden. That's all right, too. We could adjust to a fee, a super-fee, if it comes off. Possibly you'd want to stay at a distance, a freelance's distance, should Ivo have to be displaced by harsh means, the non-voting means. Pete would understand that. I'd probably understand. People like you have your poncy little standards and I'd possibly put up with them.'

'Ivo displaced?'

'Yes, you know, displaced. But if you did agree to come in with a holding, we would naturally be able to insulate you – though, again, only if you wish – insulate you from sections of the business that you might find not your style. We know you live in a manse, father-in-law a minister of the Gospel. Pete is looking at methods of creating a what could be called *cordon sanitaire* capable of keeping you out of criminal courts, should it ever come to that, which is very unlikely. Pete is a respected community councillor in his village near Sevenoaks and would not wish to endanger that or distress his wife and children. And I, likewise – sons, grandchildren who would suffer enormous shame if I were put in the dock. Daughter of the Commodore.'

Corbett said: 'As a matter of fact, I have been thinking of—'

'Do you know, I feel a real evil towards Ivo for making me go through that figures charade this morning. But he's angered people a lot more dangerous and uncompromising than myself. These are people who would instantly see the beautiful logic in owning a huge money-cleaning item like the Complex at this tricky time, and they would certainly not allow Ivo to mess it up for ancient pique. Juvenile. These are pragmatic folk, Jule. They can also be temperate and it's conceivable they'd let Ivo walk away more or less intact, as long as he did walk away from everything. I mustn't pre-judge.'

'He's not going to walk away from 76 per cent of a golden operation, is he?'

'No, he's probably not going to walk away. I do feel for his wife and children, I assure you. If he were taken out, fully taken out, or even only brought down with some unignorable disability, there'd probably be financial provision for them. But we have people in these companies whose outlook is possibly over-simple, and once they've decided on what needs to be done they'll work all out for it, removing any hindrance – forcibly removing any hindrance. Any hindrance. But, I say again, please understand, I'm not referring to you here, Jule, nor to any of your family. No, indeed. Indeed, no. You've already seen some of that sort of behaviour from other people in the Bay, haven't you? I mean, what happened to Boris Lowndes. Ah, here's the lad.' They drew in with other cars at a wooden church hall in a Chelsea side street. A small boy wearing a cap and green jersey climbed into the back of the Mercedes. 'I'm looking after Caspar while his mummy and daddy are in Colorado skiing, you see,' Laura said. 'What was it all about tonight, Caspar?'

'Flowers in the hedges. So we'll know which is which, such as campions, violets, primroses.' He seemed to be recalling a lesson: 'People should please leave the lovely wild flowers alone, not pick big bunches. It's better for Nature if they are left to grow. Nature needs the help of all of us.'

'I agree,' Laura replied. 'Here's Mr Corbett who knows Nature also, but mainly the sea, like great-grandfather. We're going to give Mr Corbett a lift home. He's been working late.'

'Sometimes I think it's dim as arseholes at Cubs, gran,' Caspar replied.

Of course, of course, what Corbett wanted now was to go back to Omdurman and show Grace he no longer occupied that pathetic fetch-and-carry position but had moved into real estate with Laura and Pete. Or soon would. Show Grace and any of the other afternoon girls who might have discussed him. Laura had brought the transformation he longed for. It had been extremely hurtful to think of Grace fucking him in the supposed special room and then, no time afterwards, describing the insignificance of his job to associates while awaiting her next trick. Oh, out of politeness she had spoken well of the £40 million botanical gardens and his connection with it. But she'd know none of that £40 million actually derived from him or would ever go to him in a sale. Now, though, the gardens would come into his interests and, in fact, be only part of them. The thought of owning a nursing home truly excited Corbett. If he had some unhumiliating disease in the future he might use the nursing home himself. He liked the idea of doctors scurrying to make sure the proprietor was pleased, and even consultants. He had not discovered what kind of property those three – Karl, Andy and Clark, the American – were into, but he would bet they did not have power over truly professional folk such as doctors.

It was evening now and Grace would be at home with her hubby and child in Chislehurst. Different girls were available at Omdurman, but he had no interest in proving his new status to them. It was the afternoon girls whose views he prized, and especially Grace's. Corbett thought he would get back to Omdurman tomorrow after lunch. He hoped Laura was right and Pete would call with the proposals in the morning. They should be able to resolve all that swiftly. He loathed greed and would probably not want to force them much above 15 per cent. Perhaps Pete would agree to come with him to Omdurman after lunch. Corbett was pleased with this idea: he would be acting as guide then, not getting shown the scene as someone from the sticks by people like Karl, Andy and Clark. Corbett saw this as in line with his new rating.

He decided it would be a mistake to ring Henrietta and tell her about these happy changes in status. His morale was up and he wanted to keep it up. Hen would start asking her bright fucking queries about how it could be done, this move into ownership: how definite was it, how would the finance be provided, how would he keep himself and her safe and her father safe once Sidney heard of the betrayal? There were certainly people he wanted enlightened about his new dimensions, but these were above all Grace and other afternoon girls at Omdurman. A total correction had to be made in their minds. He knew their response would be warm and unquestioning, especially when he put the kind of bonus their way that could come only from a man of true portfolio.

He had another reason for neglecting to phone Hen this evening. Corbett did not wish to hear an account of the missions to her love chums which she had kindly taken on. All that seemed part of the middleman era now, and he must leave it behind. Merv and Jacob were going to deal with Henrietta's extra men as a kind of minor favour from Sidney, the kind of favour Sid might do for someone he regarded as dependent, incapable and, character-wise, slight. It was like providing a flunky with private medical insurance to make sure he stayed fit enough to serve you. No longer would Hyson be entitled to regard Jule with such condescension. He found he was not interested in finding how these occasional comforters of Henrietta reacted to her warning, supposing Merv and Jacob had not already reached them: would one or both of Hen's men agree to run, refuse to run, invite her in to reaffirm their bonds despite threats? Now, Corbett felt himself a good way above these little anxieties and the possibility of measly killings and went back to the flat and slept.

Grace and he had that same room again next day and, in Corbett's view, their time together was beautiful and alight with meaning. At first, Pete wanted to join them, bringing two other girls, but to Corbett this seemed not the right kind of atmosphere. He had the idea Grace agreed, though she could hardly say so in public: at select venues like Omdurman a client's preferences must always be catered for, unless it came to brutality beyond a very intelligently defined norm. Pete had obviously been pleased when Jule suggested they should come here this afternoon to celebrate, following Pete's financial presentation in the morning. He turned out to know Omdurman, and often visited after lunch as it meant he could get the usual train back to Sevenoaks in the evening. Although Corbett had hoped he would be introducing him to Omdurman, it was not a complete disappointment to find he already knew the afternoon girls. This meant they would probably be aware that Pete had a share of a conglomerate. If he behaved towards Corbett as towards a partner, or potential partner, they would understand Jule's brilliant rank. To tell them would have seemed pushy. Quality should be apparent. He was sure Pete would treat him as an equal, because this was what they wanted him to be. It would not be like the visit with Karl, Andy and Clark.

Private in the room, Grace said she was very glad Corbett had insisted on being alone with her. Because he wished above all to avoid boasting, he did not tell her he had guessed this. 'I hope Peter's not offended,' she said.

'He'll be fine. I can take care of that.'

'I know he's important in the business – a stakeholder.'

'Right,' Corbett replied.

'You, too? Well, you're so unbothered – you might even be his boss, I suppose.'

'We're colleagues.' This would do. He did not want to make mad claims.

'Good,' she said, and Corbett felt this, too. It seemed to him he had to take her with lovely tenderness and respect. There was that noblesse oblige aspect to things now: if you possessed big powers, or the promise of them, you should be especially caring to a girl like this, not treat her as some bought trifle. He hated haughtiness. Her clothes were to be removed by him considerately, and especially undergarments, not yanked off in some crude let's-have-you style. She would recognise worth because she was being treated as worthwhile. Pushing her legs open had to be a gentle matter, too. He did not want it to seem as if this man, so splendidly placed in commerce, could have whatever he wished and when. He needed to feel she was giving this to him as him, because she wanted to, not because of his business eminence or the payment. Loins bruising should have no part in things.

He went down on her, really desired to: it was more than a token. His tongue played for minutes in the delicate furls and interfolds of her and he was glad she didn't put on any phoney ecstasy groans, just squirmed for a better angle now and then, as if what she was getting was an entitlement. Corbett could arrange his mind to expel for these minutes the idea of other men with her. He liked the feel of her thighs against his ears, like a balaclava. It was as though he was being held and given comfort while he gave comfort. She knew his business grandeur, yet also knew he was a questing, ordinary lad with an ordinary yen to eat pussy. This was the kind of impression he had to convey, this distinguished ordinariness. She must regard him as basic as well as rare. Anything other would make him vain and barbaric, and he would have really despised this. It seemed to the point to have her actually sitting on his face for a while with him affectionately mouthing her. Everything was designed to make him seem undominant here. Modesty was the core of him.

In a while, Grace wanted to reciprocate orally. Corbett did not mind this but, again, respect towards her was required and he would allow no ungoverned ramming of himself against her larynx. There had to be more gentlemanly ways of marking a business success than that, for God's sake. He abhorred presumptuousness. In any case, he had to keep in mind that the full triumph was not delivered yet, as Hen would certainly remind him in her snotty way, if he contacted her: eventually he would have to, but eventually would do. Although Pete had arrived as scheduled at the flat with his papers and a scheme early today, not everything could be concluded then. These were proposals only – good, workable proposals, but proposals. Despite his joy, Corbett knew there were mighty uncertainties still. The biggest was Ivo – what to do with him. Laura had been right about the hatreds. This morning, pre-Omdurman, Corbett and Pete had sat on each side of a rosewood table with coffee in the flat's main living room, a yellow envelope folder containing a few handwritten sheets open before them. Pete said: 'Some want him wiped out.' He blinked a bit, but only a bit this morning. There was something resolute, thoughtful and subtle about him now. Behind the pale spectacles his eyes looked full of knowledge. You could see why he might be up there with Ivo. It did not seem to worry him that the place might be wired. He spoke easily, at normal volume. 'Me, I'm opposed at this stage.'

'Wiped out financially – in the commercial sense? His powers taken away?'

'No, wiped out,' Pete said. He made a two-finger gun with his right hand and put it on the back of his neck, the SS preferred spot for executions. He was more or less unblinking now.

'Laura said something like that,' Corbett replied. 'Hinted at something like that.'

'Hard to take in?'

'I—'

'You wouldn't be asked to do it, old son.'

Old son. Corbett could not make out whether he was being condescended to or treated like a colleague. Because of his mood he decided on the second. He said: 'No, I know that, but—'

'It would be carried out in-house.' Pete leaned forward and spoke more quickly, as if obliged to give the alternative notions but determined to get them out of the way fast because, however bright they seemed, he did not accept them. 'There are company people who could handle it. Not total specialists at that kind of thing, but capable.'

'Laura spoke of them.'

'Best like this. No fee, no talking outside. Ultimately, they'd be given stronger dealerships as reward, or allowed to move up to some of our more progressive porn lines – really enticing productions, these: Laura's greatly brisked up that side of things. No, these would not be merely hit men, Jule. They'd have a genuine business identity also and we'd need to honour them in one of those ways.'

'But you, you personally, Pete, don't—?'

'There's an undeniable mystique about Ivo. As long as he were alive many would be afraid. They'd dread a comeback, with a personal gang backing him. Napoleon with his thousand from Elba? It's certainly a possibility and a bad, bad one. Just the same, I think we need him. At this stage.'

'For his name?'

'Absolutely. I knew you'd grasp it, Jule. Need him for that very mystique which scares some. Look, mystiques are not plentiful. I can supply several strengths, but not that. Nor Laura. You? Perhaps. But I'd say don't destroy Ivo for it; channel it, utilise it. I'd want him reduced, knocked out of the chairmanship, yes, but still with us. Perhaps he could hang on to the heliport. That kind of thing appeals to him – machinery, fuel stores, pop stars flying in for gigs, maintenance of the landing pad. Ivo is fine at hands-on but also adores celebrities, any celebrities – it's his gutter upbringing – he's still charmingly amazed he can meet the famous.

'Laura said something similar.'

'Oh, she's always ahead. His name's no special asset at the Complex, but it does count in all our other activities, really count, Jule. Counts among some very difficult people. Irreplaceable. The point is, we'll need maximum income for laundering through the Complex to make the investment worthwhile. Sure, Ivo can upset people, but he can also build useful, crippling terror into our competitors, Jule, and he's sunk sweetener cash with very nice care into law contacts of all ranks. That kind of facility is personal to Ivo. It wouldn't automatically pass to whoever succeeded him. Yes, whoever. My view has to be that the companies would be weaker if Ivo were killed or even so badly injured his image slipped. I'll be arguing this with other company folk; the more extreme, less patient folk.'

'What does Laura say?'

'Laura was raised in a family that held we should have blown the Jerry navy out of the water long before Munich.'

'She'd have Ivo done?'

'Probably. But she's worried that the people who actually perform – I mean, do the hazard side, the bullet side – they might want bigger recognition than better dealerships. Perhaps they'd feel entitled to board status after such a prestige slaughter. It could become difficult to contain them. She did history and knows what happens in revolutions. OK, guillotine the king and queen but then the chaos and grab and in-fighting start and the conspirators stalk one another. Robespierre, tops today, topped tomorrow. I'm very Frog this morning.'

'She'd be afraid for her life? And yours?'

'And yours, Jule, if you were with us. And I hope you will be. So, anyway, Laura might agree to my ideas on Ivo, at least for now. And, of course, she has some feelings of tenderness towards him, as I do myself. Zest, for example – he's got plenty of that. He can inspire. To leave him with a holding at the heliport fits in well with the general business plan.' Pete had drawn a couple of sheets from the envelope file and glanced at them. 'Very briefly and simply, that plan is to

divide up the Complex into four and loan-finance it as separate pieces. My advisers say it would be comparatively easy to
raise funds for such purchases. No bank would be asked to
carry all the risk, only a quarter. Each quarter would fall far
below two hundred million and I'm told this is crucial: banks
and finance houses generally are fairly relaxed on secured
loans up to the two hundred, but eyebrows twitch once an
application is for more.'

Corbett said: 'The Complex ought to be—'

'Kept together as a unit. Of course it should, and it would
be. That's the only way to maximise laundering potential –
get a real money-mix through the hotel, casino and shops
mainly, but also expenditure and takings via the nursing
home and gardens. Sid's discovered this, obviously. Well, he
created it for the purpose. I'm told it can be contractually
agreed pre-purchase between the four parties – Laura, you,
myself and Ivo – that on completion of the deal we form a
united board of ownership of our allied segments. Ivo's going
to need some convincing on this, clearly. But he'll come
round, I think, when he sees the alternative.'

They had talked detail until a little after one o'clock, then
took a pub lunch and went on to Omdurman by cab. Now,
enclosed by Grace and moving slowly and, so far, gently in
her, he felt a real satisfaction that he had not pluralised but
kept only with Grace. She deserved this and he could tell from
the way she gripped him and moved so cheerily and excitedly
with him that she was grateful. Of course, these afternoons
she'd get a bucketful of fucks and other men would probably
think her grip and movements were especially for them.
That's what coming to Omdurman was about. But Corbett
believed she had a true and unique closeness with him, and
with him as him, not as a major business entity, although this
was bound to give him added sweetness for Grace.

Pete paid. Apparently the company had an account at
Omdurman and Corbett would appear on the bill as an
unnamed contact given hospitality. Pete wanted to get back to
Kent now in time for a parent-teacher meeting at the school

where one of his children was form captain. He and Corbett were about to leave when Philip Castice-Manne came from a corridor into Reception and greeted them. 'Jule, Pete, I heard you were here. Something special?' he said.

'God, Omdurman belongs to you?' Corbett asked.

'I take it as a real compliment, Jule, that you turn up on successive days. There's a bonus in this for Grace. She's a wonderfully flexible girl. There were times today when I wouldn't have recognised you, Jule – obscured by the setting.'

'Recognised? How?'

'How, indeed,' Castice-Manne replied.

'You watch?' Corbett asked.

'Some clients we naturally like a file record of. Not for advertising – don't worry! Would we?'

'There are pictures?' Corbett asked.

'Christ, pictures?' Pete said. 'Wouldn't you know it, though?'

6

When he reached home, Henrietta greeted Corbett in the hall, her brilliantly regular face now vivid with joy, forgiveness and faith in him. Her tall body quivered in exultation. 'You've had a triumph up there, Jule. I know it, can feel it.' Her arms were around him before he put his suitcase down and her half-open mouth on his. He liked her half-open mouth in a kiss, the feel of defencelessness in it and the taste-trace of what she had been eating, perhaps something sauced with horse radish. This sort of kiss showed everlasting commitment to him and the likelihood of cartwheeling passion later. He hugged her with one arm. Hen could so often be like this, so gloriously and unrestrainedly like this. There were times when she showed only brick-wall disbelief in his hopes, and suspicion about his social life. He had expected to meet that now. But there were times, also, when a thrilling optimism and unquestioning love took hold of her, made her gleam and shout with confidence. She'd relegate her awkward brain and trust her gut and hormones. This was what helped make their marriage. This was what would always keep them together, regardless of others. Some madness in it? He didn't mind a bit of that. His cool mind could do for two. His boardroom mind could do for two. 'And I, I've had a triumph too,' she yelled. 'Triumphs.'

'Oh, wonderful, Hen.'

'The usness of us is splendidly clear, toweringly indestructible.'

'I've always known it,' Corbett replied.

Her father must have heard the jubilant greeting and came smiling into the hall at a trot, sweat bright as neon on his eyebrows. Henrietta and Jule lived with Floyd in the manse house attached to Bethel Baptist Chapel, where he had been minister for more than twenty years. 'She was so excited, Jule,' he said, 'knowing you would pull off something great.' He must have been working-out in his study when Corbett arrived and wore a singlet, navy shorts and trainers. He looked sick: terribly frail, stooped, skinny-necked, his knees two separate kinds of problem.

'As soon as she heard your footsteps in Mount Stuart Square, from taxi to front door, Henrietta knew, knew, you had succeeded, cried out to me that you had succeeded, and that she had never doubted it,' Floyd said. 'As though Scott of the Antarctic had come back a winner. "This, this, is my man," she said.'

Hen's father's real name was the Reverend Dr Rhys Gareth Llewellyn, but he liked to be called Floyd after a black boxer he admired, Floyd Patterson, first heavyweight ever to gain the world championship twice. He had his hair cut in Patterson's style, with a kind of small, tightly rolled quiff at the front, and fairly claimed it was getting to be fashionable again now with youth. Several framed fight pictures of Patterson hung in the manse hall, but none of the disastrous 1962 contest with Liston. Floyd would still occasionally weep about that during meals, tugging at his dog-collar as though to dump it, and asking repeatedly whether there really could be a God.

Corbett said: 'But you, Hen – your victory: you managed to reach them?'

'This is her despicable, on-the-side lovers you're talking about, is it, Jule? Yes, she did, she did.'

'In time?' Corbett asked.

'In time,' Henrietta replied.

'Grand. And will they get out of the country? We don't want a police involvement.'

'It's possible,' Henrietta said. 'I don't think I care much. I've done what I can. They're dear boys in some ways – well, clearly – but they must not be a burden on me now. I see my life as elsewhere. Elsewhere from them. As here, only here, Jule. The usness of us is so strong, so good now.'

'Wonderful, Hen,' Corbett said. He meant it. She was his.

'Nor a burden on you, either, Jule. I'd blame myself endlessly.'

'There's toleration for you here, darling,' Floyd replied. 'Sleep-arounds fall within the Lord's mercy, you know.'

Corbett took off his coat and they went into the living room. Although Floyd accompanied them he remained standing near the door, poised to return to his study and continue the tragic body-building. Henrietta kissed Corbett again, her lips still apart, and fondled the hair on the back of his head. He enjoyed this. It seemed very natural, truly loving. It was something neither Grace nor any of the other girls he'd been with in Omdurman ever did. Their training probably said they must concentrate pell-mell on usual erogenous areas. 'Oh, they queried things, both of them – naturally,' she said.

'I can understand that,' Corbett replied.

'Jule, you are *too* understanding. It's a middleman's bow-and-scrape habit – seeing all sides.' Floyd let his pulpit voice boom. 'They deserve nothing. They have treated you as nothing. Hen, of course, connived and more than – in that trawling way of hers, letting down her nets on both sides. Nonetheless, I see them as cock-happy thugs. The country is better without such.'

Henrietta began to imitate the men she'd called on, whining a little, snarling a little: 'Why, why did they have to go, they wanted to know. Why would someone like Sidney Hyson wish to damage them? They'd done nothing to injure him.'

'Yes, it could be a puzzle. I do see that. It's not so simple, Floyd, really.'

Henrietta said: 'But, yes, simple, simple and more simple. I told them it was because Sidney Hyson prizes my husband and is determined to make his life stressless and unhumiliating. And this is not merely that Hyson wants my husband to focus better on work for him, but out of a decent, scrupulous regard for a friend's marital happiness. Sid might be a towering villain, I said, but he also knows morality. Then I told them: "And I, I also prize my husband because he is someone who deserves to be prized, regardless of what my behaviour may have indicated recently. Unaccountable, wretched, slut lapses, pride driven – the lust for conquest. So, now, go," I said, "for God's sake and in your own interests. My interests are no longer involved." I kissed them – in a farewell-for-ever mode, no tonguing or anything like that. Nothing to make you or Sidney fret, Jule.'

'Hen described it all to me, acted some of it out. She really stuck it to them, Jule,' Floyd said. 'This is a girl who refuses to be compromised with any man, or men, on account of a few casual, uncontrollably hot-clit bonks, sought at times of genuine depression and psychological confusion. Do you remember that poem by Edna St Vincent Millay?'

'Of course,' Corbett replied.

'Called "I Being Born a Woman and Distressed".'

'Right,' Corbett said.

'She gets herself under some man but having had her itch scratched, says he shouldn't think: "I shall remember you with love, or season, my scorn with pity". Likewise, what Hen did could be seen as an aspect of the women's movement, an assertion of natural female need. Oh, St Paul and the Scriptures generally would not approve, I know, and I do listen to them, but she is my daughter and I have single-parent responsibilities since the death of her mother. I can say, bravo, Hen.' He gazed at her for a few moments, then turned to Corbett: 'And you, Jule – a bag full of wondrous deals?'

'There've been some advances, Floyd. I wouldn't claim more.'

He beamed, the grand, emaciated old face pulsing with pride in Corbett. 'This is modesty only,' he said. 'I'm sure of that. And I can feel Hen is sure of that.' Floyd glanced back at her. She was a little flushed, eyes screwed up slightly, as if straining to see a glorious objective which she knew was there, though clouded at present. 'I don't regard this as merely Mammon,' Floyd said. 'This is achievement by a very resourceful, very tough, utterly indomitable fighter.' He grimaced and straight-lefted the air as celebration, a blow that could floor a toddler. Floyd was adored by many of the older people in the Bay for his fine doggedness and idiocies. He remained the stanchion of a famed Cardiff docks community, and had corroded in step with it. Corbett guessed, sadly guessed, that neither Floyd nor his chapel here in the Square could survive the changes. He would lose the title of Bethel pastor and never win it back, as Patterson had won back his title, because in the new Bay there would be no place for Bethel. His grail training regime was pointless: even if he got his weight up from 136 to 240lbs and had something done about a knee, or both, he would never be called on to avenge Patterson for that evil first-round knockout, because Sonny Liston was dead. And dockland as Floyd had known it was dead, too. Vive le fucking Complex!

In an almost disbelieving, earnest whisper Henrietta said: 'What I sense is something that goes beyond routine success, beyond just the ace sales skills we'd all expect as standard from Jule.' She was sitting opposite Corbett in an armchair, staring at him, trying to unlock him, trying to know his thoughts. He felt it was wifely. Her dark eyes, which could be so sceptical, now glowed with love and admiration.

'Heavens,' Floyd replied.

'Ownership?' Henrietta said. It was almost not a question, nearly a pronouncement.

Corbett realised, yes, she knew he was a different Jule now, just as Grace did. Power must be ambient in him. She saw she should not try to dominate. It would be a kind of absurdity, irreverence. She realised she must defer to him. 'For a while I've felt bored with middling,' Corbett replied. 'As Floyd says – the need to suppress one's self and always see things as others see them.' And yet, despite her apparent awed friendliness, he waited for the bleak, clever, well-informed niggles to start now from Hen.

'Become a proprietor?' she asked. It was still a tremulous whisper. 'As you mentioned in the Connaught?'

'You're entitled, Jule,' Floyd cried.

'Considerable obstacles remain,' Corbett answered. He had not decided how much he should tell Henrietta, except that it would not include that interview with Philip Castice-Manne and some of his colleagues following Omdurman. This had been a session hastily scheduled at Castice-Manne's main offices off Grosvenor Square. Pete was not invited. Of course not. Pete could get home on time to the PTA. Corbett went alone and had found the meeting harsh and deeply frightening. He was relieved to quit London after it.

Christ but the Bay had become huge money. Castice-Manne was already installed there in a reasonable way and now wanted more, wanted what he called 'a true spread,' meaning the Complex added to his existing property. They were like old-time barons these people and, like Hitler, always looking to extend, always in the hunt for Lebensraum or, in these days, the laundry room. So many saw the gorgeous chance of lakeside money-cleansing through Sid's Complex. The urge had increased because of Treasury threats about the laundering of criminal gains. It was the scale of the Complex that attracted people like Castice-Manne, plus the very complexity of the Complex's finances. Hundreds of grand, possibly even millions, could be disguised and purified in the accounts of the hotel, the nursing home and the shopping mall. Wash me in the books of the Complex and I shall be whiter than snow. Ambitions to secure this boon were dark and fierce. So was malice. Possibly Corbett should not have been surprised. He was already familiar with the competition and venom.

Just the same, he had been upset by Castice-Manne and his foul, pressurising hints about the concealed, all-angle observation points in Omdurman, and the pictures; plus heavy cross-questioning on price ranges for Sid's properties. Obviously, Castice-Manne did not know Corbett was no longer looking for outside bids, that Corbett had ceased to be a spectator and would become a contender. Castice-Manne must not know it yet. Corbett thought he had just about held him and his directors off for now by promising they would be briefed at every stage of sale negotiations. And they would be briefed, briefed with what Corbett decided it was all right for them to be briefed with and when they should be briefed with it. This, then, was the first real sign of the end to middling: at last his personal interests had priority. The skills he had used for so long on behalf of others would now help Corbett shape a timetable to benefit him and Hen. She deserved this, even if she did pass herself eagerly around. Floyd was most likely right and she had not been herself at the time, times: momentarily clobbered by randiness like the lady in the poem.

Corbett remained troubled, though. It hurt to imagine Sid Hyson one day studying photographs of Jule's face, thigh-framed, at Omdurman – Sid Hyson and anyone else. But especially Hyson. It would seem a snub to him. After all, Sid longed to protect Corbett's marriage. Hyson was worried enough about things between Henrietta and Jule to order those who cuckolded him to be at least permanently wheel-chaired and possibly slaughtered. You did not put people like Marv and Jacob on to something unless intending true damage. Some events at Omdurman could never be regarded as in line with this well-meant, restorative effort by Sid. Regardless of what happened about the sale and purchase, Corbett would hate images from Omdurman cameras to stay for ever fixed in Hyson's dark mind. Although Corbett believed his behaviour there had been affectionate and natural, in photographs or on film they might appear undig-nified, comic, even reprehensible. Almost any sexual behaviour looked undignified if photographed, and some variants more than others.

Obviously, the very worst prospect was if the pictures were put in front of Hen or Floyd. Hen had an unspeakable eye for detail. She would not be tolerant, despite her own waywardness. Floyd? Several Old Testament books were very fierce on hygiene for the Israelites in the wilderness, and he might howl a harsh, reproachful text at Jule. The geography difference was unlikely to rate with Floyd. But Corbett calculated that Castice-Manne would approach Hen and Floyd only if he thought his hopes for the Complex had collapsed: solely a revenge move. While he still believed himself a candidate he was sure to hold back any pictures, as a threat. Corbett had to make sure he went on believing he had a chance, until concealment became impossible. When Jule was settled into ownership and had perhaps actually walked Hen around the penthouse, he would feel even stronger than now, and if Hen and Floyd had seen the pictures by then he might feel able to face them and argue that this had been just a larky, laddish afternoon, relief from ferocious business pressures far from home. In a way that was true. A bonding with Pete had taken place – the kind of sterling thing that often occurred when men went tandem girling. Corbett thought the Omdurman visits should be seen as one reason the grand transformation in his career had come about at all.

Floyd said: 'But I'm spare here. I expect you two will want to… Oh, I think back to days when I would come home from a Baptist mission conference in Eastbourne or Peterborough and your mother, Hen, would be ungovernably impatient for—'

Someone knocked at the front door and Floyd went out to answer. On the back of his vest, in florescent red capitals, were the words GYM MASTER. Corbett heard a conversation in the hall, the words not distinguishable, and then a little while after Floyd came back into the room with an elderly woman. 'Yes, but think of it this way, pastor,' she said, 'if your son was washed up on a beach, his face burned to bits, would your attitude be different? Or, all right, you haven't got a son but your daughter, here. Or, more likely, him, your son-in-law.' She pointed her thumb at Jule. Now he recognised her voice and attitude from the telephone in Sid's London flat.

'Mrs Lowndes, what happened to Boris is unspeakable, but in the faith to which I belong we do not pray for the souls of the dead,' Floyd said. 'Some religions do, I know. However, we believe a man or a woman must see to his or her salvation while on this earth, alive.'

'What salvation did Boris have?' she said. 'What Sid Hyson and his crew dish out is not salvation. You'll write Boris off, like the police have? I never shall. I'll hunt and hunt, but meanwhile—'

'Mrs Lowndes wants me to devote a service to asking God to look with understanding upon the soul of Boris,' Floyd said.

'I'd pay,' Mrs Lowndes said. 'I can pay and pay well. Boris left quite a bit of stacked cash around. Look, Floyd, half to the Bethel Fighting Fund against the development, and half to you personally, no mention anywhere, I promise, and these two are not going to canary, are they? These are old notes Boris put away an age ago, definitely unmarked and not traceable by serial numbers.'

She was small, daringly made up, slightly yokel-faced as Boris had been originally, her cheeks too rounded, her nose too podged. Corbett wanted to offer her a ploughman's lunch. She wore a dark red, leather suit, the skirt to knee-length, right for her age. She knew how to work an audience and switched her gaze from Floyd to Henrietta and Corbett now and then, though she was mainly concerned with Floyd, as minister.

'I can't, Mrs Lowndes,' Floyd replied. 'My congregation would know it was wrong. Word would spread.'

'But answer my point,' she said. 'If Jule was to get it – I mean, he could get it easily, the way he does his own thing and gives offence—'

'What "own thing", Mrs Lowndes?' Hen asked.

'Oh, Mrs Lowndes means just in general – the all-round middleman style, I expect,' Corbett replied.

'Does she know something?' Hen asked.

'Do I know something about what?' Mrs Lowndes replied.

'About future changes,' Hen said.

'I know what I know,' Mrs Lowndes replied.

'Oh, don't give us some deadbeat fucking jargon,' Hen said.

'I hope I didn't come to a manse to be sworn at,' Mrs Lowndes replied, her head haughtily pulled back, as though she had been struck. Corbett liked her vigour.

'What do you know that you know?' Hen said.

'I know that I am here to ask our beloved minister to do what he can for the soul of my dead son.'

'A priest at St Mark's would do it for you,' Corbett said. 'They go in for limbo and all that.'

'It has to be Floyd. Floyd is the Bay. Boris knew and respected Floyd.'

'It's many a year since I saw him in Bethel,' Floyd replied.

'All the same, he respected you. He was busy. Are you going to hold that against him, for heaven's sake? Yes, heaven's,' Mrs Lowndes said. 'All right, he sneaked off Sunday School. But this is an eternal soul we're talking about, Floyd. I want him given a better time in the afterlife than he received at the end here. He cut some corners, yes, or I would not be asking for this kind of help, but he was gentle, mild, and was content with loony, harmless projects like his history of the fridge.'

Mrs Lowndes had a red shoulder bag. She opened it now and brought out two heavy wads of what looked like twenties, tied with tape. Suddenly, she went forward and thrust them down the front of Floyd's vest. The garment was tucked into his shorts and the two packages slipped as far as the elastic waistband and bulked out the cloth of the vest in two rectangular slabs. She stood close to him, her body tense, her face under the powder solemn and irresistible. 'Please, please, Floydy,' she said. She put out a hand and let it rest for a moment in the angle between Floyd's thin shoulder and his thin neck. 'Do we let our Bay boys wander in the great Unknown without some guidance?' she asked.

'Come, then,' he said.

He turned at once and, with the money still under his vest, walked back out into the hall and opened the door leading through a short corridor to the chapel. Mrs Lowndes followed. Henrietta and Jule went after them. Corbett loved

Bethel: its plainness and modesty; its green emulsioned walls; the fine, solid pews; the undecorated, opaque windows with their protective wire grilles outside. The grilles would not stop the demolition ball. Floyd went quickly up into the pulpit, under the wall text: 'Without shedding of blood is no remission'. Mrs Lowndes, Henrietta and Corbett took seats in the front row. Floyd adjusted the money under his vest more comfortably and leaned forward, resting on the edge of the pulpit. His eyes were closed, not in a psychic or pious way, just closed. Corbett was conscious less and less of a resemblance between Floyd and Patterson at his peak, despite the haircut, and not just because Patterson was black.

'Oh, Lord,' he said, 'we are here to speak to Thee out of hours, as it were, about one who, in his youth, was a member of this congregation but who, like so many, went his own way until his own way took him to disaster. Thou art the way, Lord, and those who depart from it will not flourish in the fullest sense. Here with us, Lord, is a mother concerned for the soul of her ruined boy and who, who, could turn her away unconsoled? Not Thee, oh Lord. Thou wouldst find a way to ease her anxieties, regardless of theology and the Pharisees. This was a lad who led a deeply dangerous life for juicy fees and, as she points out, there is another who does the same present in our company now, namely Jule. These are boys who have their little talents, no doubt, but they are also boys who have been enveloped by forces bigger than themselves, so much bigger. They are but buttons in life's great sewing box. The landscape and waterscape they have known – that we all have known – is suddenly another landscape, another waterscape, and they are lost in them. But they do not know they are lost, Lord. They think they can help create this landscape and waterscape. They are weak, they struggle, they are expendable, as we have seen. Oh, protect those in that position, Lord! Oh, watch their dubious backs.'

Floyd retreated a step in the pulpit and opened his eyes. Corbett saw his father-in-law had been smart. He had not betrayed his Protestantism by praying for the dead but had prayed for him, Jule, instead, with a passing, weepy reference to Boris. On the whole, Corbett felt fucking pissed off. Hadn't he just explained to Hen and Floyd that he was not weak, not someone who struggled or was expendable? He was not a button in a box, he was very much main fabric and into major property, or would be soon. It was insolent of Floyd to speak to God or anyone else as if this was Corbett's only context – Bethel, the Bay, the manse. He had a London shagging pal, Peter – good with paperwork and member of a PTA – who would see him stupendously right – as well as a friendly daughter of a Commodore RN, Laura. Jule was not another Boris. God, he wasn't, was he? Was he?

Floyd came down from the pulpit and, decisively pulling his vest out from the shorts, recovered the two packets of notes. He did not glance at them. Mrs Lowndes was smiling. She seemed content with Floyd's prayer. It was as though any mention of Boris from a chapel pulpit would be sure to work. Corbett thought the quiet dignity of Bethel helped, a dignity easily rich enough to withstand Floyd's workout gear and exposed physique. Floyd handed the money back to Mrs Lowndes. 'This will be better used taking care of you, Vera,' Floyd said. 'A beautifully soft, leather suit like that costs and costs. Boris would want you to look right.'

She put the money into her bag without argument. 'Very well, Floyd,' she replied, 'but should the same thing happen to Jule – elimination, a beached, maltreated corpse – yes, if he is overtaken in that way, it is I who will pay for the funeral, an occasion and equipment worthy of him and of the whole dockland tradition. You said Boris could not flourish, but he flourished to some extent and I would like to use some of those gains as I've suggested. Please, you must not deny me this.' She turned away from Floyd momentarily. 'Oh, tell the pastor he must not, Henrietta, Julian,' she demanded. 'Since your prayer, Floyd, I feel Boris and Jule are for ever linked, for ever souls alike and sure of the same forgiveness and mercy through your good offices.'

Fuck off, Mrs Lowndes. I've left Boris behind and there's no soul link and no career link, either. Boris, you see, Mrs Lowndes, was only a go-between but I'm due to become one of the kind of mainsters he went between. Corbett did not say this, though. His rage he could always improve into smarm: a routine job skill. Mrs Lowndes deserved some tenderness. Her son had received none. 'Thanks, Mrs Lowndes,' Corbett replied. 'You honour me by the comparison.'

'Jule is not going to die; not, not, not, you stunted, creepy cow,' Henrietta cried. She struck the back of the pew with her fist.

'I want you to be right on that, Henrietta, really want you to be,' Mrs Lowndes replied. 'But after Floyd's kindness the least I could do is make sure there was no skimping if Jule got himself removed through arrogance and deception. A mock-wood box is so demeaning.'

'What arrogance? What deception?' Henrietta cried.

'Oh, aiming beyond what's right for himself.'

'Is that what Boris did?' Corbett asked.

'Like Satan,' Floyd said.

'What do you mean, "right for himself"?' Corbett asked.

'Right. In accord. We have our place in life,' Vera Lowndes replied. 'There we stay.'

'No,' Corbett cried.

Floyd said: 'That's the Corporate State, Vera – Mussolini-style fascism.'

'We can rise,' Corbett cried. 'We can, we can. We must.'

'Boris would definitely wish me to help Jule,' Mrs Lowndes replied.

During funerals at Bethel, this first pew they were sitting in now was taken out so the coffin could stand close to Floyd in the pulpit as he ran the service. For instance, Boris Lowndes's casket had been placed there. Gazing down on it then, Floyd had made Boris's life sound as worthwhile as he could, something Floyd always tried to do for crooks and semi-crooks from the Bay who had been brought in for a service. He referred to Boris's unstinting care of Vera and his good dress sense, never the slightest colour clash between tie, shirt, shoes and suit. Sid and Gloria had attended, of course, with Marvin and Jacob; all of them wearing top-class dark clothes in recognition. Unmixed grief was in their faces throughout. As long as Boris was dead and beyond troubling them any longer, Sidney would be generous with mourning. Sidney was a Berkshire outsider in the Bay but liked to be seen as part of local pageantry, along with his wife and colleagues. It was a kind of plus in Sid. Corbett found now that he did not want to quit this first pew, sat on it ferociously, like on some defeated enemy's neck. He imagined that as soon as he and the others had gone the pew would be removed, in preparation for his own remains. He was ashamed of such fantasising panic, but could not escape it. Would Sidney and Gloria and Marv and Jacob turn up for him, too, in the circumstances?

'Did Boris ever tell you he thought Sid Hyson might want to wipe him out, and why?' he asked Mrs Lowndes.

'Boris showed me where the cash stacks were around his flat shortly before,' Mrs Lowndes replied. 'Premonition?'

'But why – the premonition?' Corbett demanded. 'What signs had he had?'

'And he drew my attention to the uncompleted manuscript of the fridge history, plus notes,' Vera Lowndes replied. 'He said that, if I didn't mind, some of the money could be used to pay anyone who would be willing to complete this life-work for him. I ask you. As if. I inquired who he had in mind for such a sure bestseller: Stephen King? Dick Francis? I was not being unkind. I wanted to jolly him up a bit – break him out from gloomy preparations for death. The fridge project! That's what I mean when I say Boris was utterly stupid and unthreatening. Who'd kill such a hay brain? Well, we know who. I hear Sid's selling up.'

'Hardly,' Corbett replied. 'Things are too good for him.'

'He wants to retreat,' she said. 'He's afraid of the water – the same water that carried Boris to the beach. Sid knows the water will come for him, too.' She had begun to intone.

'That's crazy,' Henrietta said.

'He wants to sell,' Mrs Lowndes replied. 'But, of course, you know this really, don't you? The buzz says Jule is acting for him. Dicey. It's why I offered to do the funeral.'

'That's crazy,' Corbett said.

'I heard Hyson dreams of Boris rising up out of the tide like an angry sea god and pointing the enraged waves on towards Sid and the Complex,' Mrs Lowndes said. 'Penthouse dreams. I'm glad, glad. Actually pointing at the Gloria.'

'But this is far-fetched and heathen,' Floyd replied.

'The buzz is the banks think Sid's flipped and want their money back before he loses it all for them. What kind of security is a botanical gardens? Where are the buyers? This is what I mean about the funeral, Jule. If he has flipped he could lash out anywhere. You're very near.'

'We don't want to hear what you mean about the sodding funeral,' Henrietta replied.

'I do understand you rawness, my dear; your willingness to curse, even in a chapel,' Mrs Lowndes said. 'He puts himself in peril, he puts you in peril. Oh, there was a time when I thought they might go for me as well as Boris. Floyd's prayer for Jule might not be enough.'

In bed half an hour later, Henrietta licked Corbett busily on the chest, arms and shoulders, with the grain of his skin and across it, as though testing to see whether he already tasted of Bristol Channel saltwater. There was an uncertainty about the way she held him. Sometimes her arms seemed to cling with fierce, desperate strength, and sometimes they were slack, absurdly gentle. He felt she did not know whether he was the solid, reassuring, mighty commercial figure he knew himself to be, available for her to hang on to in her terrors and doubts; or was he a near-ghost, someone doomed as Boris had been doomed, and owed delicate handling in case he suddenly disintegrated? If he fucked her from behind, not in her actual view, would she even know he was there? He felt so spectral, so toned down. He saw that in her opinion he had declined suddenly, hopelessly. Corbett believed in the sureness of progress but suddenly his bonny confidence was smashed. It was because of Mrs Lowndes and the talk of his death. Hen had resisted these forecasts in a lovely, loyal way, but she was shaken, and he knew she saw him as shaken, too, and gravely diminished.

He wanted to yell at her that Mrs Lowndes was not the only other woman interested in him. There was a bigger context. Metropolitan women, and one particularly, had glimpsed something else, the positive. These were knowledge-able women, familiar with men and their rank and ability to pay. They had seen not extermination but magnificent status and a stock-owning prospect for Jule, and they had continued to believe in these even when Castice-Manne arrived and began his hellish threats and bullying.

Had Grace known about the observation points and pho-tography? Originally, Jule was disappointed to think this but then realised that those extreme ploys might only be used on men of undoubted power, against whom Castice-Manne needed ultimate leverage: recognising an equal, at least that. The pictures were a kind of compliment. Grace and the rest appreciated this and, as a result, would think more of Jule. He had at least parity with Castice-Manne. These girls would know what an event it was to have a figure like Jule going down on them.

But, of course, Corbett could not say any of this to Henrietta, just as he could never have been rude to Mrs Lowndes. Although his words would be factually right, they were not the kind of argument Hen might wish to hear, and especially not just now. He slipped down her long body, his mouth ready and fairly eager. It would have seemed a betrayal after Omdurman not to. If those damn snaps ever did turn up he would not want Hen thinking she'd been short-changed.

She opened her legs for him unreluctantly and sighed. He thought it sounded like expected pleasure. This excited him. Communication with Hen he cherished. She said: 'I'm think-ing of a blues number Daddy sings sometimes – His Eye Is On The Sparrow. That's God's eye, lovingly, protectively. Like in the prayer – asking Him to watch your back.'

Corbett lifted his head marginally: 'Which fucking sparrow?'

'Really, I know you'll be all right, Jule,' she replied.

'I'm some fucking sparrow, you mean?'

'That's not what it's saying, not at all. It's saying that, if God's eye is on even the sparrow, think how much more He will care for someone of distinction and potential, Jule.'

'Sound point,' Corbett replied, lowering his head again. He longed to be of useful, affectionate service to any woman he loved, and Henrietta he loved fiercely, unceasingly, regardless of blips. He did not think it worthwhile to define to himself the difference between being here like this with Hen now, and being like it with Grace a day ago. He hated what could be called hairsplitting. Obviously, he knew there was no question of getting voyeured here. He was not utterly against being on show, but privacy did have value. Floyd was probably still down in Bethel, talking to Vera Lowndes about Boris and, in any case, seemed lately to have given up listening at their door when he thought they were having it off. He might have realised his chest was growing so wheezy he could not be secret. Corbett felt sorry for him. Floyd deserved better than to be wholly excluded from their joy.

'In a way, to fuck after all these delightful prelims seems a kind of crudity,' Henrietta said.

'No. Violent but not crude.' He believed this, was not just saying it.

'No,' she said, 'I suppose you're right, Jule.'

'Right?' he replied, moving onto her. And so, the sweet violence; his, hers, unsparing. After it she said: 'Confession, Jule. I can't hide in lies after that grand togetherness. I didn't tell both of my... you know... my, well, friends – didn't tell both of them to get out of Britain because of Marv and Jacob.'

His brain was still spreadeagled after the thunder of their climax and he grunted: 'What? What you saying, Hen?'

'Didn't—'

'Christ, Hen, you—'

'I know. I said I'd warned both. Sorry. But only one, really. Foolish. Divorced. But the other… he's still very married, Jule, a family man. Was it… well… practical?'

Instantly, he decided this must be the one she thought most of. She couldn't bear to send him away, even for his safety. If he had a wife, this would make him more valuable to Hen, more challenging, more difficult to possess. They were lying naked on their backs on top of the bedclothes, their hands touching, not quite entwined.

'I regret not informing him, regret it badly, Jule.'

'You cared for him too much? Care for him too much? Hen, don't you see this is—?'

'If I cared for him I'd want him removed from danger, wouldn't I? I found I couldn't worry about him – not enough. And then the difficulties of packing up a household as well.'

His anxieties shifted. 'But you did care enough about the other to worry?'

'It was easier, Jule. I see now, though – they are both lives, both human beings, both needing to be helped.'

'They'd helped themselves.'

'Jule, I—'

'What we can't in any way afford, Hen, is to have him killed or seriously hammered now – at this crux time. It sounds disgustingly cold to put it like that, but—'

'I do understand, Jule.' She gripped his hand properly.

'This opportunity I've brought back from London – it depends crucially upon my credit rating. Oh, there are people who will vouch for me, sure – one the daughter of near enough an admiral, another familiar with the City – but even their recommendations will not do if I'm put under tough scrutiny by a bank or finance house and they find I'm the chief suspect in the vengeance killing or mutilation of one of my wife's opt-cocks. And inevitably I would be a suspect. Wrongly, yes, but it's the perception that would count.'

'We must go to him, Jule, tell him to clear out, perhaps

with his family, perhaps solo, but somehow to go, soonest. It might be hard to explain to his wife. She'll possibly resist, turn unpleasant. I don't think I can manage it alone, Jule. It will need the endorsement of another voice – a husband's voice and one who can plead a career, a fine future.'

Corbett yearned to help her. It hurt him to see Hen crushed by guilt over a mistake, however gross. This was not how he thought of Hen, nor how he wanted her to be. Hen was spirit, aggression when necessary, defiance. Yet he hesitated at her suggestion. To Corbett it looked like a mad risk for them both to visit this man. Jule had been prepared to do it earlier, but now they had so much more to lose. Yes, in Hen's words, there was a career, a fine future. These had shape, solidity since the London trip. Corbett had to consider that Marv and Jacob might have already moved. By now, this man could be missing or dead or fearfully injured. If Corbett attempted to call on him, with Henrietta or not, he would get implicated. To try to deliver the confidential warning, they might have to hang about near his house or work so as to intercept him. Corbett could be spotted there and become even more of a suspect than he would be anyway. Perhaps he'd manage to prove he had no part in what had happened, if it had already happened, but the publicity would be around at once that he was in the frame. All stature and creditworthiness was sure to die.

'Look, Hen, I have to see Marv and Jacob to report on how offers are coming,' he said. 'I'll use the meeting to feel out whether they've acted yet against your friend. It's possible they've spent the time searching for your other friend, if he has done a runner abroad.' He did not want to know their names. That would elevate them.

'But is there time, Jule?' she asked.

'I can't tell. If there is, I might be able to talk them out of it. Convince them it's of no consequence – that you don't want anything more to do with this man.'

For a while she lay quiet. Corbett listened, in case Mrs Lowndes had gone and Floyd was at their door after all. This was a very personal conversation. 'Of no consequence?' she said. She released his hand. 'Do you feel no resentment about him then, no jealousy?'

Hadn't Gloria hinted that Hen might react like this? At once, he turned towards Hen and attempted to put his face against hers. She drew away. 'Certainly I do,' he said. 'But this is the point, isn't it, Hen? It will be assumed I feel resentment, jealousy. These would be my alleged motives.'

'Assumed? Only alleged? You don't care that much?'

Oh, Jesus, did she want him to kill this bastard? 'I care enormously.'

'But "of no consequence?"'

'Hen, I am right, aren't I? You don't want to see him again?'

'I feel as if I'm being treated like a slag – someone who just goes to men when she feels like it, but it is "of no consequence."'

'No, not like that, Hen, honestly. What I'm thinking of above all is our image.'

'*Your* image,' she said. 'Mr Impeccable, I suppose. Mr Investors' Dream.'

'I want to be your dream, too, Hen. My image does not matter if it's not also yours. I want to be the husband who found the moment, clutched the moment, and took himself and you out of the piffling life that sufficed for people like Boris Lowndes and his mother, and who established us as part of the very structure and foundation of things, a glorious, secure part. We are folk with responsibilities now, Hen, the almost sacred responsibilities of ownership at the Gloria. And one of the main responsibilities is that we are clean and that we look clean.'

Slowly she laced her fingers in his. 'You sound such a man, Jule, such a thinker,' she whispered. 'Take me again. Take me. That's one of your responsibilities, too.'

'One of my privileges,' he replied.

'Enter me,' she said, 'like entering upon an inheritance. This is your due and only yours.'

Corbett adored hearing her speak like this. It would have been measly to start pressing for detailed assurances.

7

When Corbett reached the penthouse in Sid's hotel at the Complex, he found Marv and Jacob there but just about to leave. They were bright with excitement, especially Marv, their fine, double-breasted, dark suits buttoned fully, as if to bottle up all the exuberance. They invited Corbett to accompany them.

Christ they're going to kill him now. They're on a pre-hunt zing. They'd like me to watch. They want to show how much they care for me. They'll make me an accessory.

'We can talk in the car,' Jacob said. 'Your reflections on the London trip.'

'Oh, if you're going somewhere urgent, I'll come back and see you later,' Corbett replied. The fierce symmetry of the suits scared him. These were people sure to triumph. Some automatics were very slim and could nestle into a shoulder unspotted, even under such brilliantly tight jackets.

'Yes, I suppose sort of urgent,' Marv said. 'Important.'

'You'll exult in this,' Jacob said.

'I'd like to, but things to do around the Bay,' Corbett replied. 'Just minor, like tidying up, but necessary.' Dim to be dressed informally, as he was: a navy-trimmed, cream fleece. He'd look like some authentic-lover-of-the-game football fan who vox popped on TV about non-typical thugs tainting the sport.

'It would be a privilege to have you with us, Jule,' Marv said.

Corbett said: 'I—'

'Come on, Jule. Occasion of occasions, believe me,' Jacob replied. 'An epoch dawns.'

God, Corbett found he hated Hen, not just for fucking other men but for making him prey to the rotten generosity of people like Marv and Jacob and Sid. In the hotel foyer, Marv picked up from Reception a large bunch of flowers, wrapped around with transparent plastic, and a huge ginger teddy bear. He said his girlfriend had just produced a daughter and they were on the way to visit. Relieved and astonished, Corbett replied at once: 'That's wonderful, Marv. Congratulations.' He ditched his excuses, a basic middleman skill when essentials changed. 'I'm honoured to come. I guessed it must be something wonderfully positive – your obvious joy.'

'I've never seen Marv so entirely radiant,' Jacob said, 'hand on heart.' Jacob would use words that seemed a bit too strong, and he often tagged on a phrase vouching for truth, where truth wasn't doubted.

'People have been very sweet,' Marv replied. 'I rang down and said, "Get me something to take", and like true experts they come up with these.' He waved the irises and pointed at the teddy, which Jacob was carrying affectionately against the chest of his suit jacket. 'I couldn't have chosen better myself. Thanks, Edna,' Marv told the clerk. 'On my personal account, please. And here's for you.' He passed her a five with his free hand. There was a fragment of grandeur to him, despite his features. It could be fatherhood and his suit. It could be his role as stand-in for Sidney. This was a suit made for Marv, not off-the-peg, and using the wool of wools, warm, soft, terrific at the cleaners, like Corbett's London-bought outfits. Jacob had the same. Probably Sid paid for dressing them. He'd want quality near him, although Sid was not much for tailoring himself. He used to confess he was more keen on architecture.

Marv, Jacob and Corbett talked in the foyer while the car was brought around. After the first hotel burned down, Sid took the chance to get the foyer wholly redesigned, as Corbett had told Laura. Sid thought the original entrance pokey, not worthy of an hotel associated with Gloria's name. Sid would say: 'If it's to do with Gloria it has to be glorious, hasn't it? Give me a vestibule that vocalises her.' The new foyer was magnificently spacious and light, rich in proper glass chandeliers: Sid would have spat at imitation, however good.

'You've had some worthwhile London activity, Jule?' Jacob asked.

Corbett said: 'Well, very useful opening shots involving—'

'It will delight Sue if you'd come in and meet the babe, Jule,' Marv said. 'Business talk in the car is fine, but if you could actually pop into the ward as well.' 'Of course,' Corbett replied. 'Is this your first?'

'In many ways, yes,' Marv said.

'Marv sees this as a beginning,' Jacob said.

'Well, yes, the beginning of a life,' Corbett replied.

'Exactly,' Marv said. 'You've got an instinct about this kind of thing, Jule.'

'More than just a single life. Marv's very into dynasty, the foundation of one,' Jacob said. He shifted the teddy bear gently to his other arm so that more of his own round, unencouraging face was visible, in case of an argument. Corbett struggled to spot what was being said, as well as what was being *said*. 'I think dynasty is shit, myself – just a load of offspring sucking at you, take my word: sucking at your missus to start with and then you, yourself, pretty soon, when they get to need money; rest assured, greeding on your gains, like a holy entitlement, no exaggeration. Think of the Kennedy lot. What's the plus? A family tree. So?' His accent was refined, lulling. He said: 'Trees are great in Nature, don't get me wrong, or – out of reverence for Sid – trees in a botanical gardens. But do I want to make a tree as an item for me, as an individual? It's a need I don't feel. You, Jule?'

'Hen and I don't think of children yet, though certainly not ruled out.'

'In your line – yes, hellishly dangerous,' Marv said. 'As you're placed at present, that is. Which could change. Have you considered that, Jule?' Corbett concentrated. 'A child definitely needs a father. This has been proved. The worst thing is if the father's dead, obviously, but it's very bad, also, for a youngster to see his father crippled and his face reshaped by beatings – an iron bar or a piece of fence post, that kind of unsparing weapon, with or without edges. Or burning. Such a sight can affect a child for many a year, into her/his thirties, even. Psychology is subtle, Jule, always has been.'

So, have you killed, reshaped, Hen's lover? One is, was, a father, perhaps both. Thoughts only.

Marv said: 'Likewise, the name that parents give a child can have a considerable bearing. OK, I'm called Marvin. Don't tell me I'd be the same person if they'd decided on… what… say, Rory or Luke. We're thinking of Evaline.'

'Lovely, Marv,' Corbett replied.

'Take those names, Rory or Luke,' Marv said. 'What do you notice about them straight off?'

'These are boys' names,' Jacob replied.

'Oh, Christ, give him a prize, Jule, will you? What else?'

'One's in the Bible. Not the other – not Rory,' Corbett said. 'I don't think so. I suppose there might be a Rory deep in those begat lists in Numbers or Chronicles, but unlikely. Rory hasn't got that wilderness feel to it, more Irish.'

'You'd be familiar with the Bible because of Floyd,' Jacob replied.

'No, right, there's no Gospel of St Rory,' Marv said.

'Here's some mirth, I'd say,' Jacob replied, giggling.

'What?' Marv asked.

'A Gospel of St Rory,' Jacob said. 'It sounds untoward. Fig trees and sick of the palsy – not harmonious with Rory, or am I wrong?'

'They're short,' Marv replied.

'What?' Jacob asked.

'The names. Luke. Rory,' Marv replied.

'Oh, definitely,' Jacob said. 'There are shorter ones, Marv. Jo. Bo – like in Bo Derek.'

'Of course there are shorter ones,' Marv replied. He remained good-tempered, someone in a civilised debate, searching out neat truths. 'But the thing is that Luke and Rory are the full names yet are still short. Jo is not the full name. It's short for Joanna. Or Sid for Sidney. Think Sidney's brain's suddenly totally gone, Jule? In pieces?'

'What?' Corbett replied. 'Why say that?'

'I don't know what Bo is short for,' Jacob said.

'It could be Bonny,' Corbett suggested. 'Or there's Boadicia. They wouldn't want a name like Boadicia Derek across a film poster, stealing space from other stars.'

Marv said: 'The thing is with a name like Marvin, which can be said as Marv, or Sidney said as Sid – the thing is, making it briefer shows a kind of friendship. Maybe trust.'

'Julian, Jule,' Corbett said.

'Exactly,' Marv replied. 'Friendship. Trust. A name that can be shorter is an asset. It proves I'm able to be close to people, people who call me Marv. Others who call me Marvin are not always so close – not enemies, not hated or to be watched out for, or given some suppression, maybe, not at this stage, but they're not so close. You can tell this with a name like Marvin. But you couldn't with someone called Luke or Rory because these are names that are already as short as they can be. You could not call someone Ror, like Jo or Bo.'

'Ror would be stupid,' Jacob said, 'like raw meat or a tiger prowling.'

Rory, Luke: were these the names of Hen's men? Corbett had assumed them simply names Marv pulled out of nowhere as illustration. Was Marv telling him something, though? He did not want to be told it. Oh, God, don't let either of her friends get hurt. She would not forgive Corbett that, no matter what she'd said lately, and no matter if she did try, which she would not.

'Ev would be all right for Evaline. Or Val,' Marv said.

'Ev is truly short,' Corbett replied, 'and in speech it wouldn't be mixed up with Eve because the E would be said like in Ed.'

'Exactly,' Marv said.

'Yes, or in Exactly,' Corbett said.

'Evaline seemed a good one because there are a lot of the letters in it matching the ones in Marvin,' Marv said.

'Only two the same as in Susan, though, pardon me if I'm mistaken,' Jacob replied.

'Sue's not bothered,' Marv said.

'Or why not a double name: Evaline-Sue?' Jacob replied. 'This is quite a notable fashion – Mary-Lou, Tracy-Ann. It would be hard to shorten Evaline-Sue, though, for those close. Evas sounds a bit scratchy, as I see it. The pill's a beautiful facility for a girl like Henrietta, Jule. I don't feel authorised to call her Hen yet.'

'Well, perhaps for all women of child-bearing age,' Corbett replied. He and Marv were comfortable on a long, blue, leather sofa. Jacob remained standing at the Reception counter and had the teddy bear seated on it now, supported by his right hand.

'True, child-bearing age,' he said. 'Or at least, all shaggable women of child-bearing age, and Henrietta is assuredly that, no dearth of evidence.'

'This is sensitive material, Jacob,' Marv said. 'Our commission is to ease things for Jule, not emphasise the downside.'

'I love the way Jule sticks by her always – calls her Hen sometimes. That shows closeness despite everything, undoubtedly. Akin to your being Marv, Marv.'

Corbett said: 'Her other men, alleged other men – I don't know whether you've—'

'Do you think Sid's decaying, decayed, mentally?' Marv asked. 'This foyer's not bugged. Sid considered it but decided no – that it was unwholesome for a place dedicated to Gloria.'

'How do you mean, decayed?' Corbett replied.

Marv said: 'It can happen – somebody trying to run an operation like the Complex, with debt collectors at the front door and on the phone. The mind might go flaky.'

'Front doors, it being a Complex,' Jacob remarked.

The big blue Merc drew up outside the hotel and the three of them climbed into the back. Marv closed the partition window between them and Sid's chauffeur, Nightride Ambrose. Corbett sat with Marv. Jacob pulled down a hinged extra place and was facing. Corbett said: 'Although this is not strictly the report on London, I wanted to have a word – well, Jacob, you did open the topic – I wondered if you'd had any thoughts about the two men who were supposed to have, and I do stress supposed—'

'In London you'd see, I imagine, Ivo Vartelm and possibly Phil Castice-Manne,' Jacob replied. 'Also-rans in our race last time.'

'These two are definitely interested parties,' Corbett said, 'though I wouldn't stop the list there.'

'Of course they're interested parties,' Marv said. 'The Complex is for the picking.'

'How do you mean?' Corbett asked. He realised this question could become his theme.

'Castice-Manne knows the scene from close,' Jacob replied. 'Whenever he's down here from London, he lifts up his snout and scents a bargain at the Gloria across the lake, if you ask me. I've got to inform you, Jule, I don't altogether go with Marv on this.'

'On what?' Corbett asked.

'Marv and I are close, obviously, and I always address him as Marv, out of trust and friendship. But that doesn't signify I accept all his thinking. He plans for his dynasty. That's a different approach from mine, another kind of impulse altogether, please recognise this. He's thinking of provision for generations ahead. Me? Less long term.' Jacob was black, very bald, his eyes large, dark, ungenial. Now and then, Corbett had thought that if he himself took the longest long-term view, it would be Marv who would kill him, not Jacob.

'Still not clear of your drift,' Corbett replied.

'It *is* complex,' Jacob replied. He laughed. 'Or Complex with a big C.'

Corbett said: 'Quite.' How did he get past this chatter to ask them what he longed to ask and dreaded the answer to? 'But could I bring you back to the subject I raised – Hen's association with, supposed association with, the men that Sid wants—'

'Regardless of my new plans, I've got a loyalty to Sid that goes beyond just calling him Sid, not Sidney,' Marv replied.

'Oh, clearly,' Corbett said.

'Sid's paying for Sue to have the babe in this private place, you know,' Marv replied. 'Not his own nursing home in the Bay. You can see that, can't you, Jule? We're on our way somewhere else. He could have used a Bay ward and medics and saved himself a handful. But he says: "No, no, no, the Bay's beds are for the aged. Birth's not the speciality. No spot to start a dynasty." So, you'll see, I'm bound to feel a lot for him, Jule, but I still have to ask: Is Sid up to running this outfit?'

'Displace Sid?' Corbett asked. 'I've never heard—'

'Management takeover time, Jule?' Marv replied.

'He wouldn't go,' Corbett replied.

'On the face of it, true,' Marv said.

Corbett asked: 'The whole Complex? This is—'

'This would be confidential for now, clearly,' Marv replied. 'You're used to confidences, Jule.'

'I understand.'

'Middling is all confidences, that's a fact,' Jacob said.

'There'd be a full, boardroom partnership for you, clearly, Jule,' Marv said. 'We long for you to join us. Ever seen an old film on TV called *The Caine Mutiny*, or maybe even read the book? The officers have to take over forcibly when the captain falls apart in heavy seas. Water can get to people in command.'

Christ, Corbett saw he was more in the middle now than he ever had ever been as a middleman. Pete and Laura wanted him with them to help topple Ivo, fearing he might break up. Odd, Corbett had spoken to Laura of *The Caine Mutiny*, too, because of her naval family background, possibly. Now, Marv. While he talked, Marv had been watching Nightride Ambrose through the glass partition, checking he betrayed no sudden sign of catching what was said. Marv's bath-sponge face was exceptionally bath-sponge now, showing no hint of treachery or pride in the child. Nightride was known for his timeless loyalty to Sid and Gloria.

'Some of Marv's thinking I'd go with, no question,' Jacob remarked. 'My anxiety is, the genius of a man like Sid can often be mistaken for lunacy. Think of Marconi, reviled for his theories, yet those historic messages across water near the Bay, and now Walkmans a fucking nuisance on every beach.'

Marv said: 'My feeling, Jule, is OK, Jacob naturally esteems Sid and sees all sorts of special abilities there – so can we all, I'm sure. But if you joined, Jule, and recognised the possibilities – if Julian Corbett with all his experience joined – I believe this would bring Jacob in, too. Then we'd have a boardroom combination that any private-equity firm or bank or finance house would be eager to back in a take over – plainly a knock-down-price take over because we know from the inside how bad Sid's books are, and because the Complex would lose so much of its value once Sid was flung out somehow.'

'How somehow?' Corbett asked.

'"The water, the water,"' Marv replied, mimicking Sid's voice; thin, frightened, plaintive. 'Is that kind of terror sane? Yes, he might have to be neutralised totally, and perhaps Gloria as well – she's got a lot of awkward fight, that old thinker – but don't fret, Jule, you would never be asked to see to it, although you have exceptional access to him. "The water." This is another reason he wouldn't let Sue go into the Bay nursing home. He's afraid she and the child would be swished out on a tidal wave one night. All right, in a way this is a kind of consideration, and lovely. Mad, though. You've heard of the waters breaking? Sid's got his own version. But those barrage sluices are tip-top, Jule. Infallible.'

Jacob leaned forward on the small hinged seat, contemplative, combative: 'A super-gifted mind like Sid's can be in touch with things beyond the apparent,' he said, 'such as water, a basic element. Sid knows about power and natural force. They're his kin, his brethren. As I see things, anyway. There's mystery in Sid. There's pre-Christianity. Talking of water, have you seen how Sid can hold someone's head under in the grotto at Glorside for exactly the right spell when ques-

tioning a bastard who won't talk – who thinks he won't talk?
Sid's really got the touch.'

In the maternity home, Marv put his flowers in a vase and
then lifted the baby from the cot alongside Sue's bed and
looked into its face for a while, smiling. The child was awake
but stayed quiet. Jacob showed her the teddy bear plenty of
times, moving its arms in full circles and pressing the
squeaker to the beat of *Pack Up Your Troubles In Your Old
Kit Bag*.

Marv said: 'You know Jule Corbett, don't you, Sue? He's
the one Sid asked us to help by knocking over a couple of lads
who've been boning Jule's wife, though the relationships were
at different times, clearly.' Marv did a couple of slow pirou-
ettes, holding the baby happily against his face.

Corbett said: 'Yes, Marv, I wondered whether you—'

'Sid does try to be helpful,' Sue said. 'Is helpful. Look at all
this.' She indicated the large private room, rural-scene water-
colours on the walls; piss but not farcically garish.

'In one way, Sid was saying more than he knew,' Marv
replied.

'This is the nature of genius, as I understand it,' Jacob said.

'Don't spin her too much, Marv,' Sue said. She sat up a
little more straight in the bed and held out her arms for the
baby. Marv did not pass her over, though. Corbett thought
it suited Sue to have her arms wide and welcoming like
that. You could see motherhood in general in it, part pose,
but something real there, too, probably. She was fair,
almost blonde, her hair cut short to not quite skinhead, and
she might look at her best sitting up in a private-room hospital bed. The linen around her gleamed and seemed
somehow to lend Sue much of its freshness and good
quality. Judging from where her feet jutted up under the
bedspread, she must be quite tall, maybe taller than Marv.
Her neck was lovely: long and slender, not quite right for
the haircut.

Although Corbett liked tallness in women, it could make
things awkward bending to a cot or pram, but they had prob-

ably thought of this and accepted it. She had on a mauve bed jacket with large, chased-silver buttons and turned-back cuffs, the kind of thing many women with a bit of money might buy if they knew they could be whipped in for a first birth at any time. The colour gave serenity after all that pushing and yelling. Any time you liked, Corbett could read clothes. He liked her hands, clearly in sight now as she asked for Evaline. They were ringless, small, square; the kind of hands that would probably do well on an electric guitar and get the skin off a garlic clove with deftness.

Marv still did his slow, gyrating dance with the child. He was fascinated by her. It seemed monstrous to Corbett now that he'd originally imagined this to be a murder expedition. He must have drifted into egomania, believing everything centred on his life. There was another, new life here. Corbett found the positive nature of maternity brilliant, as against the prospect of slaughter.

'Sue's right,' Jacob said. 'Watch out, Marv. Evaline's brain's not anchored properly yet in her head. That isn't finalised until well, well on. This could disadvantage a child if the brain gets permanently loose.'

'Have you children, Jule?' Sue asked. She lowered her arms.

'He and Henrietta don't want any at this point,' Jacob replied.

'Are you sure?' Sue asked.

'About Hen's views?' Corbett said. 'Oh, I think so.'

Susan said: 'I wondered if, maybe, this was why she occasionally—?'

'These are sensitive areas, Sue,' Marv replied. 'I don't see any link between not having kids and Hen's getting about a bit. As far as I know she wasn't seeking pregnancy. Are we talking about Jule's possible infertility here? Hardly.'

'I don't even know the names of the men, if they exist,' Corbett said.

'It could be better like that,' Marv said. 'We were discussing names earlier, Sue – their significance.'

Corbett said: 'Were their names, are those names, Rory, Luke? These might be names that would appeal to Hen.'

'Jule's been seeing people in London that we have to repel, Sue,' Marv replied. 'You've heard of hostile bids. Repel, repel, repel.'

'Can you?' she asked. Her voice was big and warm and proclaimed, yes, Marv could repel them. Corbett considered there might be a fine relationship here. It heartened him. Marv was the sort who would not mind that type of woman's haircut. He'd regard it as witty.

Marv handed Evaline back to Sue: 'To some degree, yes, we can fight these metropolitans off,' he said. 'Depending on Jule, naturally. How he plays it. I'm inviting him to take a directorship the moment we're in control and Sid and Gloria made safe. A private-equity firm hearing Jule was in would come up with funds and help in management. We'd ask Jule to talk to any likely financier. I slip into mad rages with such people, and Jacob's full of shit. So Jule's needed.'

'If it had been a boy, I would have suggested Guillaume, the French for William,' Jacob replied. 'We have to be aware of Europe.'

Sue said: 'It was your father-in-law, wasn't it, Jule, who did the funeral for Boris Lowndes? You remember Boris? Found on the beach like that. It said something, like a message in a bottle.'

'I think we all remember the death of Boris, Sue,' Marv replied.

'Intolerable, no other word for it,' Jacob said.

'So moving, the funeral, I heard,' Sue said. 'He took a tragic situation and found some hope there.'

'Except for the Liston fight in 1962, Floyd will never allow despair to sink him,' Jacob replied.

'Were there offers in London, Jule?' Sue asked.

'Not at this stage,' he replied.

'Vartelm – his ploy would be to offer very, very low, to flatten you from the start, I should think,' Sue said. 'Getting you into a serf role and grateful for anything at all because he's aristo, Ivo.' Jacob had stopped squeaking the teddy bear. Now, though, humming quietly, Sue followed the rhythm of *Pack Up Your Troubles* as she rocked the baby.

Corbett said: 'I trust I'm not boasting, but Vartelm would never try that on me. We didn't get to figures. At this point. Just prelims – sparring.'

'That's what I mean about me and rage,' Marv said. 'If there were delays and tactics. Not my area.'

'Ivo's another of those names very difficult to shorten,' Jacob said.

'I wanted Jule to meet you and Evaline, Sue, so he'd know my view of the future. What I have in mind. I see the possibility of a lovely continuance.' Marv spoke in a matter-of-fact way, yet Corbett heard power there and worthwhile, awkward obsession. 'I see Evaline influential in that nursing home in the Complex, caring for wealthy old folk into, yes, the second half of this wonderful millennium century, and bringing on noble trees and plants in the bot gardens which might continue even longer, many trees being full of time, particularly the olive. Yes, I'm interested in a family tree, but in real trees also.'

'This is quite a vista,' Jacob replied. 'Even I must say that, despite my known feelings against the dynastic.'

Sue said: 'Ours is such a lucky babe – a father so committed, so creative.'

'To extinguish Sid and Gloria is quite a task,' Marv replied. 'When I say "extinguish", of course I mean taking the Complex from them on our terms. Important to play along very normally for the present. Follow his wishes, follow his orders. Make sure Nightride's happy.'

Nightride had waited outside. In the Mercedes again, Marv pulled the partition back and told him: 'All right, let's find our fucking target. Have we timed it OK?'

Corbett said: 'Marv, I don't—'

'This would be the loverboy, yea?' Nightride replied. He opened the glove compartment and took a cardboard-covered notebook from it. Before starting the car, he studied a page for a while.

Marv said: 'I don't want written stuff around afterwards.'

'Relax, Marv, will you? Once we've done him I'll eat the notebook.'

'You'll enjoy this part of things, too, Jule,' Jacob said, 'as much as meeting the babe, count on it.'

Nightride half turned as he drove: 'I get a role in this. Sid said I'm included. I'm carrying a definite untraceable and silenced. I'm not some fucking spectator or just a driver, Marv. Sidney knows what I can do.'

'Which target?' Corbett asked.

'Ah, which?' Nightride said. 'Too right, Jule. No choice.'

'Our fear is there's only one now,' Marv replied. 'The other guy has disappeared, maybe left the country. Alerted? I don't know how, Jule, but it's possible.'

'We took these dearies in the wrong sequence, that's a fact,' Jacob said. 'We should have realised the divorced one could just up and go as soon as he heard hints.'

'Heard hints fucking how?' Nightride asked over his shoulder. 'Who been leaking? One thing I can't abide – a mouth.'

Marv said: 'Talking to Sue and looking at the child in there I was bound to feel even more, Jule, that men who treat another's wife with disgusting casualness should expect only a harsh settlement eventually. Decent values don't look after themselves. They must be guarded.'

Nightride kept on: 'How did the other chap get warned? Sidney's going to be irritated.'

Corbett said: 'Look, it could be the situation has corrected itself – one gone abroad, the other returned to his marriage and children. Possibly we could leave him now. Marv, I think you can see the binding significance of family even more clearly than before, following this birth.'

'Letting it drop would be a problem postponed,' Marv replied.

'Sid wouldn't like that,' Nightride remarked. 'I needs to send a coded fax saying it's done – at least one of them. This might get the lesson to the other – stop him coming back to her when he feels dick-led again. It happens. As long as he knows there were two at it, obviously. Sid wants you sealed off from pain, Jule, and your marriage in with a full chance. Sid's been with Gloria so long despite everything, he truly believes in all that – marriages, I mean. It's lovely to watch.'

'Make sure Sue brings the teddy with her when she's discharged, Marv,' Jacob said. 'Things can go missing in a hospital, private as much as NHS.' They drove out of Cardiff, north up the A 470 towards Merthyr Tydfil. Marv said: 'This guy is a one-man-band, Jule.'

'Which?' Corbett asked.

'The love man,' Nightride replied.

'In what way a one-man-band?' Corbett asked. 'Running some business entirely solo?'

'In that way,' Marv replied, 'a one-man-band way.'

Jacob said: 'Worth seeing. He's got a big drum and cymbals harnessed to his back. He plays the mouth organ with his lips while he beats the drum with steel caps on his elbows. Plus, he kicks out with one foot, connected by a line to the cymbals and drumsticks. It's an art, take my word.'

'People know him. The police know him, and don't give him bother,' Marv said. 'I suppose he makes a tenner or so each outing.'

'He begs?' Corbett said.

'It's an artistic performance,' Jacob replied. 'Like street theatre. The 10p coins in the hat are fees. You shouldn't feel ashamed for Henrietta fancying him. As well as the skill side there has to be fitness – a drum that size on his back and working his elbows and foot. Some people who started with busking moved on and eventually rose to the concert platform. Dame Myra Hess.'

They turned off the A470 and drove through the long town centre of Taffmead, 'hub of the valleys', as it was called. 'He works here?' Corbett asked, staring at shoppers from the car both sides.

'Around the market,' Jacob said. 'Not yet. In an hour. Taffmead market's famous. We've got his timetable. That was half the trouble. While Nightride and I researched him the other one made a bolt – live to fuck another day.'

Nightride drove on until they came to a big, free car park. 'It's still there,' he said, 'or we'd of been real stymied.' He stopped the Mercedes and climbed out. Marv and Jacob left the car, also. Corbett hesitated. 'Yes, and you, Jule,' Nightride said. 'It's all for you, you know.' Corbett joined them. Jacob re-entered the Mercedes, but in the driving seat.

'We use the Peugeot 406, Jule,' Marv said. He pointed to a steel-grey saloon on the other side of the car park.

'Whose?' Corbett asked.

'Right,' Nightride replied.

'This was taken yesterday from a long-stay multi-storey,' Marv said. 'We'll be fine.'

'Taken?' Corbett asked.

'You know, fucking taken,' Nightride said.

'You?' Corbett asked.

'It could of been reported nicked by now, of course, but maybe not. Anyhow, so far it's OK for the job, or it wouldn't still be here.' Jacob, in the Mercedes, suddenly drew away. Marv, Nightride and Corbett walked to the Peugeot. Nightride put gloves on, did something to the lock and opened up. He took the driver's seat. Marv and Jule went into the back. Nightride provided more gloves and they pulled them on. 'We while away fifty minutes,' Marv said. 'Nightride can fill you in, Jule.'

Nightride turned around. He had the notebook open in his hand. 'He does two hours every Thursday, Friday and Saturday, three spots around the market. You can see he times himself. Two hours exact. Jacob said fit, but, even so, playing like that for a spell's a killer. Face red, sweat everywhere including the pavement, body bent, and the elbows and kicking getting weaker at the end, so the drum and cymbals sound feeble, like heard distant. People stop throwing money – they're not being given the full thing in the late part. And now and then he has to fight off kids trying to pinch the cash or wanting just to fuck up his show for laughs – kick his left leg away when he's working the cymbals and drumsticks with his right. He's knackered.' Nightride held the notebook up so Jule could see a double page. Sketched in pencil was what looked like a horseshoe of outer stalls in the Taffmead market, with three crosses at different points to mark the sites where he performed.

'This is the right man?' Corbett asked. 'I mean, supposing there *is* a man, men, at all.'

'Him,' Nightride replied.

'Sid had a watch on Henrietta ever since he first heard the whispers,' Marv said. 'We could see such behaviour might turn out disturbing for someone like you, Jule, devoted and sensitive, and Sid longed to protect you. I agreed. There were a couple of penthouse meetings about it. Henrietta was a main agenda item. In no time now, you might be in penthouse company meetings yourself.'

'Is this one Rory or Luke?' Corbett asked.

'What?' Marvin answered.

'What you were saying,' Corbett replied.

'No, no, those were just names, like illustrating,' Marv said.

Nightride grew tense. 'So who's these other two, Marv?' he demanded, his voice all at once gone shrill. 'Rory, Luke.'

'Just names we were discussing earlier,' Marv replied. 'As names, that's all.'

'Yea, but who?' Nightride asked. 'We don't want two more in on this. This is a nice, neat operation, but only one target.'

'Christ, they're nobody,' Marv said.

'So why did you close the partition? Why did Jule ask about them?'

Marv said: 'You're not going to get someone with a name like Rory or Luke as a one-man-band. He's called Felix or Eric, isn't he?'

'Eric Anthony Moyle, thirty-eight, married, two children,' Nightride replied.

'My God, how did she meet him?' Corbett asked.

'When he's out of the music clobber he can look all right,' Nightride said. 'Dark hair and burning eyes, like that actor who done the mad concentration-camp chief.'

'Ralph Fiennes?' Corbett asked.

'And he spends,' Nightride replied. 'Women do go for him. His wife puts up with it. He window cleans Mondays and Tuesdays unless it's raining, and is most likely on the Giro as well. Well, of course he fucking is. I haven't looked into that. Take as read.'

'Perhaps bumped into him in some Cardiff club,' Marv said. 'This could be before Nightride and the other boys and girls were watching her for us.'

'He do get to clubs,' Nightride replied. 'Some music arrangements he copies for his street numbers, tries to.'

An element in Corbett stirred and might have said or snarled, but did not say or snarl: Yes, get rid of Eric Anthony Moyle now, any way you like. God, Eric Anthony Moyle was a humiliation, just at a time when Jule saw possible huge improvements for himself and Henrietta, maybe with Marv and Jacob, maybe with Laura and Pete. How could Hen have turned away from him and gone to someone like Eric Anthony Moyle? Did Moyle actually wear the hat he put at his feet for coins? Oh, Jesus, what did the other one do, the one who had cleared out in time? He might be even more degrading. Some clerk in local government? Corbett thought of how it would be if the word ever got to Ivo Vartelm that Corbett's wife had been playing with a one-man-band. And then the tale would be passed down from Ivo to Grace and the other girls at Omdurman. How could they go on considering Jule propertied? As they'd see it, no wife would give herself to someone like Moyle, and possibly someone worse than Moyle, if her husband were truly eminent and established, with reliable money.

But Corbett worried for Moyle, all the same, and worried for Henrietta and himself. This was such a social stoop for Hen to take there must have been overwhelming attraction between her and Moyle. Hen did have susceptibilities: it hurt Corbett, of course, but that was Hen and he wanted her. Wasn't he one of her susceptibilities himself quite often? If Moyle were destroyed, she might be devastated, and for ever embittered, regardless of what she had told Corbett lately. Floyd said Hen's mother grew sour near the end. It could be genetic. Corbett was sickened to think he would be suspected of killing someone as farcical as Moyle for getting to his wife. And he was certain to be suspected – he had realised that from the start. Didn't Marv see that Corbett's stature and ability to pull investment funds would be disastrously weakened if the notion went around he had slaughtered a kind of vagrant, from jealousy? And what sort of man married a woman who would go off with a one-man-band called Eric? He could imagine bankers and financiers and private-equity folk in the City asking this. Yet Marv had brought him here today, wanted him to be present, put him even more at risk of blame.

Corbett said: 'My God, you're not going to do him out in the open like that, with a market crowd around, are you? What, from the car?'

'Not on,' Nightride said.

Marv said: 'Pedestrianised where he works.'

Nightride turned a page in the notebook. Jule saw a further drawing. It appeared to be a footbridge over a river and leading to an area with trees and bushes. Nightride said: 'So, he's done his music, collected his bits of money and wants to go home fast, and get the drum and brass off of his back. The footbridge and this park are the quickest way, and he takes it every Thursday, Friday and Saturday.' He pointed to the top end of the drawing: 'The park's got a patch of wood-land here, like left to true Nature, you know? We wait there. We got to hope there's nobody else about. It's not far from the road. We're into the Peugeot straight after we hit him.' He turned another page to a road diagram. He pointed again. 'Jacob's here with the Merc, about seven miles. We dumps the Peugeot and gets back to the Bay. The thing about having a private hospital room like Sue is no bugger knows for sure the

time you visited. Sue can give an alibi for part of the afternoon – maybe enough to make it seem, like, impossible for us
to reach here and do him. Anyway, why connect me and
Marv with him? For you, different, Jule, obviously, if they
find out about the affair. But you'll be all right. Look, try to
practise not twitching, all right? Moyle can't run or dodge
about, not with a lumpy thing like that on his back and heavy
boots for the link line to the sticks.'

'I don't know if you want to speak to Moyle before, Jule.'

'Speak? Before?'

'That's one reason I thought it would an be idea for you to
come with us.'

'Speak?'

'Explain to him why he's getting it,' Marv replied. 'And let
him know Henrietta is back home and will for ever be so,
possibly with children in mind for the future, once you're set
up in a true situation. Let him see he's nothing – a stray
moment.'

'Most probably we could hold him for you while you
talked, Jule,' Nightride said, 'though it will be tricky getting
arm locks on him from the back – so he's facing you to listen
proper – tricky because of the drum.'

'Nothing long-drawn-out if you do talk to him, obviously,
Jule. But it would probably settle you – settle you permanently, that is – yes, settle you if you knew he knew what it
was about – the moral side – not just some casual violence in a
wood.'

'Marv's right. Some of these bastards think they can fuck
anything, like entitled, no comeback? Well, this is going to be
an education for Eric.'

'No,' Corbett said, 'I don't want contact, no face-to-face
close stuff.'

'Well, I can understand,' Nightride replied. 'To look at
someone you been sharing her with, it's rough. Next time
you're on the job you're asking yourself is she gazing up at
you but seeing him, even though he's dead?'

'Plus, there's possible identification,' Corbett said.

'Identification?' Nightride asked.

'If you decided after all only to give him a beating,' Corbett said. 'He might be able to talk afterwards.'

'This would certainly be a point if we had decided to do only that,' Marv said.

'Sidney wouldn't feel good about just a slap,' Nightride said. 'In any case, someone with a drum and brass on his back – a beating would be tricky likewise, and a lot of noise.'

'We can move now,' Marv said. 'We'll regard it as agreed that you don't want to make a statement, Jule.'

Nightride started the car and took it slowly back through the middle of the town and then out alongside the river and park. He drove on until they reached a road bridge and roundabout and came back up on the other side of the river and park. Nightride obviously knew the ground. He pulled off the road near a picnic area with rustic-style tables and benches and the three of them left the car and made their way into the small stretch of woodland. They found themselves concealed positions from where they could watch a wide. gravelled path that led from the town-centre footbridge to the far end of the park.

Corbett wished now he had not refused to speak to Eric Anthony Moyle, but was afraid to disrupt things by telling Marv he'd changed his mind. It troubled Corbett to think this attack might seem to Moyle nothing more than a gang of louts who knew his movements and would mug him for the tenner or so in coins, perhaps to buy drugs. That could soil Corbett's status, even though Moyle would be wrong and, in any case, only have time to suspect it for a second. An avenging husband and possibly eventual father was an altogether larger role, as Marv had suggested. Even noble. Perhaps Corbett would call 'Remember Henrietta!' just before Moyle's mind and life went. Did Hen use her true name with him? In any case, Marv's suit would probably tell Moyle this could not be a group of ordinary crooked locals. It was not at all a suit for a killing in a wood to fund a habit.

This was a gorgeous spot. When the trees shifted in the breeze they caused little patches of sunlight to race across the path, glowing on the gravel. This park, with its strip of woodland, would probably be what the environmental planners called 'a green lung'. Corbett had always loathed this phrase, thinking that lungs should not be green, but today he could see more clearly what people had in mind. No wonder the picnic facility had been placed nearby. It really jarred with Corbett that such a beautiful place had been selected by Nightride.

When Moyle came into sight, Corbett thought he looked weirdly impressive, not just like someone who had pulled Hen. Moyle walked very upright, despite the drum, and his pace was steady, dogged. He could have been a symbol of what folk would do in the good cause of music. The walls of the drum were painted dark blue, light blue and cream. The cymbals glinted richly golden, like the gravel, above these bright, circus colours. Somehow, Moyle made Corbett also think of knights in their grand lurid gear passing through familiar country. Had Hen ever seen him with his drum? Did she even know about it? Could Hen get badly upset about someone called Eric? He could understand her grieving for a Rory or Luke. Moyle did have the hat on. It was a greenish pork-pie, not too bad.

Nightride went swiftly past Jule at a crouch, using the bushes and tree trunks for cover. He held some kind of silenced revolver in his gloved right hand. Where had Sid found this gifted chauffeur? When Moyle was almost abreast of Jule, though clearly unaware of him and the other two, Nightride suddenly stepped out from the trees just in front and shot him three times in the chest, a two-handed grip, arms out stiff at shoulder height like someone who had been trained. It happened very fast and when Corbett shouted around the tree trunk hiding him: 'Remember Henrietta!', Moyle might have been already dead. He had lurched to the side at first sight of Nightride and the gun, and as the bullets struck him this lurch became a stagger and then a collapse face down, his drum swaying slightly above him, the cymbals sounding gently three or four times in the fall. Marv came out onto the path and he and Nightride gripped Moyle by the drum harness and pulled him, still on his stomach, into the undergrowth where he would be better concealed. The cymbals clanged again.

Nightride and Marv unharnessed the drum and put it on its side near Moyle so it would not stick up and be obvious to anyone on the path. Staring down at Moyle and the drum, Corbett thought now not of questing knights but of films about old wars, such as *The Charge of the Light Brigade* and *The Red Badge of Courage*. That kind of movie always showed dead drummer boys with their drum lying near them in the battlefield aftermath. These images were meant to say the lot about war's useless cruelty. Perhaps Jacob's playing *Pack Up Your Troubles In Your Old Kit Bag* on the teddy bear squeaker, then Sue's humming, also made Corbett think of war. Was a war starting here now? Nightride held out the revolver to Jule, perhaps in case he wanted to put a personal bullet into Moyle for taking Hen. Corbett turned away. Marv had produced no weapon and Corbett still did not know whether the good tailoring hid a pistol. Nightride returned to the spot where Moyle had fallen and scattered some of the blood-stained gravel with his foot. Marv bent over the body and took two handfuls of coins from Moyle's jacket. He poured them into the pockets of Jule's fleece. 'This was evidently a robbery,' Marv said.

'I don't want them,' Corbett replied.

'Of course you don't,' Marv said. 'Ditch them once we're away from here.'

'Did you see what I mean about that actor, them eyes?' Nightride asked.

8

Of course, there had been frequent periods in his career when Corbett considered disappearing abroad. He didn't mind inland Spain, say Murcia or Seville. Ten per cent in cash came out of every fee he earned and was kept hidden about the manse to cover travel and a stay for at least a year, given careful living. That is, travel and maintenance for himself and Henrietta, assuming Henrietta would come. She could be pissy about Europe and, in any case, loathed the idea of what she called 'exile'. Escape funds were standard for any middleman. The money stacks Boris Lowndes had shown his mother were probably meant as escape funds originally. Christ, Boris, why, why didn't you use them? You could be in California now, polishing your history of the fridge. Boris must have felt an increasing threat or why disclose the savings? Mothers were all right, but you did not tell them about money unless things looked damn dark. Had Boris hung on, hoping he could still scheme his way clear? One of the crucial skills in middlemanning was to spot your exit time and act on it, like leaving a woman.

Nightride, Marv and Corbett abandoned the Peugeot and, in the back of the Mercedes again on the way home, Jule thought about doing a runner, say tonight or tomorrow at the latest. He was trembling but did not think it showed. If he was going to leave it might need to be quick. Load the car and get to a ferry port. He could see himself driving by night down through France towards Hendaye and Irun at the border. He would wear a white T-shirt which he had always thought gave him a good, sacrificial, victimised look, but which was short-sleeved and showed the strong development of his arms and shoulders. He fancied one of those round, brown or beige woollen Afghan hats, in case he wanted to drive with the window open.

Yes, Henrietta was almost sure to protest against retreat, in that all-brain-and-bravery way of hers. But suddenly the array of pressures had begun to trouble Corbett. And they troubled him at least as much as the situation's prospects had thrilled him not long ago. Part of Jule envied Hen's other friend, the one who had taken the early warning and gone. The trouble with middlemanning work was that so much of it could seem like ordinary, legitimate business dealing, with ordinary, financial, unviolent risks – the kind any company executive would expect – and a lulling took place. Corbett must be alert to that. Something like this might have happened to Boris, though it was clear he had also begun to sense things were turning uncontrollably bad. Lowndes could have been regarded as quite good-looking in a grandmotherly sort of way and this would probably explain the irrelevant, vindictive abuse of his face. It upset Corbett badly because he would regard himself as not just more handsome in a classical style than Boris, but with greater animation and wit in his features, as well as delicacy. Sometimes he would feel dazed and almost scream at the thought of these being blow-lamped or hacked at with Stanley knives amid chuckles, pre- or post-death. Fine and shapely, his cheekbones especially he thought, should be spared that kind of business ploy.

He sensed tough, approaching difficulties, the way Lowndes obviously had. These difficulties could encircle and throttle Corbett if he misjudged, like a rabbit in a gin, or like a middleman in the middle. Of course, Hen would never see it like that. She had this mad calmness, probably learned from Jack Hawkins in a TV war film, at least when it was Jule facing the trouble. It fucking was. There were Ivo and Philip Castice-Manne, both requiring special consideration from him, and both capable of bloody retaliation if the special consideration didn't come. And special consideration could not come to both, or even to either, supposing Corbett concentrated on his own emergence as a main man. Corbett did intend to concentrate on that, providing that he stayed. Castice-Manne had the pictures, or said he had: Corbett believed him. Pete and Laura wanted him to be part of a conspiracy which would remove Ivo, whatever remove meant. She had told him enough to make things dangerous if he refused to join them. Now, Marv and Jacob wanted him to be part of a conspiracy which would extinguish Sid and Gloria, whatever extinguish meant. These were proposals which seemed to cross the frontier between routine, very close-to-the-wind commercial practice, and sheer villainy. Floyd probably would not distinguish, but Floyd's thinking capacity had been damaged by his Baptist College training and by all those punches he had taken during fantasy rounds with Liston.

As an additional pressure, Marv and Jacob had sweetly arranged things so that Corbett was an accessory to murder, and they had it in their power to offer – or not – a possible partial alibi at the nursing home. We'll take care of you, Jule, as long as you jump the way we want. Suspicion for the killing was more likely to point at Corbett than at Marv, Jacob or Nightride. Corbett depended on them. This gave Marv and Jacob infinite leverage, stronger even than Castice-Manne's Omdurman photographs.

Of course, there were still elements in Corbett that delighted at some of these pressures – that longed for and lived for these pressures. They could be regarded as business successes. They meant he was in demand from all sides, something any middleman craved. These pressures were testimonials. He was box office, he was a star, and people wanted to hitch their wagon to him. Yes, but over everything lay one dominant uncertainty which might make all the risk-taking and stress seem absurd: would Corbett actually be able to help in raising the huge finance required by any one of the three rival firms? All of them seemed to regard this as certain. It was flattering, but this man of property hadn't actually got any yet, and might never. Give it up? Make a dash? He thought too much sun on fresh face skin like his could be ageing, but if he did choose a Spanish city as his hideaway he would make sure he bought a wide-brimmed hat, though not a sombrero because he'd look like some fucking Benidorm fortnighter Cockney.

Marv said: 'Those two with Ivo – Laura and Peter Dite. Like his Cabinet. Meet them, Jule?'

'Just formally, across the boardroom table,' Corbett replied. 'Pleasantries.'

'These two won't just sit back and watch,' Marv said.

'How do you mean, Marv?' Corbett asked.

'The Admiralty's in her veins. The jolly-tar heritage – grappling irons and boarding parties.'

'I don't—'

'Jacob's done some research on her.'

'Father was very gold leaf in the navy,' Jacob said. 'Flotillas, if not more. It's given her aspirations and a belief in invincibility. She might want to rule the waves down in the Bay lagoon. Personally, I mean, not as just an Ivo supernumerary. Ivo could be for the push.' Jacob was in the back of the Merc with them. Nightride had taken over the driving again. Marv left the partition unclosed. He would think it churlish to shut Nightride out after they had slaughtered someone together and jointly unhooked his drum.

'So there might be an approach to you from them, Jule, to join a new firm, their firm,' Marv said.

'Right,' Corbett replied.

'Play it along, maybe,' Marv said. 'For now. We know where your true loyalties are, don't worry. We trust our man.'

'Thanks, Marv,' Corbett replied.

'I know Sidney would never doubt you, Jule,' Nightride said. 'You're golden with him. That's why he gets so ratty about other men fucking your wife senseless.'

'Thanks, Nightride,' Corbett replied.

Jacob said: 'I'd really rather have wished to be there when Moyle was done, Jule.'

'Jule was great, like born to it,' Nightride said. 'Anyone call you a weak ponce when I'm around in future, Jule, they got me to cope with. This was lurking in trees and Jule lurked like he had been lurking in trees all his life, like a cheetah.'

'I adore seeing retribution meted out, a kind of natural justice, perhaps in its way greater than any other form of justice,' Jacob replied. 'This can restore belief in a good, governing, overseeing Force running Existence, in my view.'

'There's a lesson for all sorts of fucking shaggers around in the end of Moyle,' Nightride said.

'Yes, those bullets had like a text on them,' Jacob said.

'What?' Nightride snarled. 'There wasn't nothing written on them bullets. I told you, untraceable.' He moved about jerkily in the driving seat, as though wanting to turn right around for the argument but couldn't, because of the road.

'No, I meant they had a sort of symbolism to them,' Jacob replied, 'spoke a message.'

'What text on them?' Nightride asked. 'What message? You think I get fucking bullets inscribed with my initials like fucking cufflinks?'

'As if a text,' Jacob replied. 'You know, like from the Bible. About sin, and paying for it.'

'What, he used to pay her for it?' Nightride asked. 'Should you say this in front of Jule – call his wife a whore?'

'I was talking about punishment,' Jacob replied. 'A wonderful, prevailing, strict orderliness in the Creation to which, in our particular way, we can contribute. How I interpret these events, anyway.'

'Like that other black guy with John Travolta in Pulp Fiction, shouting the Bible before he killed them kids?' Nightride asked. He seemed more comfortable now.

'I believed in world orderliness a long time before any film, rest assured,' Jacob replied.

'That Bible, though – it's full of stuff, that's a fact,' Nightride replied. 'What, Jacob, you saying it's really got something in there about a cock-happy guy with percussion gear on his back?'

'Proverbs,' Marv answered. '"He that bangeth a drum and married women shall be brought low when loaded with shekels gathered in a hat."'

As soon as Corbett returned to the manse, Henrietta said: 'Did you find out anything from them, Jule, about my other… about my…?' She grew angry with herself, frowned hard. Despite her strong, long face she suddenly looked like a distressed teenager. Regardless of the foul reason for this, Corbett felt sorry for her. 'But this is damn crazy, avoiding names, as if he were not eligible for one, or as if I were ashamed of calling him by it,' she said. 'About Eric Moyle… did you discover what's happening?'

'He's the other man? The one still here? Afraid not, Hen.'

'They didn't say if they'd located him, been to see him?'

'I didn't want to ask direct in case it provoked them into going for him now,' Corbett replied.

'We must reach him, Jule,' she said. Her words were clipped, no histrionics, an instruction.

'But I got the impression they weren't so concerned any more,' Corbett replied. 'They treat it as a whim of Sidney, not much beyond that. They'll let it just fade away. Marv's preoccupied. His girlfriend's had a baby.'

'Well, lovely, obviously, but—'

'Evaline.'

'A story in *Dubliners*,' Floyd said. 'Does Marv read a lot of James Joyce?'

'I don't believe even fatherhood would stop him, them,' Henrietta replied. 'They can separate off one part of their lives from the rest. There's the family, there's business.'

Floyd said: 'Hen's been so agitated, Jule. She wishes to draw a line under this relationship, but cannot if she feels her neglect might endanger him. Do you understand? She loves him, not as a lover now, but as a human being to whom she has obligations which must be met. There's honour to this, there's nobility, no sex. I'm proud of my daughter. Shere Hite says young British women these days want sex every day. Perhaps this helps explain Hen's wanderings. She is very British. But sex is only sex. No binding hold is established. Think of that Edna St Vincent Millay poem.'

'They really said nothing about Eric?' Henrietta asked.

'Nothing,' Corbett replied.

'How do you interpret this, Jule? That he's still alive? That he is not?' Floyd asked.

'We must go to him,' Henrietta said. 'Now.'

'I wondered if, perhaps, we should withdraw,' Corbett replied.

'Withdraw from what?' Floyd asked.

'Take a holiday,' Corbett replied.

'Mrs Lowndes has upset you, Jule,' Floyd said. 'But she views things simplistically. It's natural.'

'Something has happened, hasn't it, Jule?' Henrietta asked. 'Oh, my God, they've told you something terrible about Eric.'

'The need of a break, that's all,' Corbett said. 'Business concerns bearing down a bit.'

'You're terrified,' Floyd said.

'A holiday where? When?' Henrietta asked.

'Now. Somewhere abroad. I'm not fussy. Seville? The magnificent churches.'

'This is escape, is it?' Henrietta replied. 'You need to put distance. This is desertion.'

'How can you go when you're acting for Hyson in the sale?' Floyd asked.

'Just a short break from it,' Corbett said. 'A space so I can straighten my thoughts.' They talked in Floyd's study, seated on old cane easy chairs padded with thin brown cushions. It was a square, light room containing nothing religious. There were no collected sermons or works of theology in the glass-fronted bookcase, but many volumes about boxing, including AJ Liebling's *The Sweet Science*, and *Who Killed Freddie Mills*? There was also a biography of Malcolm X and *Seize The Time*, by Bobby Seale. Floyd was in training gear again, his legs negligible beneath very short red shorts.

Henrietta stood. 'Come, Jule.'

'You want a holiday, too, Hen? Grand.'

'We'll go to see him together. I need Eric to know it is finished between him and me, and if you are present that will be clear. Also, you can speak with more knowledge than myself about the gravity of his position. He'll believe you and organise escape for himself and his family.'

'Oh, go with her, Jule,' Floyd cried. 'Help ease her heart. Perhaps I should come, too.'

'That's kind,' Corbett said, 'but—'

'Yes, Daddy has to come,' Henrietta cried.

'Father and minister,' Floyd said. He straightened out his bit of chest. 'I feel this would add yet more to the authority of your own presence, Jule. I'll wear the dog collar. This would be a pastor of the church asserting the sacredness of your marriage to Hen, Jule, but also endorsing the absolute conclusion of this bed relationship on the side.'

'I know where he lives,' Henrietta said.

'For God's sake, we can't go to his house,' Corbett replied.

'But yes, that's how it will be,' Henrietta said.

'Think of his family,' Corbett said.

'It must all be open,' Henrietta replied.

'Yes, Hen, yes,' Floyd said.

'Eric spoke so beautifully of the one long street leading to where the Taffmead pit used to be,' Henrietta said. 'There was history in his voice – the men arriving by the score for work wearing steel-capped boots and small scarves, tin boxes with their lunch. The pit and that way of life have gone now, of course. But we'll find the street, easily. And neighbours will point us to the house, I'm sure. They all know each other's business inside out in a miserable little hole like that.'

Corbett said: 'Hen, I want you to think what such a visit could do to—'

'Come,' she said. 'Let us tell him of our joy in each other, Jule, but not gloatingly. Let us also be Christian and caring and inform him of the catastrophe that could fall on him and his. I think his wife will be grateful.'

Corbett said: 'Well, I don't know, Hen. You'll be going there as—'

'She's a dim little valleys cow, anyway,' Henrietta replied. 'Eric made that clear. He craved someone vibrant and with the larger view.'

'These qualities will always be your assets, Hen,' Floyd said, 'and always your problem. Men sniff these attributes and immediately want to stuff you, out of awe.'

'He might not be there, Hen,' Corbett said. 'Shifts. What sort of work does he do?'

'He wouldn't talk about it a great deal, from delightful modesty,' Henrietta replied. 'Eric's like that. But occasionally he would let slip some facts. He's a talent scout for some of the great English football clubs. This is why he continues to live in very ordinary circumstances despite remarkable successes – so he can be in touch with the people and pick up tips about budding local players. His hours are vary various, as you can imagine – meetings with managers, attending school games, talking to parents.'

'Which clubs?' Corbett asked.

'Only the very best, I know that,' Henrietta said. 'His fees are too high for the others.'

'Hen does draw remarkable men,' Floyd said

Floyd changed his clothes and they drove back out to Taffmead, Floyd at the wheel. It was evening and growing dark. Henrietta and Corbett sat together in the back. They soon found the long terraced street and when they knocked at a door at random and asked for the Moyles, the child who answered said: 'Mr. One-man-band? Number 77,' and pointed to a house on the other side.

They walked to it. Henrietta said: 'Yes, this talent- scouting role is very much a one-man-band. His judgment, you see – only his. Many current stars of football owe their start to him.'

At 77 they rang the bell. A slight, dark-haired woman of about thirty in jeans and a denim shirt came to the door, a cigarette lit in one hand. She was pretty, in a large-eyed, sharp-chinned, breezy South Walian style.

'Mr Eric Moyle?' Henrietta asked. A girl of around seven appeared briefly behind the woman, seemed about to join her, but then went out of sight into a back room. It was as though she'd grown used to this kind of caller and could not be bothered with going over all that stuff again.

'Eric? Absent, at the moment,' the woman replied. 'Who shall I say?' She stood in the doorway, a kind of half-and-half position – half inviting them in, half not. She was friendly by culture, she was wary by experience. They stayed at the doorstep. The house opened direct onto the street. The hall or passage looked well-decorated in a light, floral wallpaper. Framed pop concert posters hung near the front door. A child's mountain bike was propped against one wall.

'Is Mr Moyle out somewhere looking for talent?' Floyd asked.

She took a big pull on the cigarette and blew the smoke in a long, pale, thin spear towards him. 'Looking for talent? It's possible, rev, if he's got a bit of money in his pocket like.' Corbett could hear music from a television set or record player inside the house.

'It's important that I talk to him,' Henrietta replied. 'His safety.'

The woman stuck her head forward to gaze a bit harder at Henrietta. There was a street light nearby. 'You one of his birds?' she asked. 'Yes, you're his type, big tits and official accent. You're not in the pod, are you?' She finished the cigarette and threw the stub into the street. 'He's mine, you know. Mine and the kids'. He won't go with you, not permanent, so don't think it, babe or not.'

'No, not like that, I assure you,' Henrietta said.

'Haven't I had others here? There's no point calling, not even with a preacher in tow and this one, whoever. He the minder?' She nodded at Corbett and giggled. 'Not that he looks like he could mind much. Or is he Mr Money? You can't buy me off, either. All right, you think this is not much of a place, not much of a street, not much of a town. But it will do. I'm not interested in your booty, nor is Eric, the treacherous swine. He leches but that's all it is. Ever heard of a lovable rogue? Well, Eric's a crud rogue. But he lives here. He comes back here, always.'

'And will he be here soon?' Floyd asked.

'As and when,' she replied.

'I don't think we need to keep you longer, Mrs Moyle,' Corbett said.

Henrietta said: 'Perhaps we could—'

'Sometimes he walks home through the park,' the woman answered. Momentarily she sounded a little worried. 'I told him it's stupid – those bits of cash aboard. The park will be shut now.' She turned away and put her hand on the front door, getting ready to close it. 'But he'll be all right. He's landed some lolly and he's off spending it, I'd bet. Like the rev said – talent, so-called. Excuse me, lady. I usually wait a couple of days. Then if he still hasn't shown we get the search going – neighbours, family – and he turns up somewhere. He'll be with your replacement, I should think,' she told Henrietta, 'giving her some rubbish career picture of himself.'

'What bits of cash aboard?' Henrietta asked.

'If he's got lucky – I mean, pulled in some extra – he might go and see if he can get lucky the other way, do you know what I mean? Well, of course you know what I mean. He got lucky with you, didn't he? He'll leave his gear somewhere and go to see if he can pull some extra, also the other way.'

'What gear? Which park?'

'Along the river.'

They left number 77 and walked down to the gates of the park. They were chained and locked. Henrietta took an iron strut of the gate in each hand and shook it, like a prisoner in a cell. She said: 'We must look for him.'

'But his wife said he could be anywhere,' Corbett replied.

'She wanted to hurt me, talking of my "replacement". I can't leave here thinking he might be in trouble in the park,' Henrietta said. Corbett saw she was weeping. 'He's like that.'

'What?' Corbett asked.

'Careless about personal security – audacious? She talks of "bits of money". He'd be walking home through deserted parkland with heavy fees from managers and that sort of thing in his wallet?'

'I know these moods in her, Jule. They are immovable.'

'I feel a responsibility for him,' she said. 'If he's hurt it's because of Jule and me.'

Corbett bent down and Henrietta, then Floyd, stood on his back and scaled the gates. Corbett climbed over after them. 'We should have brought a torch,' he said. Thank God, thank God, no.

Occasionally a bit of moonlight poked through. They could just make out the path. Henrietta led. She would stop now and then and the three of them made a search of the undergrowth on both sides. Then they pushed on. Henrietta was still weeping. In a while, Corbett thought he noticed a tiny glint of reflected light. It might be from one of the metal tags at the end of ornamental lacing on the drum. Henrietta walked past the spot and when they were twenty yards further on, Corbett himself initiated another vain undergrowth search. He hoped his keenness would shame her and help her love him more for his selflessness.

They went the whole length of the path until they reached the river bridge and then turned and made their way back. Henrietta walked quicker now, as if convinced it had all been futile. She kept to the path. She no longer wept. The moon was altogether obscured and Corbett would not have been able to locate the drum this time. They climbed the gate and headed for the car. Henrietta said: 'I'm sorry. It was stupid. I've humiliated you, Jule, using you as a bunk-up, crying disloyally like that, and asking you, my husband, to search for... well... for a man who—'

Corbett put an arm around her shoulders: 'It's all right, Hen. I understand. This was a kind and warm act, the kind of caring behaviour I would expect from you, the kind of caring behaviour I love you for.' In a way it was true. Sometimes he wished he could break out from this daft devotion to her and ignore many of her fucking mad impulses.

'You've got a gem in Jule, I hope you realise that, Hen,' Floyd remarked. 'Didn't I say Hen drew remarkable men? None are more remarkable than you, Jule.'

'Thanks, Floyd,' Corbett answered.

'Was that really his thing, Hen – big tits?' Floyd asked. 'They can be beautiful, of course, but eventually what can a man do with big tits? Hard to see them as the basis of an enduring relationship.'

9

Corbett dreaded now that Laura would appear or Peter, or both, to tell him they had arranged for Ivo Vartelm's removal and wanted Jule to join them on the next instalment of their power grab. Welcome aboard, comrade and partner. So many were saying that and would grunt their resentment if he did not respond. Grunt and more. Or, of course, Laura and Pete might want Corbett actually to help them with the disposal of Ivo. Laura had said that wouldn't require Jule. He feared it, all the same. The yearning to quit and lose himself in Europe or the United States still nagged. Lately, he had come to like the idea of Galveston. It was another port and sounded pretty anonymous, not gaudy like San Francisco or New Orleans. In a place like Galveston he would wear dark jeans and a single-coloured lumberjacket, perhaps grey or blue. But he knew he would stay.

He saw that if he tried to disappear abroad his marriage would end. The thought was terrible, unbearable. Hen would not come with him, that was plain. She had a disgusting sense of duty to Moyle, even now, after they had parted. She would never flit with Corbett while uncertain whether Moyle was all right. He's not fucking all right, Hen. On the two or three earlier occasions when Corbett considered solo escape, he had comforted himself by thinking he could secretly keep in touch with Hen and, in a while, she might join him. Alternatively, he would return after, say, a year, when the particular crisis had quietened, and she would take him back. He could no longer regard either of these as possible. She might come to despise him. He did not sob or weep at this idea because he never sobbed or wept, but his eyes lost focus for a few moments and his knees felt insecure.

The body and drum of Eric Moyle would be discovered eventually. After all, this was a public park. Children and lovers did not always stay on the path. It was awful to think of youngsters coming upon Moyle like that among harmless greenery. Corbett hated to imagine his own body lying untended for days in such a spot, his hair probably earthy and smeared down untypically. And when Moyle was found? And when Hen heard? It was certain to be big in the media. He had been a famous, indulged, local figure. Hen would have the double agony of discovering he was dead, and that he had been a one-man-band. Certainly she would pretend to herself, and to Corbett and Floyd, that it did not matter he had been a one-man-band and not a famed soccer scout. She always said she despised some middle-class prejudices. Just the same, this revelation would torture her, set fire to her poise. And if by then Corbett had done an independent hop to Murcia or Seville, she was almost certain to decide he knew something about the death. From time to time she would let her savage, clever mind out of its shed. Once or twice she had used it to defend Jule against enemies. And, although her gruff braininess could also hurt him, it was one of the qualities he admired in her, loved in her. There had to be more to a relationship than pussy. He knew it would have been impossible for him to live with a stupid, supine woman. He needed the brightness to match and stimulate his own, even correct his own when he got off beam, which definitely could occur. Now, there was a chance she would come to loathe Corbett as a possible accessory. It might excite Hen that her man could kill for her, but hatred of the brutal cruelty and Corbett's flagrant independence of her would probably be greater.

Was he her man? Oh, God, was he? Why did she fret about some casual, shag-around, lying scrounger like Moyle? Hadn't she realised how notably more accomplished and potentially established Corbett was than this slum-based cunt-hunter? Didn't she value a whole man, a man of increasing promise? He wanted only to be more worthy of Hen, and perhaps reach conditions when they could contemplate a family. He would almost certainly stop going to houses like Omdurman once he became a father, although Omdurman was in a fine area. Unquestionably he would cease giving and even accepting oral away from home. Fatherhood had to permeate the whole frame.

He supposed Hen might have wanted Moyle kept all right in case she found a need to drift back to him for a while some time. Christ, but she would be totally evil if she suspected Jule had deliberately ensured Moyle and the drum stayed hidden while they looked in the park – that he had even created decoy searches. And this was just the sort of venomous, smart-arse thing she *would* suspect. She would remember that park episode exactly. Recriminations Hen was brilliant at. Some of her clothes he thought of as like recriminations – severe, unjoyous, heavy brown or black. She would recall that sudden dud sortie by Corbett into the park undergrowth, just after they had passed Moyle and the drum. This she was bound to regard as deceitful. But, if Jule did not bolt and was still around, it would look as though nothing in Moyle's death panicked him. Corbett could act ignorant and might keep Hen unsure. Often she would try to be reasonable and fair.

Although Corbett would not bale out, he wanted to rest and avoid further involvement for the present. He considered he deserved this. He took an evening walk around the edge of the lagoon and particularly the Gloria Complex. He found he needed to remind himself of the actual sight of it, feel of it. He lusted for the tactile. At the Gloria he wanted to touch the fabric of the hotel and the nursing home, buy something boxed and wrapped and possibly heavy in one of the late-night shops, say an earthenware article. He liked the idea of handling a package with hard edges. He wouldn't have minded actually going into the nursing home and taking hold for a while of a resuscitation machine or a patient's arm. His role in the sale had become so tangled and vague and slippery that he longed for the hard solidity of structures again, to feel concrete and wood and brick and metal, even cardboard and

bone. The patent realness of these materials would proclaim
the realness of his own prospects. He did not ask Hen to
come. This was something for his individual soul. She would
hardly understand. She thought the fucking soul department
all hers.

As he strolled, Corbett tried to work out ways to stall
Laura or Peter, or both, when they called. And he rehearsed
how to downplay the significance of the Omdurman busy-
tongue photos, if Philip Castice-Manne arrived with them.
Grace's inner thighs were a gloriously luminous white and
Corbett worried that the complexion of his face, held
between them, might come out in photographs as comparatively faded. There were always hazards when looking after
the natural, all-powerful needs of women, but they were entitled to treats. Jule had hit on a phrase to counter
Castice-Manne: he would call what went on at Omdurman 'a
high-spirited romp, only'. This ought to suggest that almost
any man with some money and a little time to fill in London
might easily find himself in this kind of position, although
undeniably intimate. Corbett hoped the words might convince Castice-Manne that Hen and her father would regard
these jolly activities with tolerant amusement: crucial to convince Castice-Manne he possessed no firepower. If Hen saw
the pictures she might have a stroke. Almost certainly she
wouldn't be neutral about a husband getting his lips on
another woman's realms.

While medicinally stroking the glass wall of the botanical
gardens main conservatory, he became sure someone was
watching him. There were lights around the conservatory but
also patches of thick shadow which obscured this observer.
Corbett turned quickly, ready with the 'high-spirited romp'
phrase, in case Castice-Manne flourished those sporty pictures to shock and weaken him. Or Corbett would bring out
his let's-not-rush-things advice if it were Laura or Peter, or
both.

Ivo Vartelm said enthusiastically: 'Yes, yes, I've been doing
the same myself, Jule.'

'What?'

'Sort of inventorying it – the Complex. Reassuring myself from it. Doing a physical check. It could be ours, Jule, ours.' His normally deadpan face was livid with ambition, his voice florid.

'The three of you would make superb owners of the Complex. But this kind of deal takes time, Ivo.' Corbett chuckled: 'Well, listen to me – trying to advise Ivo Vartelm on how to run a negotiation!'

'I offered a ludicrous price,' Vartelm replied. The small eyes were sad, apologetic, yet somehow also signalled in the semi-dark that they had known glory and would know it again. He had on a very long, unbuttoned, tan trench coat over a cord jacket, and the navy trousers of what could be an old tracksuit. Probably he had made a deliberate brave choice never to wear a hat, despite his baldness. To Jule he looked like someone determined to buy a Complex.

'I saw your offer as an opening gambit, Ivo, that's all,' Corbett said.

The botanical gardens was closing and the street suddenly filled with departing customers obviously agog about the range of leaves. 'I wanted to get rid of those other two,' Vartelm said.

'Which?'

'Those other two.'

'Laura? Peter? But they're your boardroom colleagues. You just spoke of owning all this with them.'

'That pissing Laura,' Vartelm replied. 'Her daddy was some big floating warrior. He knew aircraft carriers inside out. This is supposed to bring her class. She'll play the grande dame. She's got a grandson called Caspar. Fucking Caspar! This is the woman who gossips that I changed my name to Ivo so I'd seem a toff, and she's got a grandson called fucking Caspar.'

'Ivos are always getting into the Times Court Circular.'

'Of course they are.'

'Probably more than Caspar.'

Vartelm's voice softened. 'Oh, Caspar, Ivo – I don't want to seem piffling about this. Do you see my tactics?'

'Which?'

'The offer.'

'Thirty-eight million?'

'Insane. Insulting,' Vartelm said.

'I was surprised.'

'Jule, I settle on a ridiculous figure so Laura and Peter think I'm into senility or deliberate negativeness and they start planning a coup – a takeover. Drop Ivo. At least drop him.'

'I can't believe they'd think like that,' Corbett said.

Vartelm was leaning against the thick, curved glass of the long conservatory, his baldness without glow despite the lights. He looked intelligent, in Corbett's opinion. 'When I say it could be ours, Jule, I don't mean those bastards.'

'I don't think I—'

'Ours, Jule.'

'Ivo, you—?'

'We work together, Jule, you and I. We outsmart them. They'll break away, try a management putsch. That's lovely. I don't have to fire them. This is why I say tactics, Jule. It's hard to shed directors from an organisation, you know.'

'Even—'

'Yes, even my kind of organisation,' Vartelm replied. 'The front companies are all properly registered and constituted. Their legality is crucial. I could land myself with a big compensation bill. But if they've left willingly, that's different. They've departed for their own advantage, as they see it, and as an unfair dismissal tribunal would see it. The organisation's not liable. They've deserted the organisation to create another, a replacement. How can compo be due?'

Corbett said: 'The offer—?'

'A bluff. A provocation to them, especially Laura – getting her to tout those figures. My feeling is it worked. One of them or both might approach you, Jule.'

'But why?'

'To recruit. We all see your potential worth in this,' Vartelm said. 'Your ferocious talent.'

In this partial light, Corbett thought he would probably look reserved, even mysterious, radiating complicated but authentic power. 'You'll make a revised offer?' he asked.

'Once they've gone, obviously. A proper offer. I'll have finance houses queuing to put money in when they know demented Lady Muck has gone, and her minion – Pete. He's nothing. But that's only the clean-up side. The real plus is you, Jule. My connections with the City, your name – this combo is irresistible. Can we get out of public view somewhere? People see us talking, they'll guess what's up. She could be down here – Laura – seeking you out.'

'Oh, I don't—'

'Or Castice-Manne. He's got investment in the Bay already, hasn't he? He might be around. Or those apes of Sid Hyson, Marvin and Jacob.'

They walked at the edge of the lagoon to what was once the Norwegian church, with its famous short, pointed spire and white walls. It had been turned into a café and arts centre now. They stood behind it, gazing across the water to the hundreds of lights in the Rocco Forté St David's Hotel at the far water's edge. Vartelm said: 'If they're in touch with you, Jule, I'd like to know. I think I'm entitled to that. I've been frank with you. I have to be abreast of their likely betrayal. It's possible they may have to be countered with… They can't be allowed to destroy a brilliant collection of companies by their greed and impulsiveness, Jule. Discharging them may not be enough. She is all self, all malevolence, that woman. She says at some stage her father was big in depth charges and was in the same wardroom – wardroom as Prince Philip. All right, all right, does that turn her into a marchioness? Notify me, please if there are contacts.'

'Of course,' Corbett replied.

'Sid's away, I know, but I expect you'll be talking to him by phone or e-mail. It would help us – help you and me, Jule – help us if, during such a conversation, you could sound out what is the realistic minimum he will go down to for the Gloria, and if you could also let him feel – let him feel, I don't say anything more precise, at this stage – but let him feel that in your view, the Ivo Vartelm offer is likely to be the most healthy and reliable. This is not asking you to deceive. I believe it will be that, now our investment status is so improved by your inclusion. I might go to Alchemy – that finance house who were after the Rover motor plant from BMW.' He stared out towards the Channel and Penarth head. 'I love this setting, adore it,' he said. 'Let Sidney and Gloria know the Complex would be in the hands of devotees. I can say this for myself and I know I can say it for you, Jule.'

'Certainly.'

'Gull cries over the lagoon go to my core,' Vartelm said. 'This is how Nature should be.'

'Gulls are among my strongest childhood recollections.'

'This I sensed, Jule. The name would remain – The Gloria Complex. Unless, of course, you have objections to that. Perhaps you would wish your own wife's name to be featured also, or even instead. This could be discussed.'

'Gloria has a ring to it, an historical glow,' Corbett replied.

'Or as to glow, it could become the Henglo Complex, containing something from both names, you see.'

'I'm not sure.'

'Either way, it will be our monument, Jule, when we move on. You have children, to inherit?'

'Any time now.'

'Good. They would own alongside mine and probably extend and develop the Complex to make all their portions sizeable in time. That fucking woman with her white ensign father and fucking grandchild called Caspar – fucking Caspar! – she thinks she's the only one who knows about family. I'm glad we're speaking of these things in the lee of what was once obviously a church. You did well to bring us here, Jule. It gives a kind of blessing to our plans, the authority of rightness.'

10

At breakfast time, Jule had a telephone call at the manse from Sid and Gloria Hyson in Malta. The conversation was vague at the beginning. Sid spoke first but handed over to Gloria. She said she was coming back to Heathrow at once and wondered whether Jule could meet her there with a car. Her visit would be short. It was to do with security, Sidney's security. His safety was menaced. So was Gloria's. So was Corbett's. Above all, Corbett's.

'Mine?' he asked.

'Are you indestructible?' she replied. She said nobody should be told she was coming.

Corbett asked: 'Coming alone?'

'It's necessary. We can talk about offers for the Complex as well, naturally, but above all about safety.'

Sid must be on an extension: 'I'm out here and a bit remote from it all,' he said. 'But, all right, you'll reply I chose that, for my own reasons. Do I argue? We have entire faith in you, Jule.'

'Thanks.'

'Things are not good,' Hyson replied.

'In what way?'

'Not good,' Hyson said. 'I trust you with Gloria.'

'I'm glad.'

'I don't mean sexually.'

Corbett said: 'What? Now, please—'

'No, what I meant is I'm not talking about trusting you with her sexually, I'm talking about trusting you to make sure she – We have our differences, you know, Gloria and I.'

'Differences?'

'Policy. Business. Lately.'

'Yes?' Corbett said. Oh, Christ, what was enmeshing him now?

'I'd be upset if somehow she got herself involved in a fresh alliance.'

'Alliance?'

'Policy alliance. Business alliance.'

'Oh, for God's sake, Sidney,' Gloria said. 'How could I? Would I, even if I wished it?'

'I want you to make certain of this, Jule. Obviously, I couldn't tolerate a betrayal of that sort. Policy. Business. Besides, even at our age and with the garments she wears, she's precious to me,' Hyson said.

'This is famous.'

'I don't mean sexually,' Hyson replied.

Corbett said: 'Look, perhaps some personal matters are best not—'

'Sexually, Sid's a conversationalist,' Gloria said.

'I think of the French glamour actor, Charles Boyer, killing himself because his wife died after forty-four years together, Jule,' Hyson said.

'Boyer? Corbett replied.

'I see Gloria as very worthwhile,' Hyson said.

'I know that,' Corbett replied.

'As long as she remains faithful. I'm not talking sexually. Policy. Business. Boyer didn't kill himself because of no sex. Too old. His wife's death left him solitary, that's all. I'd be left solitary if Gloria departed. In a policy sense, a business sense. I'm not saying I'd kill myself, like Boyer. No, not myself. No, that's not my nature.'

'Sex is an important aspect of life, but only that, an aspect,' Corbett said.

'I think of Gloria as a worthwhile person, to date – which can't be denied,' Hyson replied. 'She has attributes.'

'So evident,' Corbett said.

'They've noticed them in Valetta.'

'I'd expect that.'

'These are only Maltese but they can see attributes in Gloria.'

'I detest the people here,' she said. 'Their smiles and round shoulders. And tan wallets sticking from their back pockets like the island didn't have one thief. But that's not why I'm returning to the UK'

'This is urgent, Jule.'

'I can feel that.'

'I daren't come with her. I believe I'd be at risk. People want me knocked over to make the price fall. But OK, you'll reply, "So?"'

'No, Sid,' Corbett replied. 'You're right. You mustn't put yourself into—'

'Nobody but you can help me on this, Jule,' Hyson replied. 'If she pesters you sexually, remember, she's not happy in Malta, feels off key, even though it had the George Cross in the war.'

'Foreign countries can be disorientating.'

'But there's a task for her, beyond all that.'

'I'll be there to meet her,' Corbett replied.

'This will be a bonus matter,' Hyson said.

'Thanks,' Corbett said.

'Although Gloria will give it to you in cash, this in no way puts an obligation on you, Jule.'

'The job is about her safety and yours,' Corbett replied. 'This is clear.'

'And yours, Jule,' Gloria said. 'Sidney, you're so fucking offensive.'

'General attributes like conversation, decent breath and graciousness are your main things now, Gloria,' Hyson replied. 'We have to remember that. Jule's young still.'

'I'll be in Britain to look after your concerns and ease your fears, Sidney,' Gloria said. 'Think of this, please. I could really fuck you up.'

'I hope you won't, Gloria, love,' Hyson replied. 'I don't know where that might finish. I'll be in non-stop touch via Jule. Not those other two, obviously.'

'What?' Corbett said. 'Which other two?'

'Hardly,' Gloria said, laughing. 'Or why am I going back? Isn't it because we can't rely on those two to—?'

'Marv? Jacob?' Corbett asked. He had wondered when Hyson spoke of her going for new partners whether he meant that pair. No? Who? Vartelm? Castice-Manne? Did Hyson know about Laura, Peter? Did Gloria?

'She's not getting thrown out of Malta for unseemliness, Jule,' Hyson replied. 'I'd strike anyone who said that. Thank God I, at least, know what loyalty means.'

'No virtue greater,' Corbett answered.

'I'm glad to hear you say that, Jule,' Hyson replied.

Corbett, Henrietta and Floyd had only just begun breakfast in the manse kitchen when this Malta call came. Floyd generally cooked the meal. He liked to do a bit of everything – eggs, bacon, laver bread, sausage, mushrooms, tomatoes, black pudding, fried bread. It was to help build himself up and illustrate the range of God's creation. Sometimes Floyd said a grace which contained requests for better leg strength and chest development, as well as questions to the Lord about the actual nourishment in eggs. Breakfast was the meal they always tried to eat together. It was family. It was a small daily celebration. Corbett loved it. He felt embraced by a sound tradition. Engaged with the preparation and eating of a proper breakfast, Floyd could escape for a while the depression of the Liston-Patterson fight.

Floyd had gone to answer the phone and then shouted for Jule. The instrument was in the hall, but the door to the kitchen remained open and Floyd and Henrietta probably heard most of what Corbett said. He had been careful to use no names. When he went back to the table, Floyd asked: 'Someone stressed, Jule? This was the word that came to me when I heard that voice on the line, very briefly, I admit, but yes, stress. Breaking? Obviously, calls to this house are often from folk stressed. I'm used to dealing with such. Perhaps I can help.'

'Just a business thing,' Corbett replied, eating. He breathed in joyfully the laver bread's sharp sea odour and the tang of the tea. They struck him as elemental. Didn't they tell him of a probably gleaming future?

'Perhaps Sidney Hyson on the blower?' Floyd said. 'One grows sensitive not just to the tone of a voice but to its characteristics. I might recognise Hyson's. I spoke for a while with him at Boris Lowndes funeral, debating whether the death and disfigurement had been inevitable.'

'Sid's abroad,' Corbett replied.

'Yes, you mentioned foreign countries, I believe,' Floyd said. 'Tension about deals and so on would be greater, perhaps, because of distance.'

'People like that always dread a coup while they're away,' Henrietta said. 'Think of his sidekicks – Marv and Jacob… I mean, would you leave them to look after anything you valued?'

'Those two are utterly Sid's,' Corbett replied. But Gloria and Hyson seemed to suspect something else.

Floyd said: 'Is it wise – safe – I wasn't listening, naturally, yet I couldn't help hearing you speak of safety yourself just now, Jule, and about someone threatened – well, is it safe for you to be involved in that kind of, well, stressed situation – sale of the Complex, so the buzz says?' Floyd asked. 'And a sexual aspect? Did you mention sex? I think you did. Boyer? Charles Boyer?'

'People reach out to me when they're needy,' Corbett replied.

'You think you're indestructible, don't you, Jule?' Henrietta asked.

'I get that said to me.'

'Pride – the most dire of sins, Jule,' Floyd said.

'I have to look for opportunities, Floyd,' Corbett said. 'I have to construct them. This is my trade. Some risk, but I owe it to Hen to move forward. I want your daughter with a status she deserves, and in due course that status for our children, too.'

'But you'll do it by serving how many masters, Jule?' Floyd asked. He drank deep of Lady Grey from a beaker.

'I don't have masters.'

'How can he know you're reliable?' Floyd asked.

'Who?'

'Sidney Hyson,' Corbett replied.

'Sid's abroad.'

'Oh, don't piss Daddy about, Jule.'

'I'm not sure I could help defend you adequately if things turned bad, Jule,' Floyd said. 'For instance, if one of them suddenly lost faith in you, the way it happened to Boris. I'd be upset if your features were messed about with. Could I intervene, though? I train but I'm not at best condition yet. The mental attitude's right, not my reflexes.'

'People know I can be relied on,' Corbett said. 'This is my reputation. Earned.'

'"Now some are puffed up," as Paul says to the Corinthians,' Floyd replied. 'But is it harsh of me to remind you of that?'

'I have to go,' Corbett said.

'You can't tell us where, won't tell us where?' Henrietta said.

He thought it best not to. Floyd seemed to believe any contact with the Hysons was a peril. Perhaps. Corbett did not want to make him and Henrietta more anxious. He finished all the food. He believed in showing Floyd full respect, no matter how much of a prick he could be. When Corbett left the kitchen, Henrietta followed him. Near the front door she whispered: 'To do with Eric Moyle, Jule?'

'How could it be, Hen?'

'I'd like him to be all right. Just all right.' There was real sadness in the droop of her cheeks. Corbett loved Hen for her feelings, even when they concerned another man. She said: 'I don't want him any more, but I want him to be all right. Yes, all right.' The repetition made her sound earnest and pathetic. Her words were a plea, as though she believed Corbett had some power that could make Moyle 'all right' but which she was scared to ask about. He hated to see her afraid of him. This was not Hen. He put his arms around her. 'Will he be all right, Jule?' It was a kind of sob.

Should he be comforting her about a lover like this and

appearing to share her deeply obsolete worries? Floyd came out from the kitchen. 'You don't have to convince us of your reliability and therefore entitlement to safety, Jule. But it's the perceptions of others,' he said. 'Perceptions are so important. In this day and age.'

Corbett drove to the airport. When Gloria emerged from the terminal she approached the car gingerly, as if checking that Corbett were alone, no passengers crouched down in the back. She was dressed quite well for someone of Gloria's outlook. Corbett stowed her luggage and she climbed into the passenger seat with fair nimbleness. 'Not lost, Jule,' she said. 'That's my impression, not lost. Also Sidney's impression, as it happens.'

'What's not lost?' Corbett asked.

'The body.'

'Which?'

'We talk sort of half-coded and roundabout to Marv, naturally, by phone. Plus faxes from Nightride. International calls: how many snoops are listening? But our impression was this – definitely not lost. He was told lose it, lose it, lose it.'

'What?' Corbett asked.

'The body.'

'Which?' Corbett asked.

'To be permanently lost – not washed up on a beach, not turning up somewhere else. Lost. It's not lost, is it?'

'Which?' Corbett asked.

'Sidney's impression and mine was that Marv was telling us, yes, the lad is dead as agreed, and hidden but not lost. This lad was supposed to be at the bottom of an old mine shaft until coal makes a comeback, or properly anchored for keeps in the deep deep, like sea burial. But Marv says hidden – that was our impression, through the roundabout way of talking – only hidden, not lost totally. Sidney saw big peril there at once. A deliberate ploy. I'll need to go to the body.'

'Which?'

'In person,' Gloria replied.

Corbett drove on to the M4 and turned west.

Gloria said: 'Now, please, don't take this as a reflection on yourself. I'm not accusing you of indolence. But can't you see the danger to Sidney and myself in a body lying there like that? And above all to you?'

'I don't—'

'The absolute need to go through his pockets and take a real look at the ground all round him,' Gloria replied. 'Marv seemed to be saying a park death. Are we right on that?'

'You can't visit the body. Yes, a park. In the day there are people about. In the night it's impossible.'

She seemed to doze for a while. Jule did not know where he was to take her. Did she want an hotel? He went on past the Reading turn-off. She muttered something unintelligible, perhaps in her sleep. If so, it awoke her. 'You know Sidney. He can hear betrayal in a wrong cough or a stumbled word. You, me, Marv, Jacob – Sidney sees the possibility in all of us. But especially Marv and Jacob. And maybe especially me.'

'Oh, that sort of nervousness – it's natural for people at the summit like Sid. I've met it all over.'

'Not nervousness. A kind of vision.'

'Vision of what? Disloyalty?'

'He grew suddenly convinced of it, Jule. He heard this body was hidden, not lost, and saw the meaning. Oh, yes, he sees. I, too, see.'

'Betrayal how?'

'Of the sale. If we really want that. The deal. If we really want that. Or if I really want it.'

'What?' Corbett said. 'You and Sid have changed your minds about the sale?'

'Leave that for a moment. Let's speak of the immediate situation. Marv, Jacob, they intend to destroy you – you who are alight with loyalty to Sidney and with good offers, Jule. Yes, they destroy you and the deal is destroyed with you, isn't it? The negotiations you're working so well on are suddenly nowhere. The sale prospects are nowhere. So, what happens to the price? It tumbles and tumbles, Jule. That's when they move. Management buy-out. They get it all for twopence. It's why I must see the body, Jule, search the body. Scour near it. What's near it?'

'A drum.'

'What? No, I mean the terrain,' Gloria said.

'Trees, bushes.'

'Exactly. Scour. This is the kind of ground police will go over and over once he's found. I have to be there first.'

'But for what?'

'Are you missing anything, Jule?'

'Missing what?'

'Anything that would identify you. They leave something like that on the body, near the body, and how does it look for you, Jule? I mean, the police will already have you as a top name on their list, if they dig into his life and find he's been servicing your wife. Then some extra pointer discovered on the body, near the body. That's you for ever finished. Did one of them give some attention to the clothes, for instance, Jule?'

'Marv took coins from the pocket,' Corbett replied. 'To make it seem like robbery.'

'Oh, sweet. If you take something from a pocket you can leave something in a pocket at the same time.'

'I haven't lost anything.'

'It will be something small, seemingly insignificant, but enough. Something you might not even be aware of. That's why an outside eye is needed, Jule. It's why Sidney wouldn't leave the search to you, even if you'd been prepared to do it. He's troubled for you, Jule. He's troubled for the price of the Complex, too, of course. He refuses to be beaten by a pair like that. But he's troubled for you in person as well. All right, it would be like a crime passionel. But the law here is not especially tolerant to jealousy killings. You'd go down for life. It might not mean life but it would be long enough. Who's your wife banging while you're locked up like that? Where's you chance of starting kids, of creating the dynasty you're entitled to? You could be wifing someone yourself inside. This is the Sidney scenario, and I accept it, Jule. "Go to him, Gloria," he said, and I replied, "Willingly, Sidney."'

Corbett said: 'But Marv and Jacob—'

'You think they love us? Love Sidney and myself?'

'Well, yes.'

'They're hirelings,' Gloria replied. 'They're business people. They see a plum and they'll pick it. They'll try to. I've got good flashlights in my case.'

God, she might have it right. But he did not say so. Gloria seemed to sleep again. Corbett felt he was driving in the wrong direction: back into the mess and pressure. At Heathrow, he could have ditched the car, dodged Gloria and bought himself a flight to anywhere in the EU, no passport needed. Gloria, with her suspicions – or Sid's – brought more hellishness with her, more danger, more reasons for Corbett to think he was overreaching himself and would fall and fall.

Not long after Swindon, Gloria stirred and coughed. 'You were surprised when I spoke about maybe not selling after all,' she said. 'This is me. I've never really been in favour. I went along, saw some of Sid's points, was worried by the degree of debt, yes. But how do I sell something that is dedicated to me, has my name on it, my Being in it? I love to hear people speak about things "at the Gloria". But it's Sid – these obsessions. Water. He lets such dreads get to him. Call it sensitivity, call it panic. All the time he expects the Apocalypse. Sidney was brought up in a Bible-punching Sunday School that preached the end of the world was nigh. Subconsciously, he's looking for it non-stop, even now – the end for his little bit of it, anyway. Everything has its allotted span, its duration. Old Testament as well as New. The Flood. He's afraid of a personal flood, one to wipe out the Complex. It's pathetic, Jule.'

'Sid's someone who—'

'"Tries to look ahead"… "beat the market"… "forestall trouble". I know all that and, yes, it works sometimes. But it's the Apocalypse shadow, too. I tire of it, Jule. I see it as the destruction of courage and judgment. There are times when I want to drop him, Jule.'

'Drop?'

'Cut him loose with his mad terrors. And, obviously, cut these other two loose. At least that. It's going to happen anyway, after this. They're finished. But Sidney – Sidney's lost his flare. Fright runs him. Dread's his master.' She sank back against the car door. Then she said very levelly: 'I'll keep the Complex. Of course I will. I *am* the Complex, Jule. I *am* the Gloria.'

Corbett thought he remembered a line something like that from a recent showing of the Wuthering Heights movie on TV. It, too, had been spoken by a woman. Was it: "I *am* Heathcliff"? He said: 'I can see you would feel—'

'Come in with me, Jule.'

'In?'

'Own it with me.'

Oh, God, Sid was right and she had come looking for a new alliance. Policy. Business. Ostensibly, the trip was to do with the safety of Sid, herself and Corbett. Really, it was to find another partner. Policy. Business. Did Gloria realise what Sid had meant when he spoke of Charles Boyer? Sid had said he would not kill himself if he were in despair, but – Hadn't he suggested he might kill someone else?

'Christ, Gloria, this—'

'We'd buy Sidney out. Look, I'm talking a stratagem – of course I'm talking a stratagem – but only that, not violence. Certainly not. Against others possibly but never Sidney. Could I, I mean, could I propose something like that, a killing, disablement, against Sidney?'

'Never, I know,' Corbett replied. But could Sid propose this against Gloria? Or against Corbett? Sid's thinking might be Mafia thinking, when it came to reprisals for betrayal.

Gloria said: 'Sidney and I have a time-honoured marriage, for heaven's sake. You know that. Where would compunction be? And if there's anything Sidney has earned over the years it is compunction. But, Jule, you could raise the funds. You're well in with these finance people. Of course, we'd have to pay off our present bankers. They're crippling us on the Complex loans. We need new capital, Jule – eternal *cri de coeur*. It would be a recreated company. You know how to create. That's your forte. A recreated company still centred on fine and sweetly situated property, but without the liability of Sidney and his crippling dreads. Financiers would rush for that. You could get it, I know. I say "I know", "I know", "I know" about you, Jule, and I mean it and I mean more than that. I mean I have an abiding, indefatigable faith in you. Sidney, on the other hand – well, he can be a down-factor, Jule.' She was quiet, thoughtful for a time. Then she said: 'He hasn't looked after his teeth properly. His smile's an invitation to contempt.'

'It's an interesting proposition.' Corbett felt stifled by the responsibility. His breathing grew wheezy. He could sense granulated items in his lungs, even pebbly. The body always wanted its fucking say.

'You'd attract money to invest on your own behalf, plus enough to pay off our present filthy banks. You and me, Jule. But have others been after you?'

'How do you mean, "after me?"'

'To join them in a proprietor situation. Confer your aptitudes.'

'People see me as a middleman, Gloria, significant only in that I act for you and Sidney. I hardly exist. I am your frontage, yours and Sid's.' He must keep himself modest for now. This was a woman to string along.

'If people think that about you, they're mad,' she replied. 'You've had offers, Jule.' It was blunt, not a question.

'I don't understand. What kind of offers?'

'Naturally you've had offers. You're made for bids. But think of it like this, will you? I already have ownership. I'm in situ.' Corbett found it hard to consider this ramshackle, wrinkle-skinned woman as a foundation stone. She said: 'With me, you'd be working from an established status, from tremendous strength.' Her voice banged at him, its assurance merciless. 'Not like with Marv and Jacob, or Ivo Vartelm, or Castice-Manne or – well, you'll know the other names if there are any. What's common to all of them is they start from nowhere. They want you to help with a grab. No need for grab if it's you and me. You see that? We've got it. We hold on to it, that's all.'

'It's certainly… well, interesting.'

'He's afraid of me.'

'Who?'

'Sidney. I don't want it. This is a husband. There should not be fear.' Corbett realised he had felt the same about Hen and him. 'But Sidney knows I'm thinking my way to a different outcome,' Gloria said. 'He knows I'm entitled to think my way to a different outcome. It's what a brain's for. But, yes, he's scared. That's why he'll try every way to diminish me, Jule – talk as if I'm just old lust let loose on a final swoop.' She put her small, thin hand lovingly on Corbett's thigh, only his thigh, and let it linger there for about half a mile. Then she withdrew it. 'You see? I can be wholly moderate, contained. He knows that. But it doesn't suit him. He has to find intemperateness in me, absence of control, wild juice, weakness. This comforts him, makes him feel superior, despite his fanship of doom.'

'Look, Gloria, I worry what might happen to you if—'

'Yes, Sidney's aware he's finished. Do people with a future go to Malta? And he's aware I won't collapse with him, regardless of undoubted wonderful bonding in the past. I'm still looking for a future, still climbing.'

Still climbing. At the park gates, Gloria transferred two flashlights from a case to her handbag and hung the bag around her neck. She had on grey flannel trousers, flat black shoes and a zip-up fleece done in a mix of triangular shaped forceful colours: purple, turquoise, scarlet, tan. Corbett bent double again and she managed to scramble onto his back, clawing at his jacket frantically in a couple of useless attempts and eventually settling herself on her knees first before standing. Oddly, he felt powerful crouched as a footstool. He was also the platform. He had solidity – that foundation-stone solidity Gloria herself tried to claim. He might be the rock base of their enterprise, if he decided to join her. Someone with an over-fast, bullying mind like Hen would not be able to see the strength in his present position. She would fix on only the simplest symbolism – Corbett degraded, minionised.

On the gate, Gloria could not do the next stage and pull herself to the top and over. She pushed down fiercely on him with her little feet, trying for some spring, but failed to get launched. He would thrust up with his back, too, when he thought she was ready. It didn't work and they abandoned this method: too much for a sixty-year-old. Although she looked sinewy, the strength in her arms was poor. As Sid said, Gloria had attributes, but they did not include surmounting tall park gates. Corbett visualised her trying to break out over the high fence of an Eventide Home and pitiably giving up, her spirit screwed. The thought almost made him weep. Gloria jumped off Corbett and leaned against the gates, gasping and cursing herself when she had the breath for it. It always troubled him to hear elderly people sucking madly at street air for oxygen. He'd been sucking for oxygen himself not long ago, but that was not at all similar, just a quickly passing crisis.

Gloria's dyed blonde hair had come adrift in the struggle and hung down over her forehead, obscuring her eyes. She looked like the back hem of a tattered dress. Although it was late, Corbett felt uneasy at being on show like this. Somehow, the handbag swinging from Gloria's neck made her appear unprincipled, like someone flippant about possessions. Corbett hated that kind of casualness. If a police patrol found them and looked in the bag, her torches might tell them a search was intended. And they would possibly do one in the park themselves to discover what the interest was.

Corbett scaled the gate, dropped on the other side, then climbed back so he was leaning over towards her, his feet on a metal crossbeam. The vertical rails of the gate had ornamental arrowheads at the top, but the spikes were mild and he could take them in his chest without injury, even when bent forward. Did he see a curtain move an inch or two in a house along the road? He could not worry about that. He leaned down and Gloria held up both hands. It made him think of sea rescue, of pulling someone from the waves into a boat. Perhaps Sid lived with that kind of desperate vision all the time. Gloria's fleece would be useful in an ocean rescue, making her stand out against the dark waters, supposing she floated. Corbett would never have pushed her under and held her there, despite everything.

He took her skinny wrists and tugged her up. She had next to no weight, was even skimpier than Floyd. She felt like a bag of plastic cutlery for a Whitsun Treat meal. Spasmodically, she worked with her feet against the struts to help push herself towards him. Her feet might be her toughest fitments. At the top he had to drag her over and carry her under one of his arms, the handbag hanging beneath them. As to the twitched curtain, anyone seeing these two stuck there at this hour would have a job working out what was happening. He must look like a night-exercise soldier climbing an assault course net, and carrying a lumpy piece of gear.

Corbett could tell she loved the adventure of it. He felt her body try to respond to all his moves. She did not moan or complain but kept muttering, 'Good, Jule, good. Team.' For a time she was more or less horizontal in his grip. Then he let Gloria's feet slowly swing downwards, like the big hand on that Harold Lloyd clock on the skyscraper. Corbett lowered her as much as he could and released her. She dropped and remained standing. 'Good, Jule, good,' she muttered. 'Team.' He jumped off the gate and joined her. He did not mind too much being close and associated with Gloria. But he had the impression that nobody attempting to foresee the details of his career ten years ago would have suggested he might be walking now through a riverside park at after 2am, looking for his wife's dead lover and a drum, and accompanied by an elderly woman with her hair hopelessly ragged. Some people spoke of a university education as having not much to do with subsequent jobs and he thought it true that his own degree hardly ever seemed relevant to his work.

He considered his memory naturally very good and his sense of place: no need for training on those, university or otherwise. Despite the darkness and the gap of time since he was out here last, he reckoned he would be able to find Moyle instantly. Wanting to watch her bafflement when confronted by the trees, thick bushes and heavy shadow bordering the path, he let Gloria get a little ahead. She would not even know which side of the path to look. She depended on him and he liked that. But, of course, she had to lead. Appear to lead. This, after all, was Gloria, so blazing with instinct and cleverness that she'd expect to go straight to the spot. When she found she couldn't, he would leave the path, pick his way quickly through the undergrowth and wait for Gloria to join him. He would not call out to her. That might seem like arrogance. Oh, look what I've discovered. He loathed crowing. He would just stand there by Moyle and the drum as if it were only natural that he should do the discovering. And it was. She had to be taught this, though. She had to learn to be secondary.

Oh, Christ, what if Moyle and the drum were not there? But they were bound to be, weren't they, *weren't they*?'

'Here!' Gloria turned around to speak to him. She pointed and left the path, wholly confident, like entering a shop with a wallet full of Gold Cards. 'There's been a bit of trampling. The sods might actually want him found.' She disappeared behind some bushes. Corbett followed her. In a few seconds they were standing by Moyle and the drum. She brought the flashlights from her bag and handed them on to Corbett. She bent down and began systematically to search Moyle. 'Scan the ground, Jule,' she ordered.

'What am I looking for?'

'What? Anything that says you, of course. Anything that proclaims the previous presence of Jule Corbett. Did they steer you through brambles – so there'd be fibres from your clothes left behind, or a hair? They can do all sorts with a hair these days – tell you the kind of marmalade your grandmother liked best. Have you given any papers with your writing on it – say, reports about offers? All that's needed. It will nail you. Go, Jule. Toothcomb it. Find…. Oh, look, I make you sound like a gundog. Sorry. But find, anyway. So this is the boy who cut you out with your wife.' She let her flashlight rest on Moyle's face for a second and gave it a survey. 'Lumpen, yes, but there's something to him, even with those dead eyes. He could never have known he was upsetting not just someone like Jule Corbett, but Gloria and Sidney Hyson. I'm really glad we decided to take care of you, Jule. I'll certainly continue this in our new set-up. I must keep you credible, bankable, not someone cuckolded by fucking drifters. Yes, fucking. Finance people can be a bit funny about possible Aids in borrowers. They refuse to take the wider, more humane view.'

That kind of view was what Corbett always tried to take, not necessarily concerning Aids, but in general. He felt upset a little by Gloria's coolness in dealing with the Moyle body. This, after all, was a man who had been loved by Henrietta. All right, he had stolen Henrietta and perhaps Corbett should have shown at least as much coolness about the death as Gloria, or even taken joy in it. He could not do this. If a man had been valuable to Hen he must have qualities, and Corbett felt he should respect them. In fact, hadn't Gloria said she could spot something special in his face herself? And yet she still treated him as not very much, an object to be scrutinised, that was all, in case he included something to implicate Corbett, endangering a business pact. He grew very vigorous in his scouring of the ground near the body and drum in an effort to distract Gloria from her investigation of the ins and outs of Moyle personally.

11

Now, Castice-Manne developed a new method of getting at Corbett; the object, as ever, to force Jule to push Castice-Manne's bid with Hyson. Plainly, Castice-Manne could not know Jule had decided to push no bids for the present. He had himself to think of, and had grown committed to this lately.

Down in the Bay during a visit to his existing property, Castice-Manne called on Corbett for a talk at the manse. It was another of those conversations where Jule had to work out what was meant behind what was said. A business meeting.

After this conference, Corbett came to feel it appallingly disloyal to Hen to be worrying as much as he did about a girl like Grace, even though Grace was associated with such a fine London property as Omdurman. The killing of a tart – even the projected killing of a tart – always set up complicated reactions in Corbett, and probably in others also, he would admit that: it was arrogant to imagine oneself unique. Obviously, you had to feel sad about the savage death of any girl, but tarts went knowingly into terrible risk, so it would be naive to give them all-out sympathy, as you might to a murdered child or murdered company chairman. Corbett had been surprised to hear from Castice-Manne that Grace sometimes worked outside Omdurman, where she would have safety and even comfort, to a degree. Chatting quietly at the manse, Castice-Manne told him several of the girls did occasional street beats as well, mostly in expensive corners of Mayfair. They worked there between Omdurman shifts, to build earnings. Grace was an afternoon girl at Omdurman, to fit in with family commitments. But perhaps those home commitments forced her occasionally into night work. Chislehurst, where she lived, was very expensive suburban property. Although Castice-Manne said it would be bad for the girls' image and for Omdurman's if it got around they sidewalked, going with anyone who had the cash, he could not prevent it. This kind of part-time market was often unpimped, which meant all payments went to the woman. Someone as attractive as Grace operating in, say, the area close to the Dorchester, International, Rock Café and Hilton, could probably ask anything up to two hundred pounds for full, and plenty more for kinks/unprotected. All the danger went to the woman, too, though.

'She's been hurt? Worse?' Corbett asked.

'No, not yet, thank God,' Castice-Manne replied.

'Yes, thank God,' Corbett replied. 'She's so lovely.'

'True. What gives me anxiety, Jule, is a girl like Grace, whoring it in cars and God knows where else with all sorts – these are surely the circumstances for slaughter and abuse, as always. I don't ever want to mention the Ripper in this kind of circumstance because it appals me so, but I must mention him. It happened.' There was a bit of blare to Castice-Manne's voice, even now while he spoke mildly. Like Hen, he had been to one of the best public schools, possibly Charterhouse, as Corbett remembered it. Or perhaps Uppingham. Somewhere they had a fives court, anyway. Castice-Manne sometimes mentioned that. So, not Cemetery Road Comp. His hair was piled up thick and fair on a weakish-looking body and he came over as baby-like. He could do sincerity with convincing detail.

'Probably Grace is experienced,' Corbett replied. 'She'd know how to take care.'

'Jule, I'm sure, utterly sure, she's careful, as are her colleagues who street-tout with her. But what carefulness is of use against a punter with a knife or screwdriver or garrotte cord? This is the agonising question that will not let me relax, or possibly you. And perhaps more than one punter at a trick. Girls like Grace, looking for a swift massing of capital, will take on two, three men in an untraceable car or unknown room.'

'I—'

'What happens if she's found somewhere, jabbed and cut to death or strangled?' Castice-Manne replied.

'But, God, Philip, this is alarmist, isn't it?' Corbett began to realise a little later that he had not been picking up the threats in what Castice-Manne said, threats to Corbett as much as Grace. More.

Castice-Manne answered the question he had himself put. 'What happens if she's found dead somewhere, Jule, is that the police go around to her place and turn it over, looking for leads to her contacts.'

'A girl like that writes things down?' Corbett asked. 'I wouldn't have thought so.'

'No, probably not, probably not. Have you given gifts?'

'Only money.'

'In cash?'

'Of course. This is in addition to the Omdurman house charge – but, look, Philip, I don't want to land her in any bother.'

'She's entitled to take loot or anything else from you. You're wise to keep it to cash.'

'She hasn't got my name, anyway, not my real surname, and, obviously, no address.'

'Of course not,' Castice-Manne replied. 'Are you an infant?'

'So, I don't really see the crisis.' Now and then you had to give guidance in coolness and self-control even to people as big in commerce as Castice-Manne.

'Photographs, Jule.'

Corbett almost screamed. He brought the volume down just in time to a gasp and hellish frown. 'What – she's got copies?' He had become used to the idea of Castice-Manne himself holding bedroom pictures. That could be regarded as usual business practice, like a flask of water in front of board members. But those prints shouldn't be in possession of one of the girls.

Castice-Manne said: 'Perhaps I'm remiss and soft in this. These girls take a special shine to some clients, Jule. But, of course, you know that. Grace admires you and has very understandably admired you for such a long while. Your career and potential career. She was keen to have a selection of portraits of you so that—'

'Selection?'

'Just as a commemoration of lovely and loving times together. This kind of request does occur now and then, and I feel I'd be heartless to refuse. That's what I meant – possibly it's soft of me.'

'My God, you're talking about filched blackmail pictures, not Happy Snaps,' Corbett said.

'We call them Reference Photos, Jule – simply to back our business records. Yes, Reference Photos, like, say, actors' pictures in a theatre directory.'

'Fucking theatre?' Corbett yelled.

'Right. But clearly Grace wanted shots where you were recognisable, not your face half obscured by legs and so on. Those wouldn't remind her of you, not specifically of you. I'm not saying she'd frame and hang these photos, but for an album, perhaps.'

Jesus. 'Jesus.'

'The police would soon identify, I should think, cover name or not – you're already a business notable, Jule – and they'd make something of this kind of closeness between you two, if she became a victim.'

Now, naturally, Corbett did see where Castice Manne was going. 'Philip, are you saying that your heavies might—?'

They were talking in the manse parlour. The door opened and Henrietta brought in a tray with a teapot on it and cups, saucers and delicate slices of cake. She was wearing one of her long brownish dresses made of some very good but heavy material. Corbett often wished she would discover other colours and a different style, less abbessy. The parlour was a pleasant, light room with a beige-to-tan moquette suite and a couple of additional chintz armchairs covered in material decorated with mediaeval hunting scenes. There was a long, possibly Regency, mahogany sideboard and a Pembroke

table. Corbett always thought of it as a neutral room. It contained, of course, no religious decorations or books. There
were few anywhere in the house. When Corbett termed the
parlour neutral, it was because no photographs of Patterson
or boxing in general were displayed. Tame original water-
colours hung on the walls, perhaps done by members of the
congregation. They were all sea scenes, a couple featuring the
Bay barrage. Floyd followed Henrietta into the parlour and
helped arrange the crockery on the Pembroke table. 'Did we
hear you call out "Theatre", Jule?' Floyd said. 'Were you discussing *Much Ado* at the New? I love Dogberry and Verges.'
Floyd had on old, calf-length, navy shorts, a thick, yellow
sweatshirt and stained plimsolls. He and Henrietta both
knew Castice-Manne. During landlord trips to his Bay office
block he would occasionally attend a Bethel service, to prove
links with the established community. Corbett did not mind
all that. Integration was a discipline.

Floyd said: 'I can see humility in you, you know, Philip.'

'Thank you, Floyd,' Castice-Manne replied.

'This is someone who, despite great, and greater, prospects
as a property man, will come to give a little gesture of recognition to our church and to those who live and serve here,'
Floyd said.

'I wouldn't feel complete, Floyd, if I were in the vicinity
and neglected to make my call to Bethel, and to you,
Henrietta and Jule, Floyd. What does the Psalm say: "It
restoreth my soul."'

'Not for me to poke into mighty business matters,' Floyd
replied, 'but I have the conviction that, if the Complex is
truly up for sale as rumoured, and you, Philip Castice-
Manne, are its likely new owner, then the Bay is indeed
fortunate.'

'Thank you, Floyd. Yes, I think it might come my way –
less from anything I am or have done myself but because I
believe Jule favours my bid above others, and Jule is a man of
unparalleled influence. On his say-so many a company
depends.'

'If Jule favours your bid it is entirely because he knows it to be the right bid for the Bay,' Floyd replied. Castice-Manne was head of a firm whose work in building and communications went back more than two hundred years. Corbett had been to the London offices off Grosvenor Square and seen unquestionably ancient furniture there and pictures of workmen laying roads for troop movements in the Napoleonic wars. Corbett thought an unusual name like Castice-Manne was bound to embody good history. Castice-Manne would know through his genes how to piss definitively on all opposition.

Hen poured tea and handed the cups and saucers and plates around. She distributed cake. 'Have you got some hold on Jule?' she asked Castice-Manne.

'Hold?' he replied.

'What are you here for?' she asked genially. 'The way he's sitting. I can read Jule. He's fearful. Poor little Jule. Are you trying to get some leverage on him, Philip, so he'll do what Daddy says and back your offer to Hyson – cut-price offer, I wouldn't be surprised?'

'How would he possibly have leverage, Hen, dear?' Corbett replied, laughing for a fair while: not a dry, hard laugh but with plenty of spit and genuineness around his lips.

'It's wonderful to have your recommendation, Floyd,' Castice-Manne said. 'I know Jule will listen.'

'All right, but we're looking for a full partnership in any future company, you realise that, do you?' Henrietta asked Castice-Manne. 'Jule considers his crawling, scurrying, middlemanning days are gone. That's another thing I can read in him. And I suppose I approve. Yes, I do.' She did not rush herself nor sound apologetic for lassoing the conversation. This was so like Hen. He loved the bluntness and general acumen, even though he thought she might not be playing things altogether right for now.

Corbett said: 'Oh, Hen, I don't consider—'

'We're probably stuck together, Jule and I, you know, Philip,' Henrietta said. 'I mean a permanency, I mean exclusively. There's been some outside interest in me now and then, which perhaps you've heard of. Disgusting rumour, but, OK, a fragment of truth. It was inevitable. People wondered whether I would stick with someone like Jule. Though there are certainly plus aspects to him, I did have to wonder myself about continuing. But that doubt's finished now, on all fronts.'

'Great, Hen,' Corbett replied.

'My own feeling – shall I tell you my own feeling, tell all of you?' she asked.

'Often Hen can pick up the flavour of a situation, without being given anything specific,' Floyd said. 'It's remarkable.'

Corbett said: 'Hen, this is not the kind of topic to—'

'My own feeling is someone's dead,' she replied. She was still standing by the table, pouring herself tea, and looked bulky and commanding, her profile meaty, imperturbable and bright.

'Dead? Hell, this is awful,' Castice-Manne replied. 'Who?'

'I don't know this – don't *know* there's been a death,' she said. 'It's what Daddy mentioned – a feeling. But you see the implications, I hope. If I'm to be isolated with Jule because someone else – say a friend of mine – is dead or gone abroad, I'll need a proper status for Jule. This is not greed or pride, it's a demand for a settled commercial role to match the now on-and-on-and-eternally-on character of our marriage. I can't have Jule penny-boying any longer. It would be a reflection on me.'

'Henrietta is inclined to cut right through things to what's called the nub, Philip,' Floyd said cheerily. 'She's always been like this, even as a child. When a little girl of six or seven, she'd say: "Daddy, we must find the nub."'

'How do you mean, Hen, "someone's dead"?' Corbett asked.

'Don't mess me about, Jule.'

Castice-Manne said: 'I'd be prepared to discuss a full—'

'I've done an inch-by-inch evaluation at the Gloria,' Henrietta replied. 'That's my kind of work, you know – I'm in Securities at the bank.' For a moment, her face was a banker's face then, denatured, unimpulsive. Corbett admired her for the worldliness of it. She said: 'But not the kind of bank that takes a stake in spreads like the Complex, I have to tell you. My costing – even allowing for flood risk and possible pollution stench and disease potential from the lagoon – would put the price at £210 million, and that's minimum. Sidney is going to know this, and certainly Gloria will know it. She can count.' Henrietta turned and gave a bright, challenging grin to Castice-Manne. 'You're able to come up with real money, Philip? If not, you might be wasting our time. That's my time, Jule's time. The botanical gardens, for instance. All right, there's another down West Wales, but West Wales is a long way. This is the capital's botanical gardens, the Bay's botanical gardens, and that carries cachet. I can't put a figure of less than £32 million on it. And this is only for starters, isn't it – the hotel, casino, nursing home, shops and the rest as well? All right, Philip, you'll obviously do a second mortgage on the Bay office block, and you've had some fair appreciation there. What, fifteen per cent, even twenty? That does give you a basis, I'll agree. But between you, you and Jule will still be looking at the need to raise, say, £150 million, £160 million, of finance. Although Jule's good, is he that good? Consequently, I asked about leverage. You've got something to make him try the impossible and keep trying?'

Corbett laughed again, for at least as long as last time. 'I have to ask once more, what sort of leverage could Philip possibly try, Hen?'

'He's pressurising you, is he, to use every contact you have to produce that sort of investment, Jule?' Henrietta replied.

'I don't see it as pressurising,' Castice-Manne said. 'I see it as treating Jule like a mature partner, a partner with astonishing talents and experience, and a partner whose talents and experience are admittedly crucial to our enterprise.'

'So we hear the word "partnership" at last,' Henrietta replied. She nodded a couple of times triumphantly over her cup.

'Of course. It's been central to the whole conversation, surely,' Castice-Manne said. 'It is assumed. It doesn't have to be spoken.'

'Hen's one who'll demand that terms are spelled out and unblurred,' Floyd replied. 'I remember saying to her when she was only a very young child: "Hen, you always demand that terms are spelled out and unblurred."'

'This kind of negotiation can be a strain,' Candice-Manne said.

Floyd was sitting with his cup and saucer in one of the moquette arm chairs. He put the crockery down and stood, a bit skinny-necked and ungigantic. He fisted his hands. 'Strains are what I personally was brought up to cope with as a standard piece of life, and I hope I've brought Henrietta up to cope with strain as normality, too,' he said. 'We are a gutsy family, a family which does not waver.'

'I think I'd take your figures, Henrietta, give or take ten mill,' Castice-Manne said. 'We spend big, recoup big.'

'And Jule is built into the firm?' she replied.

'Of course he is,' Castice-Manne said.

Floyd unclenched his hands and then slowly sat down again. He smiled. He'd believe he had scared Castice-Manne into extra compliance by the fighting pose. Corbett adored Floyd for his delusions, feebleness and unwanted bravery. In a while, Henrietta piled up the dirty crockery on the tray and she and Floyd left.

Corbett said: 'You're telling me Grace could be targeted by your gutter people when streeting and vulnerable if I don't push things for you with Sid and Gloria?'

'I was touched that Floyd should regard me as the best new owner of the Complex,' Castice-Manne replied. 'And gratified that Henrietta so instantly saw the benefits of your taking a partnership, Jule. This is a woman with a grand brain – I mean, her understanding of the investment strategy, and appraisal of the botanical gardens. I quibbled about the figures, but really that was only a gesture to show I did know something about property.'

'Grace.'

'She's a splendid, emotional girl and I—'

'She's not to be hurt,' Corbett replied.

Castice-Manne smiled. 'Or you'll turn the Rev Floyd on me?'

'This isn't just about the pictures.'

'Of course not.'

Corbett said: 'I couldn't bear to think I'd—'

'This is a splendid, emotional girl. I understand your concern and think it creditable.'

'A girl like that, who's got herself accidentally involved in a—'

'I will try and talk to her again about outside tomming,' Castice-Manne replied. 'Pictures like those in front of Press people – they're bound to be inconvenient, Jule, I do see that, and your father-in-law a Baptist minister, wife in Securities. All right, to an extent they're pictures showing you glamorously raffish, I suppose, and sexually damned inventive, but overall the impression would be rough. And, yes, probably a shadow on creditworthiness and any possible partnership. Henrietta would be upset over that aspect, I'm sure, quite apart from the revelation of your behaviour. If someone might offer a view of this from a detached spot, these are photographs which would definitely not help with the kind of positive attitude to fidelity in marriage that she seemed to be speaking about now that her lover – lovers, perhaps? – is out of the reckoning. What did she mean there about someone's death? Do you know anything of that, Jule?'

'Hen has a brilliantly precise mind but at times it can become lurid,' Corbett said.

'Oh, brilliantly precise,' Castice-Manne said.

12

Corbett decided he would fly to Malta. There were obvious dangers to that, but he would try to scheme his way around them. He believed he could. So much of his middleman experience had been concerned with neutralising real perils, for the sake of ultimate progress. All right, so, as a middleman, Boris Lowndes had failed to manage that. But Boris was Boris, perhaps momentarily slack in some way, perhaps even deep-down dim: as his mother said, would anyone but a dope want to do a history of fridges? Jule would always resist being classed with Boris. Jule hugely admired that motto of the Special Air Service Regiment: He who dares wins. He would never mention this to Henrietta because she would probably tell him he was pretentious and melodramatic, but he accepted the truth of those ringing words all the same.

Gloria's scheme seemed to Corbett the best of all those put in front of him and he must talk to her about it. She had already returned to the island. Corbett had not given her a decision but said he would mull things over and then be in touch. It was the kind of answer he had given to many people trying to incorporate him. He thought he understood their eagerness. He could offer so much. In the week since Gloria's return to Malta, Corbett had come to see her project as very practical, more practical than any of the others.

He wished to talk to Sid face to face, as well as to Gloria. Although Sid had made his hinted threats to her, and perhaps to Jule himself, Corbett felt he could reason him away from those appalling, primitive notions of vengeance. After all, there had been that wonderful, enduring marriage between Sid and Gloria. How could he abruptly reject this, or behave as if it had never existed, for God's sake? Naturally, Gloria and Corbett would cut Sid and his pathetic flood jitters right out of the Complex proprietorship eventually, but it must be done with consideration and tact. Tact came instinctively to Jule, even without his middleman training. As he saw it, someone's seemingly mad terrors – for instance, Sid's about the tide – were nonetheless real to them, and one should move with true sensitivity. Corbett revered business protocol. In his opinion, if protocol were not desirable it would never have developed as a standard element in commercial life.

There must be some sort of lavish compensation for Sid. Although Gloria did not seem to envisage this, Corbett would insist: strange, really – the wife is indifferent or hostile and it's the outsider who has to apply some humanity, and some thought for her safety, as well as his own. Corbett liked to regard himself as always hot on humanity issues. After all, Sidney had a true status from decades back. He conducted an undoubted empire and was settled in beautiful Renton Park, a splendid, historic, Berkshire country estate, now, of course, so touchingly renamed Glorsid. He deserved respectful treatment, honest treatment, disarming treatment, when possible. No question, Sid could get vindictive if he felt betrayed and humiliated, despite all those fine years of marriage. Perhaps Marv and Jacob might no longer be trusted to act for him, but he could hire other enforcers. Clearly, Sidney would be betrayed and humiliated, eventually. But care had to be shown, care and that supreme quality, in Corbett's estimation – humanity. These would definitely be qualities Sid had heard of. In fact, hadn't he kindly tried to exercise them himself on Corbett's behalf by ordering the destruction of Hen's cuckolding lovers? But for Sidney, Eric would not be dead in that park with his drum, nor the other man forced to run abroad. Corbett believed he owed Sid a decently grateful response, alongside the nice coup to fling him out. Negotiations had to be frank and face to face. Corbett shunned furtiveness except, that is, when unavoidable.

What had gradually won Corbett to Gloria's proposal, despite the risks, was her central argument that she already part-owned the Complex which carried her name. In situ counted for a lot. Her age and appearance and sex drive were grim nuisances but not fatal. This was the kind of partner to work with, if possible at arm's length but, in any case, to work with. Corbett would ask for a midday flight and, on the previous evening, might stay in London and try to find Grace tomming around Mayfair. Plainly, Corbett did not want to look for her at Omdurman. This had to be private from Castice-Manne.

Corbett knew that locating Grace on the streets would be chancy. Castice-Manne had spoken as if she traded there only rarely, when faced by money crises at home. Did she have children as well as a husband? School fees? Riding? Phone bills? Corbett felt he must try to get to Grace, though, to discuss things, probably only that. He did not mind talking to a tart in a one-to-one, non-sexual mode if it was really necessary. He took an extra £300 in twenties with him to cover her lost tricks time. That was only basic politeness.

Corbett felt quite gratified by the way the girls around Shepherd Market and Curzon Street evidently regarded him. It thrilled him that their instant assumption was, yes, he had come out from one of those magnificently select hotels in Park Lane or Piccadilly on a pussy quest. They thought he clearly belonged to that unusually pricey setting. Corbett believed he did have this kind of bearing. It might be the way he walked or held his head, or the clothes he wore and, more vital than that, how he wore them. He felt he had the knack of making even cheap gear seem stylish, though in a non-flagrant manner. His mother had always stressed to him the importance of bearing. Any of these girls would be proud to be taken up by him because they could see at once he was a payer, and would never need to stint on body lotions and deodorants. He wore a lightweight grey suit with a real sheen to it for Malta. His shoes were tan slip-ons which had cost him £175, and that in a sale. He was not staying in Park Lane but in the Regent Palace Hotel, off Piccadilly Circus. This had its own character, he thought. His blue-check shirt had been tailored for him and his tie was silk. His cufflinks were gold but not lumpy, flashy gold. There were muggers about, here and in Malta probably, but, in any case, he had always been keen on restraint in his dress from a taste, not just a safety, point of view. Ostentation his mother and he despised.

He could see that other girls were terrifically disappointed when he would not go with one of them but insisted he must find Grace. However, he promised two or three that the next time he was in the area he would make himself fully available over a period of hours. He hated any woman to feel he had been offhand or, worse still, cold with her. Even this sort of woman tonight was entitled to kindliness if at all possible. Corbett revered gallantry. Never did he forget that concept, noblesse oblige. He was convinced that girls – and not just professional girls – longed to get fucked by a man with class, and more than that: a man whose distinction he was born with, not had to slave for.

Towards midnight he found Grace. He was happy to note she maintained her appearance of elegance even for street work and had on a beautifully cut, light blue suit. Blue was probably her colour. This was a Queen Mother shade. He recalled that neat, simple dress at Omdurman. Tonight, she did not seem to recognise Corbett at once and this enraged him. You would expect that if a woman had due appreciation for you and your career she would keep you continuously prevalent in her mind, even while banging other punters. Corbett found it insulting that she would clearly have taken him on as a street client regardless of who he might be, as long as he looked loaded and had no neck blood on his canines. Of course, he knew already that she had to accept whatever good offers came. This was the game. Just the same, he disliked seeing such sharp proof. He found it cruel when she greeted him with that bleak, sing-song, formula invitation: 'Good evening. Looking for business?' It was chilling to hear a relationship described as business when you had had your head in all kinds of areas of her. In Omdurman, she would never have used that word. In Omdurman, of course, she had recognised him. Perhaps she did not associate Corbett with outdoors. Things at Omdurman were wonderfully civilised and affectionate, apart from the secret cameras. 'Business' was a terribly accurate transactional term. In a special way it was business that he wanted with her now, but in his opinion this only made the expression, when used by her, more gross.

'Grace,' he replied. Spoken softly by Corbett, her name itself – its lovely religious meaning – carried, he thought, a reproach, and rightly. It was like slapping her about with a New Testament.

She recovered at once. This offended him. It made Corbett think such a situation had happened before: the failure to spot a regular customer and a need to cover the error damn fast. 'Oh,' she said, 'Jule, how wonderful to see you again. It's the street lighting. I couldn't make you out properly. You seem taller.'

He'd had that impression himself lately, although there was no question of boosted shoes. He felt taller. He felt emergent. It was a spiritual matter but perhaps reflected in his physique the way, conversely, depression could make you stoop. 'Grace, we must talk. I'll pay for it.'

'Talk dirty?'

'I want us to get away from here. You might not be safe.' He looked about urgently but saw only other girls, patrolling, waiting; watching Grace and him, in case he wasn't satisfied with her and would require an alternative. In their trade they had to be doggedly hopeful, poor kids. 'There's a pub around the corner,' he said.

'They won't let me in there. I mean, any of us. Thugs on the door.'

'A restaurant?'

'Some are all right.'

'One of those, then.'

She took him to a Chinese place and he ordered dim sum and Chinese bottled beer for both of them. It would have seemed wrong to start right off about the Omdurman photographs, as though he were driven only by personal fear. A girl breezily helping herself to appetiser dumplings from the steaming, round, bamboo containers was entitled to sweeter treatment than that, surely. He thought she ate very nicely, her mouth closed while she chewed and no noise. He could see why she would want to live in a spot like Chislehurst. She was fair-haired, with a slightly angular, though not bony, face and very fresh skin. Her eyes were green-grey, undeadened yet by the work. You could meet a girl like this controlling ticket queues for Eurostar or selling time-share. In his view, if a stranger saw them eating together he would not necessarily spot Grace as a whore. The cravate-style thing she wore with her suit was quite a subdued dark blue. In fact, Corbett felt reasonably proud to be at a restaurant table with her. By training most likely, she gazed at him almost all the time, as if with interest, even devotion. He did not often get this from Hen. The egomaniac cow demanded it for herself.

'I'm afraid I might have accidentally involved you in a rather deep situation,' he said. This seemed to him a reasonable, and at the same time positive, way to describe matters. It made him sound what he was: a man important enough for rather deep situations, a man partnered by mystery. To be as troubled as Corbett felt, you had to have status. Grace did not stop eating, except to take a swig from the beer bottle. Even this he thought she did delicately, the angle of the bottle suggesting moderation, not some gulp and get-it-down session. Sometimes he felt he wanted to pluck Grace not just from the peril she was in via Castice-Manne and his people, but from her career as a tart. Trite? Was he the Salvation Army?

'I'm all right,' she said.

'All right for now,' Corbett replied.

'"For now" is all there is.'

'Really?'

'How I see things,' she replied.

It infuriated him for a second to be existentialised at by a hustler, but he remained mild with her while she ate. 'You could be targeted,' he said.

'By?'

'I don't know that I'd want to say at this stage, but—'

'Phil Castice-Manne?'

'It's a very big-money project,' he replied.

'So, yes, Phil Castice-Manne,' she said.

This angered him, also. When he told her it was a big-money project he had wanted her to say, or at least think, that this was only what anyone would expect if the project involved Corbett. 'They might want to get at me through you,' he replied. He did not mind giving her this sort of reflected status, even though she could be so damned tactless.

'I don't understand that,' she said. She stared across the food at him, her eyes still full of admiration and very intent.

'Hurt you to hurt me.'

She stayed puzzled, he could see this. 'Why would they want to hurt you?' she asked.

'It's a threat, to make me do something they're keen on. Only a threat so far, but about buying and selling some property.' He kept it vague. He did not think she would be able to grasp all the intricacies. Her career was so basic. If you fucked for a living what could imagined flooding of a botanical gardens mean to you?

'Sorry, I still don't get it. Why do things roundabout?' she asked.

'Roundabout?' he said. It might have been a conversation between people speaking different languages.

'If they want to threaten you why not make it direct? How do I come into things? That doesn't sound like Phil. He wouldn't muck about.' She spoke very precisely, very thoughtfully, like a financial adviser querying some proposal.

'At this level things are subtle,' he replied.

'Which level?'

It might be difficult for her to appreciate the scale. He wanted her to know this was not a situation comparable with, say, using a threat or two to get girls at Omdurman into line. But it would be rude and callous to say that outright. Subtlety needed subtlety. 'This is a deal running into hundreds of millions,' he said. He could have added, 'not a day's

shag takings or even a week's', but he would never have
treated a woman like that, especially not while eating in a
restaurant together. Corbett regarded it as almost a spiritual
affirmation to take a meal with someone. He supposed it
must be the Last Supper lurking, hidden away but powerful,
in his consciousness.

'Look,' she replied, 'it's lovely food, and the beer, but – this
sounds fucking grasping, I know – but it's not enough for my
time off the—'

'I've got a couple of hundred in cash,' he said.

'That's probably all right. The thing is, Jule, this part of
the night I can do three, maybe four, blow jobs and—'

He had an idea he would prefer not to hear this. 'Or possibly a bit more in other pockets. Say £250.'

'Jule, I'm sorry to have to mention such…. Someone
dealing in hundreds of millions – I suppose it seems trivial.
But the bills pile up at home. My hubbie's little plane, and
airport charges. Flying, such an obsession with him. He'd be
less without it.'

'You have your work,' he replied.

She seemed to think about that for a while. Then she said:
'So, is it like this – they lean on you by threatening to tell it
around that you go to a girl occasionally? Yes?' she asked.
'But you were up in London for important company meetings, weren't you? It's what men do after such sessions. They
need to get some action, need to relax. Are they supposed to
sit in their gorgeous suites and basket weave or watch telly?
Would your wife really get bothered about a bit of wind-
down at Omdurman, or your colleagues?'

'It's more than that,' he said.

'How?'

'They could hurt you.'

'Hurt?'

'Or more than hurt.'

'What do you mean, more than hurt?'

'More than,' he said.

'Oh, God.' She lost a little colour.

Perhaps she was starting to realise that if you fucked someone considerable like Corbett, the problems coming after might be considerable, also. He said: 'And when that happened I'd be on the blame shortlist. I felt I had to come and tell you to be watchful.' He could be on the blame shortlist for Grace, the blame shortlist for Eric Moyle. This was middlemanning.

She drank, staring above his head along the bottle. 'How can I be watchful?' she asked, when she finished.

'I know.'

'I spend my work time under men I've never met before.'

Sometimes he did find the way she spoke too graphic. Perhaps it was their fashion. 'Yes,' he said.

'Are you worried about me or about you?'

'About you above all, naturally. But what happens to you could affect me.'

'How?'

He did not want to say. If he gave it to her in detail, that look of happy adoration on her intelligent face was almost bound to slip and be replaced by fright. He enjoyed the adoration, especially when it was on view in a public setting where food was served. Hen in a restaurant could be more interested in other customers than in Corbett or anything he spoke about. She loved to eavesdrop or speculate on what people were saying to each other at distant tables. Occasionally, she'd seem to want to efface him. While neglected at those times, Corbett used to think that if his mother had ever watched Hen behave like that, she would have been damning.

'Do you mean if I was killed?' Grace asked.

'The photographs.'

'Which photographs?'

Christ, had Castice-Manne been lying, to swell the threat? Corbett realised he could appear stupid here. 'Omdurman photographs.' It was tentative. He came down to not much more than a whisper for the words, in case she appeared puzzled.

'Oh, those,' she replied.

'If the police saw them they'd come looking for me.'

'You mean, if I was dead and they searched the house and found them they'd come looking for you?'

'I'd be a suspect, no question,' he said.

'Why?'

'These are… well, in a sense… in a sense, intimate photographs.'

She laughed. 'Yes, in a sense.'

'That's what I mean.'

'What?' she said.

'I'd appear to them as a principal contact of yours.'

'Why?' she asked.

'It's obvious.'

'Why would they pick you out from all the rest?'

'"All the rest"'? Humiliation began to bite at him, big, tearing bites, and anger returned.

'Did you think you were the only one, Julian? Really?' She put out a hand and touched him lightly for a second on his. She spoke as if conscious of how much the truth might hurt him but aware she must clarify, anyway.

'Castice-Manne said—'

'These are identification pictures,' she replied. 'I shouldn't be telling you this, obviously, but things have begun to sound dangerous. When a man comes back to Omdurman wanting a particular girl – say me, for instance – it's important I can recognise him and remember some biog. The re-meeting might seem sordid and heartless otherwise. These are clients paying a lot of money and it would offend them to feel they've been forgotten. Some regard themselves as uniquely gorgeous lovers, bound to leave eternal grand memories. All right, you'll say I'd forgotten you just now in the street. But in the street is so different from Omdurman. In Omdurman we expect to have regular clients, and it's only a matter of making sure we sort out one from another.'

'You have a lot of men's pictures?'

'Some. We all do. Par for the course. For the intercourse.'

Corbett detested puns from women when the subject was serious.

'With a couple of notes about each – their work, holidays, childhood if they've gone on about that,' Grace said. 'Many do – to excuse why they're at Omdurman. Neglected by their mother. A sibling preferred. It's vital to recall all that kind of self-pitying stuff. They consider they've given a glimpse of their tender soul.

'But these are photographs taken when—'

'They might show special tastes and kinks, yes. They are important, too. It's a rounded profile. These are a client's personality.'

'His soul. You keep them at home?' To Corbett it seemed unbelievable.

'They're under lock and key, naturally,' she replied. 'Phil won't have them at Omdurman, in case the house is raided. He's right. Photos like that could betray very prominent clients – church and synagogue honchos, politicians; obviously – courtiers; obviously – judges; hair stylists supposed to be queer and liable to lose face and business if it came out they're hetero rams. Phil says confidentiality is the crux of the business, more even than unslumped arses.'

'You study the pictures at home?'

'When everyone else is out, obviously. To keep customers vivid in my mind. You never know who's going to turn up at Omdurman.'

'Honestly?' Like school revision. He objected to the notion of being in an album with all sorts of nationalities and so on, and among men with all sorts of kinks, as she put it, so damn matter-of-fact. He was merely a topic among other topics, not someone uniquely precious to her. He had longed to be that. Weak? Deluded? Disgustingly naive? 'I was going to ask you to destroy the pictures,' Corbett said.

'Ah, you are worried about yourself, aren't you, Jule?' She stood up. 'I ought to get back.'

He stood too, and called for the bill. She walked to the door and waited while he paid by card. Outside he said: 'Please, be careful.'

'We've dealt with that.' He felt for the money in his breast pocket. 'A hundred will be fine,' she said.

'No it won't.' He gave her all of it, the three hundred. 'Couldn't you go home now?' he asked.

She took the notes and kissed him on the mouth, not much more than a touch, but with a meaning to it, he thought. Maybe she longed for him. Perhaps he had become special to her. She said: 'I believe you do worry about me – as me.'

'Yes.'

'Why don't I take you somewhere? To be crude, you've paid for it, Jule. It's quite near and comfortable and camera-less. You're entitled to the full service. Then I'd go home.'

He had wondered about this. 'I don't think it should be like that between us, not tonight,' he said.

'No, nor do I, really,' she replied. 'The talk hasn't been that kind of talk, has it?'

'Go home,' he said. 'Please.'

'Yes, I might. Honestly, I might.'

'Couldn't you just do Omdurman? I mean for a while, until things are a bit easier? Safer. Weeks. Even a month.'

'Yes, I might. Honestly, I might.'

Corbett did not mind iced soup. Malta was a hot little country, despite that damn mistral wind blowing from Africa, and iced soup was obviously one way of dealing with the temperature. He liked the history of Malta and he knew Sid liked the island's past, too, although Sid dwelled mainly on the last war, when the island was besieged and bombed by the Italians and Germans. Things a bit further back than that impressed Jule. In fact, Corbett often felt that if he had not come into his present kind of work he might have been an historian. He thought he had the right scrupulousness about accuracy, as well as the instinct for comprehending a far-off period. He had bought a booklet about Malta at Heathrow and enjoyed the tale of how Britain took the island from France after Napoleon. The Maltese had wanted this. The British were really respected then. It was Corbett's aim to help bring back by his work some of the spirit and grandeur of those times. He had the idea that several staff and other passengers at the airport when he arrived guessed from just a glance at him that here was someone on a rare and crucial mission, and entirely able to manage it. This was a small island with less than half a million people. Corbett thought they would probably not have seen many men of his kind; that emergent, yet, above all, sensitive kind.

Sid and Gloria had a big, square, cream-walled villa just outside Valetta, beautifully air-conditioned, windows permanently closed against mosquitoes. It was rented furnished from an American academic. A maid and cook came in daily. Besides iced soup, the cook produced an excellent fish course for them this lunchtime and they drank Italian white wine. The villa stood in its own grounds and flower gardens and a lawn seemed well looked after, so perhaps they had help there, too. The flowers were brilliant and plentiful, great banks of red, pink, blue and yellow. This was true, abundant Mediterranean growth. It would have been simple to hide a body and drum there. A water sprinkler revolved slowly. It comforted Corbett that Malta had sprinklers. He loved to see facilities spread worldwide, as would anyone with an uninsular mind.

He had the feeling that Sid appeared settled here, even if the property was only rented. He would want to test the area before committing himself to a buy. Sid was still twitchy off and on, but Corbett sensed contentment too. Distance from all the enmities and competition might please him. Perhaps the arrangements for ridding the Complex of Sid would be easier than Corbett had thought. Sid's worries might have squashed all fight.

He must like the nearness to Valetta on account of the port's famed connection with the Navy and merchant convoys in the war. Sid loved the sea as long as it was bygone sea, the sea in tales or War Museum records, not sea unlacing the Bay barrage now, or tomorrow night, brown, estuary sea with his fucking nursing home's name on it.

They ate inside in a cool, long, white-walled room, the table genuine wood, no cloth. The doors also were unpainted real wood. Beautifully planed and varnished wood with the knots highlighted always gave Corbett the good sensation of contact with noble skills. Some knots looked so stark and unmanageable, yet they had been reduced and brought into a table or door by patient carpentry. Mankind had its triumphs. He saw the process as similar to middlemanning: rough difficulties smoothed away by the calm and positive abilities of people like himself. These skills with wood here had probably been around since Malta was occupied by the Knights of St John, in the 16th century. Corbett invariably felt awed by decent tradition. This was a facet of his love for history.

Sid feared bug stings if they lunched under the garden awning. He had heard of someone who died and of another whose face had swelled to double its usual size and stayed like it, making him twice as liable next time he ate out of doors. 'This could go on and on, Jule, am I right,' Sid said, 'and faster, a kind of geometric progression, because there would be increasing flesh for the insects? People would notice a face like that, even in Malta.' Through a lowered venetian blind, Corbett enjoyed the sight of the flowers while they ate. He thought a view typical of a locality could often add significance to the already major significance of a meal. The pink and the red flowers quivering in a small breeze had a kind of jollity and mischief to them, not like those filthy, fucking smug red and pink ones in Britain waiting to be funeral wreaths. Hen detested such flowers, too, and would punch or kick the heads off them in parks, like martial arts, then trample the petals, knees high and Hunnish. You could never forget Floyd had put her through a top British public school. The attitude towards certain flowers was one of the things that had drawn Corbett and Henrietta together. They often said it was not a mere matter of wanting to shag each other, which would have been damned ephemeral.

'I know what Gloria thinks. I need to know what you think, Jule,' Hyson stated during the gazpacho soup. In his eating, even of soup, Sid was as noiseless as Grace. He did not look as though he would be, especially in view of his teeth, yet he was. Sid was not the kind to pretend to be upper class by getting loudness into the sucking of soup. His eyes stayed on Corbett, dark and blank as street pools.

Corbett said: 'I'm not sure I—'

'That's why you're here, isn't it, to tell me how you regard it?' Hyson replied.

Corbett said: 'I don't—'

'Squeezing me out,' Hyson replied. 'Like I'm fucking finished.' The stare was still on. Had he talked in this style to Boris Lowndes?

Corbett said: 'Oh, Sid, I haven't—'

'I've explained things to Sidney – our intentions,' Gloria said. She spoke in a bold, unarguable voice, like a placard.

Jesus. Was that safe? Corbett had come to Malta expecting to be subtle and, above all, humane with Sid. She had simply told him he was out. Could it be so easy? Did she understand the risk?

'An early, very early, point in the discussions, Sid,' Corbett replied. 'Nothing settled.'

Gloria said: 'Well, I think we—'

'You don't come with offer figures, do you?' Hyson asked.

'A foolish one, an insulting one from Ivo Vartelm, that's all,' Corbett replied. He would have to edit, obviously.

'And you haven't flown out here to tell me about that, have you?' Hyson said.

'I've explained to Sidney that selling is just a mighty fucking error and if he can't see it, it's time he fucked off,' Gloria said. Her tone continued to announce the death of that prized friend of Corbett, tact: possibly peacefully at home after a long illness. Women could be like this. Henrietta could be. They said what they thought, seemingly without thinking that what they thought might need some thinking about and decking up before they said it. Perhaps this was why Corbett had never come across a middle-woman.

'You agree with that, Jule?' Hyson asked, 'Selling is wrong at this point?' He spoke mildly, as if it were an academic debate. What had happened?

'Of course he fucking agrees with it,' Gloria replied. 'Would he spend time in a dump like Malta if he didn't agree with it?'

Corbett said: 'Well, now, I—'

'I can see why you'd be confused, Jule,' Hyson replied. 'I'd never think of you as totally treacherous and evil.'

'Thanks, Sid.'

'It's the whole structure of things, isn't it?' Hyson said. 'Marv and Jacob setting you up that way with the body. Potentially.'

'I've dealt with that, Sidney,' Gloria snarled. She was fiddling with a dinner knife on the table.

'Yes, I know, but all the same, Gloria—'

'Haven't I told you I've dealt with that? Jule couldn't be more in the clear. I spruced that corpse.'

'What terms?' Hyson replied. 'For me.'

'Terms?' Corbett asked. They were onto the fish. It was in a great, sharp sauce which Corbett thought probably regional and handed down like the skill with wood. He loved regional food served on a strong, plain table. Together they seemed to take him even further into a tradition. Obviously, he did not suddenly regard himself as Maltese – that would seem stupidly premature – but he felt appreciative. Ambience hugged him like an aunt.

'I've said we'll look after Sidney as well as we can, Jule,' Gloria replied.

Corbett was brilliantly comfortable with things as they appeared to be working out. They matched what he had hoped. Gloria seemed to have assessed Sid well. She knew his terrors and weaknesses. Of course she did. Together, she and Corbett could triumph endlessly. Sid without Marv and Jacob, and above all without Gloria, was a fragment. Some people expanded from being stung. Sidney shrank. He had on khaki trousers and a green, open-necked shirt. The shirt suited him, went well with his handsome, beaky face, like a hefty bird in foliage. He looked as he almost always looked, powerful and lucky. He was not. The motto on the gates of his Berkshire place said in Latin: 'We survive, we continue.' He had inherited that motto, which obviously made it out-and-out balls. The Renton Park people before him had not survived and continued and Renton Park became Glorsid.

And now, in turn, Sid himself would not survive or continue. Perhaps Grace had it right after all and there was only 'for now'. Sid was not for now. Corbett and Gloria were for now and what came next, especially Corbett. Gloria certainly had a brain and will suited to now, but the rest of her was not really up to it. Her face and body were not for now. They might have been for now in about Harold Wilson's time. Her clothes were not for now. Corbett could not say when they were for. He wondered about the period of the Potsdam meeting between Churchill, Stalin and Roosevelt. As to gates, she could not get over them unhelped. Castice-Manne had quoted Psalms and Floyd used to repeat a bit of that book of the Bible, too: 'By my God I leaped over a wall.' It was not God who got Gloria over those gates in the night but Corbett. She would want him to carry her in this partnership and he would, but only at first, obviously. What he wondered about was a gradual fade-out for Gloria, something like this fade-out for Sid, and an invitation in to Hen. Probably she could be kept tolerable, or almost, as a boardroom partner. Her brain and general contempt for others would be vital.

'A consultancy for you, Sid,' Gloria said.

'Oh, at least that,' Corbett said.

'What capital aspects?' Hyson asked. 'There's capital of mine in the Complex.'

'Of course there is,' Corbett replied.

'Jule is going to take away your burden, Sidney.'

'It sounds like a Gospel chorus,' Hyson replied. 'The dear English language is so full of suggestion.'

'The debt burden,' Gloria replied. 'There'll be new capital from fresh backers on the strength of Jule's reputation. He's going to attract good funds and we pay off the sods who are dunning us. Some of these finance houses employ damn dangerous people as bums. I'd rather not tangle. They could follow us here. The equity should be a fair bit bigger than the debt so there'll be a surplus. And we buy you out with that, some of that. In due course.'

'How much is some?' Hyson asked.

'Some,' Gloria replied. 'Enough. You'll be fine and worry-free, Sidney.'

Sid took a while considering this. He ate systematically. moved his shoulders about a bit inside his shirt to suggest something pent-up. 'But if I fight it?' he asked.

She'd heard a bell and came out of her corner immediately. 'If you fight it you're fighting me. I don't want that. Jule and I don't want that.' She leaned forward over her plate and gazed, not at him but just past him, as though he certainly mattered, but could matter more.

'Certainly not, no, I don't want that,' Corbett replied.

Hyson said: 'I don't want that, but—'

'I don't want that, Sidney,' Gloria replied.

Corbett knew what she was telling him in these clanging, repeated words. If Sid accepted this business arrangement, the personal arrangement between her and Hyson could continue. That is, the marriage. And would continue. But if he opposed her over the Complex, she would fight Sid back and cut him out of her life absolutely. Could he take that?

'And the flood burden will be gone too, Sidney,' she said. 'Your worries about the channel and the barrage sluices – those terrible depreciation anxieties and the impossibility of insurance. All these totally understandable concerns we shall take away. Peace for you. You've earned it. And then there's our busy Chancellor of the Exchequer, Gordon Brown, making a real intrusive fuss here and with EU finance ministers about so-called money laundering – wanting to extend what it means. You don't need this kind of persecution, Sidney.'

'But you, Gloria, you will have these anxieties still, and I will see these anxieties in you and I will feel them, also,'

Hyson replied. 'How could it be otherwise? We who are so close and have been so close for so long.'

'Jule is immune to these anxieties. I'll draw strength from him and this I will impart to you, Sidney, like milk from tits. It will happen slowly, gradually, but it is sure to happen, because of Jule's infectious confidence.'

They both seemed to have gone into drama-speak, a sort of ham dialogue meant to be flung passionately towards the stalls' back row. Abruptly, though, it changed. Hyson said starkly: 'I'm out, then?'

'Not out,' Corbett replied at once. He laughed, a laugh shaped to reassure. Although he had hoped the transference might be easier than he'd originally feared, the speed of the process now scared him. It did not sound like Sid. The cracked voice did not sound like Sid. 'Not out in any sense,' Corbett said. 'Think of it more like taking the presidency of the company, a move into a less hands-on role but still an esteemed and guiding figure, while others, under that good, ultimate leadership, do the routine, day-to-day stuff.'

'Yes, we might talk to you now and then about items, Sidney,' Gloria said. 'Yes, now and then. Or probably less than that. You'll get so you won't want to be troubled. But yes, occasionally talk to you about an item, maybe. Ashtray styles for the hotel – that kind of thing.'

'President?' Hyson said. He sounded pleased.

'That's how we see it, isn't it, Gloria?'

She did not answer for a while, then said: 'Along those lines.'

Corbett said: 'We'd treat any continuing investment by you before buy-out as a fixed fraction of the total, Sid, so that whatever enhancement we eventually get on the property through inflation and go-ahead management would be reflected in your pay-off. If it was a quarter it would stay a quarter, regardless of how the Complex appreciated under our control.'

'When?' Hyson asked.

'What?' Corbett replied.

'When will I get it?'

'In due time,' Gloria said. 'It's to your advantage not to rush us. This will be a growing investment.'

'And, obviously, a business arrangement only,' Hyson said.

'Absolutely,' Corbett replied. 'As far as I'm concerned this has no implications about your... well, about your marriage.'

'As far as you're concerned?' Gloria said. 'You're *not* concerned, are you?'

'No, that's what I mean,' Corbett replied.

'So don't be so damn eager to say it,' Gloria said.

'And then these pictures,' Hyson said.

Corbett had finished eating and gripped the very authentic, consoling wood of the table with both hands. 'Which pictures?' he asked.

'Omdurman,' Gloria replied. That same unholy curtness. A woman came in and set bowls of fruit on the table, then withdrew with the dirty plates.

'Castice-Manne sends these pictures, evidently wanting to smash things between you and Gloria,' Hyson replied. 'Gloria's supposed to reject you, through jealousy, because of how you're... well, placed in some of these photographs. Yes, placed. They came addressed to Gloria, though she's not secretive. Castice-Manne must have somehow got an idea you and she might want the Complex. Perhaps it was obvious to him. Perhaps I should have sensed things, too.'

'How did he get your address here?' Corbett asked.

'Sent to Glorsid. The staff redirected,' Hyson replied. 'They probably didn't open the package.'

Only probably. Oh, great.

'You don't go there very often, Jule,' Hyson said. 'I'll see there's no giggling if you do come.'

Gloria said: 'Pathetic. Does Castice-Manne really imagine a sex portfolio is going to upset me? We all have to wind down, don't we, Jule? You'd had tough commercial meetings just before these photographs. You're entitled to some carry-on.'

'Grace said that,' Corbett replied.

'Grace is the slit and so on?' Gloria asked.

'Yes.'

'There you are, then,' Gloria said. 'And I can't think these are photographs to damage you creditworthiness, Jule. If anything, the opposite. This looked like damned expensive pussy.'

'How in God's name can you spot that in a snap?' Hyson asked. 'Pussy's pussy.'

'Quality of the photography,' Gloria replied. 'The sharpness. The depth of expression caught in Jule's face. These are fine cameras.'

In the night, Corbett was awoken by somebody entering his large, beautifully furnished bedroom. There was no lock on the door. He had looked for one. He hated sleeping in an unlocked room when the setting was strange to him. Oh, Christ, it's the other aspect of the partnership. He thought he heard suppressed sobbing. Had some of what he had said hurt Gloria? Had he seemed to put distance between her and Corbett by being so considerate to Sid? Or had she merely pretended not to be jealous and upset by the pictures? Must he comfort her? He did not want her in his bed, and he especially did not want her in his bed when Sid was so close. Sid might already have been made jealous by Castice-Manne's sending the photographs, as though there were a sexual element between Corbett and Gloria, and the pictures intended to destroy it.

Hyson said: 'I had to throttle her, Jule. It's what you'd expect, isn't it, given that degree of betrayal? All-round betrayal. I did try to warn her. You've heard me.'

'Well, yes.'

'I should think she'd expect it herself, despite her loudness. That's a partial consolation.' Hyson came and stood near the bed. It was dark. As far as Corbett could make out, he had on a blue, zip-up boiler suit, which presumably he slept in. Corbett remained lying flat and attempted to run through in his mind the layout of the room, in case something could be used as a weapon. Yes, Sid was weeping, but with some control. 'Policy. Business. She would have deserted me in those respects, Jule. I see it as like Charles Boyer being left alone by his wife through death. But suicide well, suicide is not me somehow, Jule. It would have been another betrayal. A betrayal of myself by myself.'

'I see.'

'And so it had to be Gloria. Do you understand?' Corbett thought there might be an anglepoise lamp on the other side of the room near the door. It was solid metal. 'Tragic, Sid,' he replied.

'I can't blame you, Jule,' he said. 'She drew you on. I don't mean sexually. Or not necessarily. Policy. Business. No, I can't blame you. I need you, Jule.'

'Yes?' Corbett abandoned thinking about the lamp, about weapons. He sat up a little. He despised cowering other than when it might be a help.

Hyson said: 'The confidence she spoke of – your confidence in the barrage, all that.'

'Yes, Sid?'

'Perhaps it will come to me, come to me direct, not through Gloria, as she mentioned. It can't come through Gloria now. Nothing's going to come through Gloria now. If we work together, you and I, Jule. It could come through you.'

'Well, yes,' Corbett replied. 'You mean you're not going to sell the Complex?'

'She could be right on that, after all. If she would risk so much, there must be a good point in it. She was very bright, the dead darling. Perhaps the Complex still is a supreme investment.'

'Well, yes.'

Hyson switched on the overhead light. Corbett sat up fully. 'Luckily, I met a few useful people when Gloria was away in the UK with you,' Hyson said.

'Useful?'

'Locals.'

'Ah.'

'Hireable.'

'Yes?' Corbett replied.

'People who are not altogether into law and order.'

'Right.'

'They'll know how to dispose of a body. This is an island, for God's sake.'

'Certainly,' Corbett said.

'Gloria would have humiliated me, but that's been dealt with. I don't want to retaliate further by being casual with her remains, Jule. No. Now, I want her treated with as much dignity and respect as can be, given that it has to be quick and secret and most probably off a small boat at night. Dignity for her is important in a foreign country with one-time grand links to the Crown. Would you like to see her?'

'Well, yes,' Corbett replied. Sid seemed to want him to come. In any case, it was important to know whether he was lying. And Corbett recognised a tribute aspect: if you had been almost into an important business arrangement with a woman who had searched a corpse on your account, it was most likely a duty to view her when a corpse herself. Protocol remained dear to Corbett. He left the bed and they went across the landing together. Corbett was naked and did not put anything on, wanting to indicate to Sid he felt tranquil and at home. He had hoped there would be a serenity about Gloria in death, her appearance more like sleeping. That would seem right for someone of her age. In fact she had obviously fought Sid, and really fought him, before he managed to kill her. Corbett recalled his image of her coming out of a boxing ring corner to oppose Sid, but that had only been in argument. Although her strength at the park gates had not been enough, despair and rage might have helped her now. She had sinew. She was on her back, wearing a long, black nightdress. One leg stuck out on the right and was not at a proper angle. It might be broken. Corbett hated to see limbs askew.

There were vivid throttle marks on her throat and bruising to her face, as if Sid had needed to knock her out, or almost, before he could get his fingers in place for long enough on her neck. Her mouth and eyes were open. Corbett had heard nothing. There could have been no screaming or yelling, just the struggle. That was magnificent of her if he had actually broken her leg. Corbett truly admired bravery and restraint in elderly women. It was not as rare as many thought.

Hyson wept quietly a little more. 'She so wanted a future, Jule,' he said, 'but fair's fucking fair, wouldn't you say?'

13

Corbett felt brilliantly gratified that Sid Hyson should have changed his views on selling the Complex because of a new, total confidence in Jule. This was the way with so many people, and Corbett did not feel totally surprised. They grew assured of their future as long as he was with them. Didn't he see it in Vartelm, Castice-Manne, Laura, Peter, and even Marv and Jacob? At times, in fact, the competing attempts to ally with Jule became almost a nuisance.

Perhaps Sid's sudden belief in him was the most remarkable, though. Hadn't it been enough to make Hyson ignore in Jule exactly the kind of plotting which had led him to kill Gloria, a cherished wife, though admittedly with almost crippling sorrow? Jule and Gloria were, after all, part of what Sid might have seen as a conspiracy – almost certainly did see as a conspiracy, yet only one of the conspirators had suffered, while the other was welcomed into fresh, buoyant partnership. It would have been foolish for Corbett to deny his own huge business worth. How could he when there were so many testimonies to it? Just the same, he found this attitude of Hyson's exceptional and immensely to the old thug's credit. Corbett decided he could agree to join him. Sid deserved it for his talented recognition of Jule's worth, and for Sid's brave willingness to accept Jule's judgement on what had been hugely unsettling topics for him, such as the water. Also, many of the arguments that had favoured an alliance with Gloria clearly applied in the altered conditions to an alliance with Hyson. Above all, Sid was still in ownership of the Complex, that priceless in situ element. This was now even stronger for Sid. He held virtually sole ownership of the Complex since Gloria's death and the apparent break with Marv and Jacob. All right, admittedly there were mortgages.

But Corbett knew he could deal with these creditworthiness issues. No more accomplished expert at that kind of work existed.

He came back alone from Malta. Sid remained anxious about his personal safety in Britain, and the dependent value of the properties. Kill or injure Sid, kill or injure the Complex's price. That was how he still saw things. On top of this, he did not wish to leave the island when his wife had so recently and inexplicably disappeared. He feared he would seem to be doing a runner from guilt. He saw his role as remaining in the villa and talking pleasantly to the police whenever they wished. Sid and Gloria were known about Valetta as a delightful couple, and he felt sure there would be no trouble for him. As he said earlier, people in Malta had noticed her attributes, and he would speak feelingly of these to the police now. He had asked his local helpers to ditch, unfindably, some of Gloria's clothes with her and a couple of suitcases, though not in a manner which in any way impaired the respectful tone of this unofficial funeral. It grieved him that he could not attend. He had told Corbett he sent some of her favourite flowers from the garden with the disposal party, to be scattered in an unobvious manner somewhere above the body. He would be able to inform the police that Gloria had only recently returned from an unaccompanied visit to the United Kingdom and might have formed some sort of friendship or relationship which made her secretly leave home now, possibly a friendship or relationship which she could not discuss with her husband.

Corbett's task now was to notify all who had been interested in the Complex sale that it would not take place, and to begin preparations for the running of the business by one former director and one emergent one – Jule. He would also approach the Complex's banks and let them know he was moving into a major boardroom position. They would deduce from this that the outlook was sound and would ease their repayment pressures. Excitement and self-belief were hot in Corbett's veins. He had won, or almost. Those fucking photographs, around the finance houses or in the manse, could still do foul damage. Not everyone would regard them as merely evidence of a forgivable, even admirable, virility and spiritedness. He must speak to Castice-Manne. Although there could plainly be no question of allowing him into the Complex partnership, Corbett thought he might be able to assure him that, as long as he kept the photographs private, Corbett would do everything he knew among Bay acquaintances to guarantee that Castice-Manne's existing property there was never torched, as Sid's hotel had been before completion. Protection remained quite a workable concept in the Bay, time-honoured in its way.

Corbett forced himself to forget the photographs. That untidy possibility must not destroy his joy and optimism. In any case, wouldn't Castice-Manne be afraid to give those pictures too wide a showing? Suppose copies somehow found their way to the police. Might questions arise about where the camera-work had been done? Would he casually endanger Omdurman and his other Omdurmans? He would be pushed back onto that kind of business even more now that he was definitively excluded from a takeover of the Complex.

Corbett revelled in his new situation and longed for Hen and Floyd to revel in it too, especially Hen. But he knew he would meet some doubts there. He did not resent this, did not allow their scepticism to hurt him. He must be patient. Eventually, events would convince them. When Sid returned, they would see. But Corbett did not really want to wait that long to share his happiness with them. It was a happiness not simply about himself and his prospects. His notion was that, in time, he might be able to bring Henrietta in with him to the Complex boardroom. She had a grand business brain, trained in large-sum accounting and investment strategies. He would convince Sid she was an asset. That should not need any big debate. Sid was getting old, might want to withdraw into a nominal position after a few years and settle, for most of the time, in Malta. He had seemed attracted by the title of president. There would be room on the Complex board for Hen.

In the manse, they were eating breakfast again, Floyd busy at the stove. Corbett said: 'Hyson wants me with him at the Complex. He's remaining in Malta for now but when he returns it will be myself and him, refinancing the Complex and resisting all bids.'

'The sale's off?' Floyd asked.

'One was able to talk him out of it,' Corbett said.

'One was?' Henrietta replied.

Corbett did not get angry at this bitchiness. It was just Hen's instinct to react like that, a sort of tic, nothing more. 'Sid hadn't realised I would be prepared to work for him,' Corbett said. 'I mean, work for him as long as one... as long as I had a full directorship, of course.'

'That clinched it, I suppose?' Henrietta said. 'Haven't we reached this spot before, Jule – the "certainty" of a transformation, and then back to the usual? I admit I believed in it myself once or twice. But this? Sidney Hyson and Gloria taking you aboard? Oh, don't, Jule. Imposs.' Her eyes did not have that friendliness they sometimes showed towards Corbett. She was eating bacon with a kind of savagery, he thought, not soothing to watch.

Floyd said: 'They'll never let you into the Complex, Jule, not as an equal. That boardroom's basically family – Sid, Gloria. Even Marv and Jacob are only tokens.'

'Developments. Gloria might drop out,' Corbett replied. 'Will drop out. Has dropped out. I replace her, thanks to my clout with the finance houses and general reputation. And then, later, almost certain, Hen, a place for you.'

'Please, Jule, don't give us rot,' Henrietta replied.

Floyd said: 'Gloria drop out? Oh, no, if anything she's the one who—'

'I know how it looks,' Corbett said. 'She seems the strong one, the tough one. But she's actually very scared, Floyd. Insurance problems, depreciation. And the Chancellor's drive against money laundering. I don't mean the Complex does money laundering, obviously, or would I want to be associated with it? Lord, no. But the Government and the EU will widen the meaning of laundering into blurred areas. She's afraid they could be caught – even framed. I think she might stay in Malta as pretty well a permanency. Yes, that. And in due course, Sid will want to retire back out there himself, and at that stage we bring in Hen. Sid would be a sleeping partner, taking a profits share but leaving management to me. And Hen. Sid loves Malta. The genuineness of things – real wood in the tables and doors. That's a minor example but typical and important to Sid. In time he'll build up resistance to insects.'

'They dangle things in front of you just to keep you toiling away for them, don't you see that, Jule?' Henrietta asked. 'It's how the powerful stay powerful.' She was ready for work, wearing a dark, silk jacket and navy skirt. He liked this sort of outfit on her. She looked intense, like some animal accustomed to bringing down prey under one sudden, clawing leap.

'I'll be powerful, Hen,' he replied. '*We'll* be powerful.'

She finished the bacon, downed her coffee and stood up. She took her cup and plate to the sink and washed them. 'You're a born middleman, Jule,' she said. 'Sid Hyson knows it. His wife knows it.'

'No,' he cried. He found she upset him so much with this that he did not want to eat any more, but he kept on so as not to offend Floyd.

'A sensationally gifted middleman,' she replied, 'but a middleman for ever. We've pretended otherwise, haven't we, but we know it, too, don't we, Jule?'

'Not so, not so,' he cried.

Henrietta left. He heard her car draw away.

'That's not her true view of me, Floyd,' Corbett said.

'Yes, it's her true view of you. She and I discuss the future sometimes. Always she assumes you'll stay as now, or get killed like Boris. There's a true fear of that in her, Jule – your death. She dreads you'll be cut down for trying to get bigger than you are. When you spoke about a director-ship I could see it terrified her. And so the sniping, Jule, the insistence that you should not try to rise where you have no right to rise, like Lucifer, like Faust. She foresees the appalling punishment.'

Corbett had intended walking down to the Complex this morning, just to look at it again, handle some of the struc-tures once more, this time with the charming certainty that it would soon all be his. He meant to call in to the hotel pent-house boardroom and tell Marv and Jacob the sale was off. Let those sods be the first to feel the power of his definite new status.

But what Hen and Floyd had said knocked the jauntiness from him, scared him for a while. Always he took notice of what Hen thought and said. He reverenced her mind. Was it, then, stupid of him to imagine Sid would bring him into the firm as a partner? It looked preposterous to Hen. Of course, she did not know Gloria had been removed and that there was a new place on the board. But he felt Hen would have regarded his hopes as stupid, even if he had told her about this change. She might not know about Gloria but she obvi-ously thought she knew Jule. Did she? Couldn't he break out of that fucking bleak categorisation? Perhaps she was right, as she generally was, and he couldn't. It took him until the late afternoon to shake off this miserable verdict on his status and reconvince himself he was as able as so many people other than Hen and her damn father believed.

Then, towards three o'clock, he did walk over to the Complex. From the Pier Head, he thought it looked magnifi-cent, undoubtedly worthy of his ownership. There was scale to it and there was a lovely wholeness and balance. The name 'Complex' seemed to him now not altogether suitable, sug-gesting as it did a complicated, even baffling, layout. To Corbett, the development had a wonderful simplicity and ele-gance. The buildings complemented each other – hotel, casino, shopping mall, nursing home, botanical gardens. The hotel reared high and the other constructions lay cleverly grouped below, as if guarding its foundations and ground floor. The sun in the west caught the great stretches of glass in the botanical gardens, causing it to gleam like a triumphant declaration of taste and soil scholarship.

If Gloria had picked the architect for the Complex, she had done magnificently, and Corbett could utterly understand why Sid would be so distressed at having to beat her into unconsciousness and then slaughter her. Corbett wished he, also, could have sent some flowers to the committal. For a true bond had existed between him and Gloria. He hated to think no emblem from him accompanied her finally, say when she was given with good weights to the Mediterranean. He was sure that if she had been able to state a view on whether to retain the Complex and, if affirmative, whether it should be Jule to replace her, she would have said yes to both propositions. Hadn't she longed for him to come in with her as owner? Absolutely: it was the reason she had been killed. She would have known that Jule's abilities were still unparalleled, still unbeatable. This kind of imagined approval was vital to Corbett. He would hate to flout any wish of Gloria. He yearned also for the actual approval of Henrietta. Floyd could be right and her seeming contempt for his achievements might spring only from fear. Just the same, Corbett felt an enormous disappointment, especially as whenever he thought about ownership of the Complex it was in conjunction with Hen.

He did not entirely accept Floyd's analysis of her attitude. Corbett thought there was also jealousy present. Never had Hen been able to concede for very long that Jule might outshine her in a competitive world. Yes, occasionally she would appear to reach a proper, awed regard for his achievements. It had happened once or twice recently. This was not sustained, though. Always there came a return to cynicism and even abuse. She assumed ultimately, didn't she, that his intelligence and flair were minor, less than her own? Possibly some of this arrogance derived from her public school. Corbett might have encouraged her in the past by kowtowing to her brain.

He still admired it. But this morning he had started to feel powerfully for the first time that her disregard for what had been accomplished was unjust. He resented that she should speak to him as to an inferior, *de haut en bas*, as the French put it. He was not *bas* – not low – however high she might feel herself to be. He had come to wish she should be brought down a little – at least a little – and so better situated to appreciate his triumphs. This would teach humility, greatly to her own, ultimate advantage. It should enable her to enjoy much more heartily the promise he had given that, in a while, she would join him as a director of the Complex. If she were coming from a deflated status, the elevation would be even more thrilling for her. In any case, Corbett believed himself entitled to get back at her for the damned inconsiderate shagging around she did.

Walking towards the Complex from the Pier Head, he went into a public phone booth and gave an anonymous tip to the BBC Wales Newsroom about the location of Eric Moyle's body and drum. He saw no danger of being implicated when the investigation began: hadn't Gloria admirably scoured the ground for possible clues?

This development could produce a real chastening sequence for Hen. Clearly, it would pain her to discover as fact that he was dead. In a way, Corbett could feel sorry for her on this account. She probably had some genuine affection for Moyle. It was not only a lust job, most likely. But what would really get to her was the revelation that she had been giving herself to a kind of hobo, almost a farcical figure in his locality, not some genius football scout who only lived an under-class life so as to stay in touch with his material. Although Hen had been to a public school, she was not out-and-out snobbish or class-obsessed, but Corbett knew she would hate to be associated with a street entertainer, and especially a street entertainer in the sort of streets where Moyle entertained. Probably she would not like to visualise, either, the comically undignified way he drove his body to produce the music: eyes bulging, leg stamping, lips locked on the mouth organ. Of course, everyone's occupation had gross aspects to it, yes, even his own, and he might tell her this if she became too distressed. Probably, though, she would regard that as patronising. He wanted to patronise her. There were not many chances to patronise such an effortlessly brass-necked companion. Her disgusting randiness had produced this opportunity, and in his view she would have deserved whatever he brought against her. But he still could not allow himself to take undiluted pleasure in hurting her, this eternal, gifted, adored slag.

The fact that Moyle had been a one-man-band might not turn out to be the whole of the humiliation. The woman Moyle lived with had hinted that no properly organised search for him took place since he was known to disappear for long periods now and then, usually because he was temporarily involved with a woman and had moved in. If this also earned publicity on discovery of the body, it was certain to upset Hen. She would look like one of a stable, and there would be an impression of hygiene risks. Corbett vowed he would never speak of these to Hen, though, or allow them to chill their bed. This would be cruel. He knew that, for her, it had always been important to believe any affair she was involved in had a bit of depth. It resembled Hen's and Corbett's certainty that their marriage was based on more than the sniff of flesh, such as the shared enmity towards particular flowers.

Again, as he put the phone down, he pitied her to a degree. There was still part of him that needed Hen to be aloof, even proud. After all, these were qualities that must have helped draw him to her originally. But he could no longer tolerate those moments when she treated him dismissively, as someone with a very basic skill in a very basic trade and stuck there for keeps.

He walked on. At the nursing home he stood for a while with his left cheek pressed against some of the cement brickwork. He wanted communication. He needed the contact with materials, materials which already felt his. It was as if he experienced a special chummy warmth in the texture, and the slight smell of the mortar seemed personal and inviting, the way certain animals give off a scent when about to mate. He knew some would regard his behaviour as far-fetched, but he saw it himself as a kind of gloriously reciprocated, brilliant empathy. He could imagine these buildings had been waiting for him, as him. He felt like crying out, 'I am here. At last, I have come to you.' This he did not do, though. There were people about, and some might already think it odd that he should press himself against the wall. They would probably decide it was some kind of building survey, but not if he began to yell. His habit of formulating thoughts but keeping them inside took charge.

He found Marv and Jacob in the boardroom at the hotel. He walked in without having Reception ring up to inform them. That's how it would be now. He had the run of the place and soon the running of the place. They had better know it.

He didn't want to be crude with them, not crush them with a blurt of new facts; he did not aim to be confrontational at all in a direct way. He would like the realisation that things were now different to come to them slowly. It was more effective like that, deeper. People had time to appreciate the scale of what was happening when you used this sort of technique, and to understand they could not resist. It was a procedure he had often employed in middlemanning: although he was moving out of that role now, it would be absurd to forget some of its gorgeous skills. He loved to spot on someone's face during negotiations the gradual acknowledgement that they had been left behind, a mounting awareness that their posturing and wriggling and bullshit were too late. Now and then Corbett thought he would like to give guest lectures on Master of Business Administration courses.

'The Complex is looking magnificent,' he said. He did not deliberately use a tone that also said, 'And it's mine, mine,' but he knew his voice might have contained this without his being aware of it. Corbett hated pretentiousness, even with

shits like Marv and Jacob. They had their identities. Marv
was a recognised father. 'How's the babe, Marv?' Corbett
asked, with decent warmth.

'That fucking Mrs Lowndes,' Jacob replied.

'What?' Corbett said. 'Boris's mother? Why?'

'That fucking Mrs Lowndes,' Jacob replied.

'What?' Corbett said.

Marv and Jacob were standing over near the long boardroom window in their suits and glancing down now and then
towards the lagoon and the road. Corbett found he agreed
with one of the potential bidders – was it Vartelm? – anyway,
the one who had said he would keep the penthouse boardroom if he took over, even though it could have been turned
into God knew how many revenue-producing guest suites.
The penthouse in its lavish spaciousness was style, was affirmation. Corbett knew it suited him. He strolled across the
boardroom towards Marv and Jacob. The sun caressed the
lagoon and four or five small sailing boats dawdled there.
This was how life ought to be always, Corbett thought: two
turds like Marv and Jacob due to find out they were utterly
fucking finished, and as background a sweetly picturesque
sight of serene, grubby water and happy yachting.

'This time I want my child to have a lasting father,' Marv
said.

'Certainly,' Corbett replied.

'It's important,' Marv said.

'This is recognised,' Corbett replied.

'Does Mrs fucking Lowndes take that into account?'
Jacob asked.

'How come you just walk in, Jule?' Marv asked.

'I thought you'd be here,' Corbett replied.

'Yes, but how come you just walk in?' Marv said. 'Do I see
signals?'

'You've been out there on the little island with Sid, yes,
Jule?' Jacob said.

'Some discussion points,' Corbett replied.

'Does he know about Mrs Lowndes?' Jacob asked.

'What?' Corbett said.

'He's out there, but she can touch him as well, you know,' Jacob replied.

'What's she done?' Corbett asked.

'We were acting to orders, that's all,' Jacob replied.

'You sound like fucking Nuremburg,' Marv said.

'Somebody should have had meetings with Mrs Lowndes. Either money her, or take her head off,' Jacob said. 'Who'd have thought it, an old cow like that? This is motherliness, I suppose, fuck it. Marv speaks about how important a father is, and I don't argue, but a mother can be a feature, also. Don't think Sid can stay nice and comfortable overseas, Jule, whatever you two have been cooking.'

'To walk in here like that – they've taken you aboard, haven't they, Jule? You're a partner, yes? We're nowhere. The sale's off, is it?'

'They want to revise some aspects of policy,' Corbett replied.

'Has he got any notion what's going on here?' Jacob replied. 'Have *you*?'

'What?' Corbett asked.

'Digging, digging, digging by her,' Jacob replied. 'In a quite real sense it's damn intrusive. She should have been thrown down a good flight of marble steps right at the start. She and Boris ought to have been treated as one target. Jule, we're victims of poor planning here, Marv and I.'

'What, you're the new force in the Complex, are you, Jule?' Marv asked.

'Sid and Gloria want these adjustments I mentioned,' Corbett replied. 'Like fine-tuning.'

'Fine-tuning that means stop the sale, get rid of Jacob and me, give you eminence?'

'They see new directions,' Corbett said. Always he regarded Marv as the more dangerous. Someone who would acknowledge a child as his and go in for a settled relationship with the mother was bound to have an extra quota of ruthlessness. As Jacob had said, Marv might want a dynasty and, obviously, one means of attaining this was by destroying others. These two would know Corbett never went armed.

'Which one was touting for you the most?' Marv asked, 'Sid or Gloria?'

'It seemed joint,' Corbett said.

'She'll want your dick,' Jacob said.

'I don't think so,' Corbett replied.

'You're telling us she loves your mental power?' Jacob asked.

'He hasn't moved her on, has he?' Marv asked.

'Moved her on?' Corbett replied.

'That was always a possible,' Marv said. 'He looked for betrayal. He thinks we've given him betrayal, does he? Did you mention something there – the buy-out project?'

'Of course not,' Corbett replied. 'Would I?'

'Is she gone?' Marv asked.

'Who?' Corbett said.

'Gloria.'

'How do you mean, gone?' Corbett replied.

'She's gone, is she?' Marv said.

'You didn't do it yourself, did you?' Jacob asked.

'Who, Jule?' Marv replied, laughing. 'You're Sid's new prince, are you? Well, there might not be any king or prince very soon.'

'That fucking Mrs Lowndes,' Jacob said. He glanced down again to the road. 'Here's Nightride now with the car. We have to go, Jule.'

'Where?' Corbett asked. It enraged him that they would use Nightride and the car. Corbett had planned on returning to the manse in the chauffeured vehicle. He was convinced Sid would approve. Hen could respond to that sort of symbolism. Corbett would have sat in the front with Nightride and not expected him to jump out and open the door for him at the manse. Corbett believed in showing consideration to underlings, especially one who had killed a man on Corbett's behalf for banging Hen. Marv and Jacob left then.

At the door Marv turned and threw him some keys. 'You might as well,' he said. 'It won't be for long.'

'How do you mean?' Corbett asked.

'No. That fucking Mrs Lowndes,' Jacob said.

Corbett stood at the window and watched them come out from the hotel, climb into the car and get driven away. He found a floor safe under the desk well and opened it with one of the keys. It contained between £2,000 and £3,000 in big-bill cash and three account books. He ignored the money and spent the rest of the afternoon working through the books, trying to get a full notion of the Complex's debts and mortgages, and the size of the job he would have in convincing banks and finance houses that the properties could still be a sparkling positive. Then he walked around all the buildings, going inside each this time, not simply running his face flesh against an outer wall. He wanted people to read from this thorough tour that he had taken on responsibilities. He was wearing the same suit he chose for the meeting with Sid and the others that day when sale of the Complex was first mentioned, but a different tie, a purplish tie with very small, beautifully tasteful medallions on it. The hotel staff and the nursing home staff and the shop managers and botanical gardens attendants and croupiers would almost certainly see the significance of these inspection visits, particularly when they all talked to one another later about the benign but dauntingly shrewd way he gazed around, and about the suit and tie and his black lace-ups.

When Corbett reached home in the early evening, he sensed at once that Moyle's body must have been found and the discovery made public. Hen and Floyd were sitting in front of the television set as though still dazed, Floyd attempting to comfort her. Corbett saw she had been crying. Floyd was properly dressed in a lightweight jacket and dark trousers for some Bethel function later. The television was switched off now but Floyd told Corbett of the local news item about Moyle.

'Oh, but this is appalling,' Corbett said. 'In a park, you say?'

'And apparently not a soccer scout at all – a busker,' Floyd said.

Corbett went and squatted near Hen's chair and stroked her arm. He longed to restore her. He was determined to be positive. 'When we're placed as I visualise us being placed before very long, episodes like this will seem insignificant, Hen,' he said. 'They already seem insignificant to me, but I can see you're hurt for the moment.'

'The TV reporter said a witness told police he saw a man carrying a woman and scaling the gates to the park very late at night,' Floyd remarked.

'Carrying?' Corbett replied.

'Under one arm,' Floyd said.

'What can it be, Jule?' Henrietta asked.

'A caper of some sort?' Corbett said.

'I suppose there might have been many a woman carried over those gates,' Floyd replied.

'This was an elderly woman,' Henrietta said.

'Just the same,' Floyd replied.

'They're trying to trace the man and woman in case of a connection,' Henrietta said.

'It's all immaterial to us, Hen,' Corbett said.

'When they start looking at Eric's life, I mean really looking, are they going to come to me?' Henrietta asked, almost weeping again. 'You know what they can be like – horribly thorough and crude.'

'We can withstand it,' Floyd replied.

Abruptly Henrietta said: 'I've thought of running abroad myself. I will. Yes, I will. I can't endure things here. The shame. My life will be blazoned throughout the tabloid press.'

Gazing at her sympathetically, Floyd said: 'I fear I could not come with you if you ran, Hen, Jule. Bethel needs me. I have to face up to those demands the way a boxer climbs into the ring and faces whatever has been put against him. Destiny.'

Corbett recalled thinking of Gloria as like a boxer, too. Some boxers were destroyed. He said: 'Oh, Hen, to run now would be so inappropriate.'

'As ever, you think of yourself only, Jule.' She sounded weary, understanding, contemptuous.

'I think of you, of you, Hen,' Corbett cried.

'You're afraid that if they name me as a lover of Eric and you've bolted overseas it will look as if you killed him from jealousy and have fled,' Henrietta said.

Once they had been considerations, just as they were considerations for Sid in Malta after Gloria's death. 'Inappropriate because we should be here for the changes,' Corbett told her. 'This is all I've ever worked for. The move into power and ownership must be smooth.'

'And, yes, I do see you must be here for that,' she replied.

'There's a place for you, Hen. This is my dream and plan.'

'When I said run I meant run alone,' Henrietta said.

Corbett was puzzled, devastated. 'No, Hen, no,' he said. They had never spoken of her going solo. The thought tore at his spirit.

She said: 'I wouldn't expect you to come. Wouldn't want you to come. I'd be running to someone.'

'What? How?'

'I've a friend who has already withdrawn abroad, haven't I?' she replied. 'You remember that? Because of those apes, Marv and Jacob. I'm in touch with him. He will welcome me. Oh, such a welcome! He wants me. Wants me. Do you understand, Jule? In Toulouse. This is no cheap street turn. This is an honours graduate and Phd, a former university teacher.'

'Oh?' Floyd said.

'Yes,' she said.

'Really?' Floyd replied. 'From one of the newer universities? Some jacked-up Poly? But never mind. Comparatively acceptable – if there has to be adultery. I can understand why you'd go to him, Hen. I mean, in preference to Moyle.'

'He's started a translation business,' Henrietta had replied.

'Certainly one-up on scrounging with a drum,' Floyd said.

'You mustn't go,' Corbett said.

'He wants me,' Henrietta replied.

That damned, imperative, hungry word. 'I want you, really want you,' Corbett said, 'What I am about to achieve is nothing without you, Hen.'

She looked at him and smiled, a smile with so much suffering in it: 'Do you know, Jule, when I was speculating just now that the police might think you'd killed Eric out of jealousy, I found I wished you had. The idea was only momentary. But, yes, it happened. Disgraceful, I know. Yet it would have demonstrated as nothing else could that you really want me and want me exclusively for yourself. No more of this ghastly, casual tolerance, this feeble broadmindedness and sweet reason, instead of blood. Blood I need, Jule, blood, blood.'

Hadn't Gloria said something like this right near the start, the bright, dead, old seer?

'Hen's always been that way,' Floyd remarked.

Corbett realised he must hold on to her. Never had he realised anything so clearly. She had to be his and only his to receive the gift, the tribute he had won for her, a share of the Complex, the struggled-for, deserved step into ownership. 'Yes, I killed Eric Moyle,' he said.

She snorted. 'Oh, God, come on, Jule. She wagged a hand at him, a teacher's reproach to a manageable infant. 'You couldn't. I appreciate your saying it but it's not in you.'

Those giggling jerks, Marv and Jacob, had said the same. She went on: 'That kind of storming, raw ferocity is not part of our thing together and never has been, has it?' Henrietta asked. 'In a way, that's praise, of course. You're not violent, not malevolent, Jule. Good for you. But in another way… Oh, I need, need, need to be violently wanted and, yes, that is why I'll run now to Toulouse and Charles.'

'Some of these new universities are surprisingly high up the achievement tables, you know,' Floyd replied. 'Not all that much under the halfway mark.'

Corbett said: 'I can tell you exactly how Moyle was lying among bushes and tall grass, the drum to his left, on its side, the river near, also on his left.'

'Ah, it's in the evening paper, is it?' Henrietta said.

'No,' Corbett replied. 'This is from my personal knowledge.'

'They announced the television news item as exclusive,' Floyd said.

'It was I, I, who climbed over the gate with a woman tucked under my arm,' Corbett replied. 'I think I can reasonably say it's the sort of thing I might opt for late at night.'

'Why?' Floyd said.

'Who?' Henrietta asked.

'Gloria,' Corbett said.

'Why?' Henrietta asked.

'Because my calibre had to be proved to her, as it has to be proved to you, Hen,' Corbett replied. 'I was showing them the body. They needed to see what I could do before they found me a place on the Complex's board.'

'The Krays used to do that sort of thing – insist people proved themselves with a killing,' Floyd said. 'Sid Hyson learned from all quarters.'

Corbett said urgently: 'Floyd, you're a minister, conscious of your duties to God and the law, but you must never speak of what I've just told you. I revealed what I revealed only for the sake of your daughter.'

Floyd's reply offended Corbett: 'I won't speak of it, Jule, because I don't believe it. This was a skilled execution, utterly beyond you.'

'No, Daddy, no,' Henrietta cried. 'He does seem to know the details independently.'

'Oh, yes.' Corbett saw she longed to believe him, would believe him. Gloria had been right.

'To let herself be carried without dignity over a gate?' Floyd replied. 'Gloria would never do that, nor give up a place in the Complex boardroom.'

But Henrietta bent across the arm of her chair and gripped

Corbett by the wrist. 'Killed him because of an overwhelming rage in you, Jule?' she asked.

'Ungovernable.'

'Possessiveness. Supreme jealousy,' Henrietta said.

'Need,' Corbett replied. He craved to preserve his new, wonderful, resoundingly phoney link with her.

'This was a terrible but splendid courage and rage you found, Jule,' Henrietta murmured, still holding his wrist.

'Never go from me again.'

'You believe this eyewash, really, Hen?' Floyd asked.

'No, I mustn't go from you, Jule,' she said. 'Jule wants me, Daddy. I can see, see, Jule climbing a gate with a woman under his arm,' Henrietta replied. 'The ease, the boldness of it. Jule has the physique, the determination.'

'Well, I think I know something about physiques,' Floyd replied, flexing himself in that way of his. There was a knock at the manse front door and he stood up and went to answer. When he returned, Vera Lowndes was with him, in tan and yellow. She seemed vibrant with joy. 'I had to come and thank you for the prayer the other day, Floyd,' she said. 'It has been so marvellously effective. But, then, I imagine you would expect it to be, or where's faith?'

'Effective?' Corbett asked. Apprehension hit him.

'I stuck with my inquiries, you know,' she replied.

'Into Boris's death?' Floyd asked.

'And I have been fortunate,' she said. 'Or perhaps I should say God directed me.'

Corbett suddenly understood Marv's and Jacob's anxieties. 'You've found evidence, witnesses?' he asked.

'There are two men who work for Sidney Hyson,' she said.

'Yes?' Corbett replied.

'They did it,' she said.

'You have evidence?' Corbett asked. 'Real evidence?'

'The police say it is real,' she replied.

'Bravo!' Floyd cried.

'I've talked to people, and endlessly talked to people – to people who believed only in silence, silence as a condition of safety, until now,' she said. 'What's known as "omerta". But a mother's pleas, a mother's persistence, can reach them, can bring them courage. Some small piece of information came, oh, hopelessly small at first. But it led to another piece and then another and then another, until the whole wall around this crime crumbled.'

'Bravo!' Floyd cried.

'And it is evidence that does not stop at those two minions,' Mrs Lowndes said. 'It implicates Hyson. He gave the instructions. This can also be proved.'

'Bravo!' Floyd cried.

Corbett saw starkly then the sudden and complete annihilation of his new status at the Complex. That fucking Mrs Lowndes. He glanced at Henrietta and read in her beloved, intelligent face that she, too, understood it was all finished. She had a real mind, Hen. So, Sid would be brought back under extradition and charged and convicted and probably jailed for the rest of his life. Perhaps they would get him for Gloria as well. As soon as he started to go under, the banks were sure to move in on the Complex to recover their loans before values crumbled, like that wall Mrs Lowndes spoke of. They would not be asking anyone who had been close to Hyson to help them by offering directorships, not even Jule. They would probably install their own expert team and run the Complex themselves, perhaps buy it for next to nothing from the Receiver. There'd be no general invitation to outside bidders, not immediately, at any rate. The banks would want time to get the Complex's reputation and worth back up to the top. Vartelm, Castice-Manne and the others were due for a wait, if they remained interested.

'So, thank you, thank you, thank you, Floyd,' Mrs Lowndes said. She carried a large, beige, rectangular handbag on a shoulder strap. Pulling it around in front of her she opened the flap and put her hand inside. 'Please, I must give you a contribution. The money will not be needed now for Julian's funeral. That threat has gone.'

Floyd said: 'Nothing. We do not sell prayers.'

Once again she looked disappointed, even hurt. She closed the bag and sighed. 'Ah, well,' she said.

'And the police have acted?' Floyd asked.

'The buzz is that those Hyson aides got a hint somehow and did a runner in the firm's limo. But they'll be found. Floyd's prayer will take care of that, too, I know. And when they're found they will what's known as "sing", you see, and implicate Sidney Hyson – even if we didn't have witnesses.'

Yes, they would. They were not likely to show loyalty to Sid when he had discarded them. Christ, would they sing about Moyle? Corbett thought probably not. Why should they make things worse for themselves, and for Nightride, who was apparently not involved in Boris Lowndes' death? Corbett hoped his reasoning was right. He would hate to be shown up to Hen and Floyd as only a big mouth. Oh, God, not, not, to Floyd.

When Mrs Lowndes had gone home and Floyd left for his meeting, Henrietta said mildly, almost cosily: 'It will be eternal middlemanning then, Jule.'

'For now, only for now, I promise, not eternal. I have plans. Please stay with me, Hen.'

She stood and took him in her arms. He felt marvellously protected and cared for and dependent. 'Yes, I'll stay with you, Jule,' she said, 'didn't you kill for me, darling?'

'You're so wonderfully worth it, Hen,' he replied.

Also by BILL JAMES, published by THE DO-NOT PRESS

Split

First in a brilliant new series from the creator of Harpur & Iles

ISBN 1 899344 73 X paperback (UK £6.99)
ISBN 1 899344 72 1 hardback   (UK £15.00)

Simon Abelard – black Manchester graduate from Cardiff's dockland – was recruited by British Intelligence to be a spy. But since the Berlin Wall came down he finds that he's working as a glorified cop.

Then Abelard is given the dangerous job of 'bringing back' a colleague who's changed sides. But Julian Bowling has not defected to the Russians, the Chinese or the Iraqis. Instead, he took advantage of his security service training to become a big-time crook. Now, he's taken millions of dollars belonging to the crooked syndicate he helped create, and the ruthless drug-dealers he robbed are after his blood.

As the bodies begin to pile up, Abelard finds himself fighting not only for his own life, but for the lives of his loved ones.

In the 21st Century, the spying game is changed forever.

"As a thriller writer James is in the very top bracket."
Crime Time

'British mystery fiction's finest prose stylist'
Peter Guttridge, *The Observer*

Also published by THE DO-NOT PRESS

Kiss Me Sadly
by Maxim Jakubowski

A daring new novel from the 'King of the erotic thriller'
– *Time Out*

ISBN 1899344 87 X   paperback (£6.99)
ISBN 1899344 88 8   hardcover (£15.00)

Two parallel lives: He is a man who loves women too much, but still seeks to fill the puzzling emptiness that eats away at his insides

She grows up in an Eastern European backwater, in a culture where sex is a commodity and surviving is the name of the game.

They travel down separate roads, both hunting for thrills and emotions. Coincidence brings them together. The encounter between their respective brands of loneliness is passionate, heartbreaking, tender and also desolate. Sparks fly and lives are changed forever, until a final, shocking, epiphany.

Also published by THE DO-NOT PRESS

Double Take
by Mike Ripley

Double Take: The novel and the screenplay (the funniest caper movie never made) in a single added-value volume.

ISBN 1899344 81 0 paperback (£6.99)
ISBN 1899344 82 9 hardcover (£15.00)

Double Take tells how to rob Heathrow and get away with it (enlist the help of the police). An 'Italian Job' for the 21st century, with bad language – some of it translated – chillis as offensive weapons, but no Minis. It also deconstructs one of Agatha Christie's most audacious plots.

The first hilarious stand-alone novel from the creator of the best-selling Angel series.

Also published by THE DO-NOT PRESS

Mr Romance
by Miles Gibson

An epic tale of love, lust, jealousy, pain and purple prose

ISBN 1899344 89 6   paperback (£6.99)
ISBN 1899344 90 X hardcover (£15.00)

'Miles Gibson is a natural born poet' –
Ray Bradbury

Skipper shares his parents' boarding house with their lodgers: lovely Janet the bijou beauty and Senor Franklin, the volcanic literary genius. Life is sweet, until one night the lugubrious Mr Marvel seeks shelter with them.

Who is the mysterious fugitive and what dark secret haunts him? Skipper sets out to solve the riddle. But then the astonishing Dorothy Clark arrives and his life is thrown into turmoil. Skipper falls hopelessly in love and plans a grand seduction. He'll stop at nothing. But Dorothy is saving herself for Jesus…

Also published by THE DO-NOT PRESS

Pick Any Title
by Russell James

**Chairman of the CRIME WRITERS' ASSOCIATION
2001-2002**

**PICK ANY TITLE is a magnificent new crime caper
involving sex, humour sudden death and double-cross.**

ISBN 1899344 83 7   paperback (£6.99)
ISBN 1899344 84 5   hardcover (£15.00)

'Lord Clive' bought his lordship at a 'Lord of the Manor' sale
where titles fetch anything from two to two hundred thousand pounds. Why not buy another cheap and sell it high?
Why stop at only one customer? Clive leaves the beautiful
Jane Strachey to handle his American buyers, each of whom
imagines himself a lord.

But Clive was careless who he sold to, and among his
victims are a shrewd businessman, a hell-fire preacher and a
vicious New York gangster. When lawyers pounce and guns
slide from their holsters Strachey finds she needs more than
good looks and a silver tongue to save her life.

A brilliant page-turner from 'the best of
Britain's darker crime writers'
The Times

'The Godfather of British noir'
Ian Rankin

'When it comes to crispness of plot and
tightness of prose, Russell James is king'
Time Out

Also published by THE DO-NOT PRESS

First of the True Believers
by Paul Charles

'The Autobiography of Theodore Hennessy'

ISBN 1899344 78 0 paperback (£7.50)
ISBN 1899344 79 9 hardcover (£15.00)

THE BEATLES formed in 1959 and became the biggest group in the world. Among other less celebrated Merseybeat groups of the time were The Nighttime Passengers, led by Theo Hennessy, who almost replaced Pete Best as drummer of the 'Fab Four'.

First of The True Believers tells of a decade in the life of Theodore Hennessy, intertwined with the story of The Beatles. It begins in 1959 with his first meeting with the beautiful and elusive Marianne Burgess and follows their subsequent on-off love affair and his rise as a musician.

The Beatles provided the definitive soundtrack to the '60s, and here novelist and musicologist Paul Charles combines their phenomenal story with a tender-hearted tale of sex, love and rock 'n' roll in '60s Liverpool.